DEPTHS OF DECEIT

A JAMIE RUSH MYSTERY

LAURA OLES

Depths of Deceit
Red Adept Publishing, LLC
104 Bugenfield Court
Garner, NC 27529
https://RedAdeptPublishing.com/

Cover Art by Streetlight Graphics[1]

This is a work of fiction. Names, characters, places, and incidents either are the product of the author's imagination or are used fictitiously, and any resemblance to locales, events, business establishments, or actual persons—living or dead—is entirely coincidental.

---

1.   http://StreetlightGraphics.com

For Anna

"No, I don't miss you... Not in a way that one is missed.
But I think of you.
Sometimes.
In the way that one might think of the summer sunshine
On a winter night..."
—Sreesha Divakaran

CHAPTER ONE

The mermaid in the truck bed was what caught Jamie Rush's attention.

The cast-iron figure peeked over the hatch, her carved, flowing hair and demure smile in view. This was supposed to be a standard identify-and-repo job. Jamie was certain she hadn't seen a mermaid on the itemized paperwork. Brody Rutger, in addition to hiding from creditors, had added theft of a local celebrity to his resume.

The day had started strong, with a lead on Rutger and an opportunity to catch him between fishing charters, using a boat he'd quit paying on months before. Suddenly, Marian the Mermaid was caught up in the mix.

And something was going on with the weather.

The month of November normally brought a steady stream of long-term vacationers from the north—affectionately called Winter Texans—who fled harsh winters for the promise of more tepid temperatures. Those who'd already set up residence in Port Alene were likely to be disappointed. Port A, usually quite predictable in her warmth, had suddenly changed her mind. That day, she was trading humidity for frigid air, and the wind, once laced with a warm, salty breeze, was offering only a cold shoulder. The palm trees lining Island Main bristled from side to side, and the town seemed to have turned inward in response. The icy wind whistled in the gap of her Tahoe's window.

Jamie shuddered at the weather's frigid downturn, while her partner, Cookie Hinojosa, all but cursed Mother Nature. He believed anything under seventy degrees was downright blasphemous.

Jamie tilted her head toward the gray sky and welcomed the sting of air on her cheeks, her head briefly popping out the driver's-side window. Cookie glanced over and shook his head.

"You're very grumpy this morning," Jamie said. She gave him a once-over, taking note of the large Dallas Cowboys logo on his chest, the silver star claiming almost all the space between his shoulders. "I see you found your favorite winter hoodie. Probably more fun to wear when they're winning."

Cookie turned to her and scowled. "Et tu, Brute? You're going to dump on *our* favorite team? Really?"

Jamie reached over and gave her partner's meaty shoulder a squeeze. "They need to earn our love by playing better. And we've been damned patient." She rubbed her hand up and down his sleeve, noting the fabric felt cold. "You should probably break down and buy a proper winter jacket."

"This is South Texas. Only snowbirds wear 'proper' winter jackets." Cookie dismissed the idea of wearing anything that added additional bulk to his substantial frame. "My Hawaiian shirts are sad from neglect."

She had to agree. A long-sleeved Hawaiian shirt would look ridiculous on anyone. She rubbed her hands together and hoped the cold snap would soon dissipate, returning the balmy temperatures Port Alene normally delivered.

"I'm going to pull back a bit," Jamie said.

Their skip of the day, Brody Rutger, owed their client, AAA Repo Services, $15,027. Brody had ducked all attempts at collection, so Jamie and Cookie had been hired to locate him and return the boat.

Jamie and Cookie specialized in skip tracing, which essentially meant finding people who didn't want to be found. They worked skips but also some surveillance—which paid well but was boring beyond belief—and some divorce cases, which also paid well but renewed Jamie's resolve to never get married. In Jamie's experience, if a person disappeared, the reasons involved money, private information, or violence. And secrets—always a secret.

Highway 361, a two-lane road with a narrow shoulder that no sane human should ever travel in a golf cart—though many visitors had—gave way to Port Alene proper. The island town came into view, and an extra lane appeared, encouraging cars behind her to claim the extra space. Brody's truck remained in the left lane, prompting Jamie to tap her brakes, allowing another car to come between them. She didn't want to be in his rearview mirror.

"He's going to take the ferry," Jamie said, following the line of cars ahead of her taking a left on Avenue G. "Thank God for that hideous paint job. Makes him easy to tail."

Unlike the endless stream of black, white, or gray trucks so commonly found cruising the main streets of town, Brody Rutger had no such desire to blend in with the crowd. His paint job was certainly custom, and Jamie wondered if the artist who'd painted the vehicle suffered from color blindness. A shiny silver surface had been shamefully assaulted by ragged flames of red, green, yellow, and purple. She was amazed that Brody had kept under the radar so long with a ride like that.

Jamie nudged Cookie, whose thick elbow rested on the rolled-down window as he tipped his head now and then to survey the traffic ahead.

"Looks like dragon vomit," Jamie said. "You think he had Rudy do that?"

Jamie knew Rudy Vallero from around town. Rudy considered himself an artist, and the guy had some solid talent. Unfortunately, that talent was sometimes compromised by too much weed and the necessity to cover rent.

The silver star on Cookie's hoodie shook with a laugh. "It definitely screams, 'Look at me.' Maybe not the best call if you need to hide out."

Jamie, driving her own unassuming Chevy Tahoe, the dark paint showing signs of peeling from years of being exposed to the hostile Texas sun, followed Brody's violated F-150, careful to stay a few cars behind on the two-lane road.

Brody was two cars ahead, the row of vehicles snaking along a specific lane designed to feed each driver into the ferry line. Four men in bright-yellow vests waved their arms to direct each car into the appropriate lane, alternating vehicles until they were evenly placed. Jamie glanced his way while her SUV idled. Once the ferry had docked and released its current load of travelers, Jamie's group began entry, each car driving over the metal ramps that linked ground to water. Her Tahoe was guided to the side opposite Brody's, the boat's center cabin serving as a divider between them.

With Brody's truck no longer in view, she turned her attention to the Corpus Christi channel and the seagulls standing by on wooden posts protruding from the water as the wind picked up, tunneling through her open car window. The afternoon sun struggled to offset the chill in the air.

Cookie shifted in his seat, his body turned toward Jamie. The whir of the boat's engine filled the cabin, prompting him to raise his voice to be heard.

"You think we'll find it?"

Jamie reached behind her head and tucked several stray hairs underneath her ball cap. "I think so. I know his friend has a place in Rockville Heights. It makes sense." She pointed out the passenger-side window. "Enjoy the view. Maybe you'll see a dolphin this time."

It was a running joke between them. Dolphins were regularly spotted by travelers on the ferry, but although Cookie had lost count of how many times he'd taken the waterway, he rarely got that lucky.

As he pretended to look for dolphins, Jamie contemplated the importance of their job. Their receivables had escalated, with many cases going unpaid for months at a time. Cookie had warned that they needed more payment up front, but many of their clients were the sort who needed their services in order to get the money owed them. They wouldn't have the cash until the job was done, and Jamie hated leaving people with few resources without any help.

Their policy was good for the soul but bad for the wallet.

Jamie loved taking the ferry. The rocking of the ferryboat on the waves and the sight of gulls soaring and landing on nearby piers soothed her worried mind, at least for a few moments. Even the unusually cold slices of air didn't detract. She closed her eyes and exhaled.

This job was different. Payment for services rendered, if all went well, would help Jamie and Cookie get square with their own accounts. Owing anyone a debt was the one burden she couldn't stomach. She hoped her luck was turning. She could get even and breathe a little more easily.

Ten minutes later, the twenty cars taxiing across the channel arrived at their destination. Rockville Heights was also considered a coastal town but with a much different personality from Port Alene's. The sister city offered more sprawl, clusters of nice neighborhoods with shopping centers, and fast-food stops punctuating the main road.

Jamie likened Rockville Heights to Port Alene's more buttoned-up older brother. But that town, too, had a dark underbelly, one Jamie knew all too well. Rockville Heights' waters were rumored to be the final resting place for several bad actors who'd simply disappeared one day.

The tales those waters could tell, she thought.

Brody's truck took one of the first exit spots after the ferry docked, the bright flame of ill-chosen colors traveling along the lane.

Jamie waited for the ferry attendant to remove the metal blocks around her front tire and usher her to exit. After several turns, she found herself in an older neighborhood with small single-story homes with substantial space between the lots, some with fences, many without. As Brody pulled into the driveway of one such house, a small, square brown-brick number with an open back lot, Jamie stopped several lengths back and across the street, keeping her distance.

There it was.

A Boston Whaler Dauntless 270 rested on its trailer, the kind of fishing boat certain to make Brody's friends jealous. Maybe that was the point, to impress friends or girls, but the one thing that remained unimpressive was his credit history. He had a reputation for skipping on his bills, his mouth unable to cash the checks it wrote.

"She's a beauty," Cookie said.

"I see what you did there," Jamie replied. "Nice Tubes reference." Speaking in eighties song lyrics had become a kind of shorthand for the duo, even though the decade preceded their childhood.

"Should I back in and load her up?" Jamie asked, craning her neck to examine the boat and her immediate surroundings. No other vehicle was blocking the trailer hitch, and she was oriented the right way.

"Let's do a quick walk around, and then we'll back in."

Cookie was always the more cautious of the two. Jamie, as he often said, "liked to lead with her face." He sometimes described her as more speed than direction.

The two made it to the Dauntless and took a quick inventory. She was a beautiful vessel in a girl-next-door sort of way. The light-blue paint was clean and even, her fiberglass neat and cared for. It was certainly washed down properly each time she returned ashore. No random trash or miscellaneous debris had been left anywhere. Brody might've been a delinquent customer, but he knew how to care for a boat.

Jamie checked the trailer base and the hitch. "I think we're good. Let's do this before he comes outside. We're already working on borrowed time."

No sooner had the words left her mouth than the sound of a large truck demanded her attention. She turned to look over her shoulder, and Cookie did the same, squinting at the vehicle coming closer.

The black dually stopped short of Brody's house, executed a three-point turn that was nothing short of impressive, given the truck's extended bed, and backed up to Brody's boat. The engine remained running as a man stepped outside the truck, his thick black boots hitting the pavement. He was well over six feet tall, his salt-and-pepper hair cropped and clean with a trimmed beard to match. He wore a heavy black leather jacket with more miles on it than Jamie's Tahoe, faded jeans, and a heavy silver chain that led from one back pocket to the front. He made eye contact but offered nothing else.

"Alastair Finn," Cookie said under his breath. He walked closer to Alastair. "What the hell are you doing in town, and more important, what the hell are you doing here on our job?"

Alastair didn't look up, his body hunched over as he turned the crank to level it to his trailer hitch. "Not sure what you're talking about. This is my job. Brody owes big, and I'm here to collect."

Cookie shook his head. "This job is ours. He owes on this boat, and we've been retained to return it to AAA. Don't tell me they hired you too."

Jamie stepped close enough to Alastair to cast a shadow over his bent frame. "I'm sorry. Who the hell are you?"

"I'm someone who knows this town a lot better than you do."

Jamie stifled the urge to slam Finn's head down into the trailer bolt. That took enormous restraint. The fact that he was half a foot taller than her was also a consideration.

In the middle of the standoff, Brody emerged from the house, his face confused in the way one looks when they've been woken from a fat nap. He rubbed the back of his head, looking at the trio of people in his front yard.

"Get away from my boat," he said, the conviction in his voice completely lacking any teeth. He was a child telling a grown man to give back his ball.

"Brody, you've been burning through a lot of money for all of us to be here," Jamie said. "You want to explain yourself?"

"Not really."

Well played.

"Possession is nine-tenths of the law, and it looks like the job is mine. Besides, if you have any conscience, you'll let this one go." Finn crossed his arms after finishing securing the Dauntless.

"Don't think I need a morality lecture from someone who swooped in and stole our job." Jamie turned to Cookie. "Can you explain this man to me?"

"Finn and I go way back. And not in a good way." Cookie's eyes, normally wide and playful, were daggers. He turned to Alastair. "So what's your story with Brody?"

Finn glanced at Brody then returned his attention to Cookie, making full eye contact. "Brody used this boat as collateral on a loan he took out with my client."

"Who's the client?" Jamie asked. She stood next to Cookie, arms crossed and eyes narrowed.

He answered but addressed Cookie. "Louie Marchese."

Cookie gave a low whistle and turned to Brody. "What the hell are you doing getting in debt with Big Louie?"

"He doesn't like being called that." Alastair leaned down and checked the trailer hitch one last time. "Brody here defaulted on his loan, so Mr. Marchese just got himself a new Dauntless. I'm sure he'll put it to good use."

"Sure. It'll come in handy for tossing bodies into Rockland Channel," Jamie quipped. She inched closer to Cookie and leaned in. "You know what this means, right? If something happens to Brody..."

Jamie and Cookie exchanged a glance as Alastair studied them both. Cookie waved a hand toward the boat. "Take it."

"Not that I needed your permission, but good choice."

"No need to be an asshole about it," Jamie said, adding, "unless that's your normal state, then carry on." She then gestured to the stranded mermaid statue in the back of Brody's truck. "We're going to take Marian back home. I'm sure Sandy's Shell Shop would like to have her back."

Alastair shrugged. "Help yourself. No mermaid on my papers." He smiled. Then he pulled his keys from his pocket and said, "See you around town."

"I really hope not" was Jamie's reply.

"I'm not so bad," Alastair said. "Just stay out of my way." He slid into the driver's seat and waved through his open window as he drove off.

Jamie responded in kind by waving her middle finger. Cookie grimaced at her like a disapproving parent, but then a smile emerged.

"I just did what you wanted to do. You remain the more digni-fied partner in our relationship." She looked at Brody, who had stood silently while the boat disappeared into the distance on the back of Alastair's dually, his head hanging.

"Really? You stole Marian too?"

"Things got a little rowdy last night. You know how it is." Brody wrinkled his nose like a scolded schoolboy, stuck his hands in his pants pockets, then turned on his heels and disappeared into the house.

Jamie sighed, frustrated that their payday had quickly become a bust. She glanced at Cookie, who was still nursing the sting of failure. "I'm really going to hate telling Carl that we lost the boat." She pointed at the statue. "Let's get her back home."

Jamie tried to push aside her concerns about Alastair Finn, but he lingered in her mind as she walked to her car. That morning, she'd had no idea who the man was, but he currently seemed to be her biggest problem.

Cookie reached into a pocket and checked his phone. "Some good news. We may have another job," he said. "I'll check in and get more details."

"I hope it comes with a good hourly rate," Jamie said. "We needed this job."

"I hear you," Cookie replied. "Broke and defeated wasn't how I planned on the day going."

They loaded the stolen statue into the vehicle and drove back toward the ferry in silence. Jamie wondered how far Alastair would go to claim their territory. And she considered what she was willing to do to protect it.

CHAPTER TWO

As Jamie opened the front door to Hemingway's Pier, she glanced back at Cookie, who was lagging behind, wrestling with his backpack. He grimaced as he hoisted it onto one shoulder. She could see he wasn't in his normal frame of mind. Alastair had gotten into his head too. It had been a long day for both of them.

"After you?" she asked as she held the door open.

He made it to the entryway and gestured. "Ladies first," he said as she walked through.

"I've been called a lot of names, but I don't hear that one much," she joked, working to lighten his mood.

Jamie's eyes took a moment to adjust to the dim lighting of her favorite bar, and she searched until she spotted the owner, Marty Scout, serving a trio of regulars on their stools. She wondered if the post office delivered their mail there.

Marty made eye contact and gave her a nod. They claimed their seats at the far end of the bar.

"C'mon, I'll buy you a beer," she told Cookie, "and we can devise our master plan to rid ourselves of this Alice guy." She placed her phone on the bar and her bag on the floor.

"Alastair," he corrected her. "Alastair Finn." He said it with a sense of resignation that was unfamiliar to her. Cookie was rarely anything other than optimistic.

Marty stood at the ready, awaiting their orders.

"Alastair Finn is back?" Marty asked.

"Why does everyone else know who this guy is?" Jamie asked.

Marty winked at her. "Well, even though you think you've lived in Port Alene a long time, believe it or not, lots of things happened before your grand arrival."

Cookie turned to Marty. "The usual," he said, glancing at Jamie to confirm that's what she wanted.

She nodded, dropping her bag on the floor underneath her stool. She rubbed her temples. "I think this day has given me one hell of a headache. How did the Rutger job unravel like that?"

Marty returned and placed two beers in front of them. "Here, this should help." He grabbed a white dishrag from underneath the bar and began wiping it down.

"How do you know Alastair Finn?" Jamie asked Marty. "And how can we get rid of him?"

"I think you're going to have a hard time with that. He's got family here."

"Family? Then why haven't I seen him around before?"

Marty kept wiping down the same spot over and over. "Well, not family. Just his dad, who I heard has been sick with some sort of cancer."

Jamie felt a momentary pang of regret for wishing Alastair physical harm. He still annoyed the hell out of her, and she was still determined to boot him out of her business, but the guy's dad was sick. Maybe she'd swing with a softer bat.

Maybe not.

"How do you know all of this?" Jamie asked.

"Lived here a long time," Marty said. "The cliché is true. People tell bartenders everything." He winked again. "And I'm really good at eavesdropping."

Cookie had been silent during this exchange, and while the man was known for many things, a quiet nature was not among his attributes. He wasn't sulking, exactly. Jamie wondered if he was being contemplative or licking his wounds or plotting the demise of a nemesis.

She reached over and put her hand on his shoulder, giving it a small squeeze before letting go. "Hey. You okay?"

Half a beer down, he took another long draw before answering. "I don't like that guy, you know?"

She nodded, taking a drink from her glass. "I can see why. Not a lot of personality, and what he's got is nothing to brag about. Like sandpaper on a baby's ass."

Cookie cracked a smile for the first time in hours, which was a relief to witness. "Alastair was that guy who always bested me when I got started. I gave him a run for it when I got more experience, but those first few years were painful. He was always in my business, taking my business, that stupid smile on his face."

This was a side Jamie hadn't seen in her partner. He wasn't one to let someone get under his skin and make him question his abilities. In their work and friendship, he was the line, and she was the kite. But right then, he seemed adrift.

"You have a secret weapon now," Jamie said as she finished her beer. "You've got me."

Cookie grinned at her, taking a sip from his glass. "He's going to hate you."

"Only if I do it right."

Jamie signaled to Marty, who had busied himself with the growing crowd of locals streaming into the bar. He quickly brought two more drafts then returned to his other patrons. A rare tourist would find their way into the place now and again, but they never stayed long. Hemingway's had a very specific vibe. It wasn't the kind of place to bring a date or parents or anyone wary of bar fights, profanity, or a greasy kitchen.

"I heard you saved Marian," Marty said.

Jamie nodded. "You'd think Sandy would figure out a way to tie her down to keep her from getting stolen. This is, like, the third time this year."

Marty held his hands up. "Sandy's got a lot going on, and besides, I think she secretly gets a kick out of it. Marian always makes it back home. I'm sure she'll get a nice write-up in the paper."

"Changing the topic to the case you mentioned before," Jamie said, turning to Cookie, "what's the deal there?"

Cookie pulled out his phone and opened the text. "Here."

She read it then placed the cell facedown on the bar. "Renata? From San Juan's Taqueria?"

He nodded. "I've known Renata and her sister since I was a kid."

"Tell me more of your young folklore," Jamie said, leaning back and tilting her chin toward the ceiling. "I love to hear stories about families with parents who were nice to them."

Cookie's eyes lit up when he talked about his family. They made him nuts, to be sure, but he truly loved their shared crazy DNA. Jamie couldn't relate, but she basked in the outer circle of association whenever possible.

"Renata's mom, Sylvia, was one of my mom's best friends a long time ago. My mom babysat Renata and her little sister, Leah, when they were little. They knew each other the way most people do here—island town, all that. Sylvia worked in Corpus, and my mom ran a little day care back in the day. My mom would pick the girls up after school and bring them to our house. I was a few years older, so these little kids were kind of a bummer, but Renata was always nice. Smiled a lot."

"What about Leah?"

"Don't remember much other than she always looked like she was trying to figure out how to jump the fence and escape."

"I can relate."

"I bet you can."

"And where's Sylvia today?"

"She passed away a couple of years ago," he said. "Breast cancer."

"I'm sorry," Jamie said. "Cancer sucks."

"It does."

"And her husband?"

"He passed away when Leah was little. Car accident of some sort, from what I remember." Cookie took a deep breath and sat for a moment. "So it's just the two sisters now, but Leah's gone quiet. That's what Renata thinks. She thinks it's not just Leah being Leah."

"Meaning... she doesn't check in a lot?"

"She thinks something is different this time," Cookie said, one hand up like a caution signal. "Here's the thing. Renata says straight out that she can't pay us, and she's already been to the PAPD. Just doesn't know where else to turn. I know we can't keep taking these freebie cases, and it's always more complicated when it's people we know."

Cookie was right. Taking on cases as favors was something they didn't have the luxury of doing, given their current state of bottomed-out brokeness, especially since the paycheck for the Rutger case had disappeared with Alastair and the Dauntless. And doing favors for friends often changed the nature of the friendship, because information about loved ones had to be delivered, and that intel was rarely positive. Taking a case for a friend often meant being willing to sacrifice that friendship if things went south.

And they sometimes did.

"Renata and Leah are family to you in an extended way, yes?"

Cookie nodded. "Yeah, but bills..."

"We'll pick it up somewhere else" was her reply. "I'm in."

Jamie figured that the case, like many missing-person cases, might end up being less of a mystery than expected. Leah might have just decided she didn't need her older sibling updated on her every move. Several of their cases resulted in the discovery that someone simply needed other people out of their business, and ghosting them was the only way to do it. An effective strategy, although painful for the haunted.

Cookie glanced down at Jamie's phone, which kept vibrating on the bar surface. "Which family member are you avoiding now?"

She knew she should've put the cell back in her bag. "Alex. He's been persistent lately."

"Your father usually is when he wants something," Cookie responded, reaching for a bowl of peanuts. He took one, peeled the shell, and left it on the bar, popping the nut into his mouth.

"You know better than to eat those," Jamie chided. "Probably older than you."

Marty's kitchen knocked out some quality bar food, but the snacks were always an afterthought.

"You need to call him to, you know, get him off your back." Cookie finished his draft as she followed suit.

More locals were ambling in, checking off another day of working at the boat docks or fishing tours or their own restaurant shifts. Port Alene catered largely to tourists, and with only three thousand locals, the economy fell short on high-paying gigs in anything other than real estate. If only entertaining vacationers provided a better living wage... Most people lived there because they loved island life even if the cost meant abandoning the idea of climbing the career ladder.

Jamie's thoughts on Port Alene career opportunities were interrupted by the crash of glass and multiple men yelling. She swiveled on her stool just in time to witness Marty with his hands around the neck of a man who was six feet tall and almost as wide. Marty, sizeable himself but smaller than his brawling patron, had the advantage of many years of breaking up bar fights. He quickly separated the man from his foe, who was much smaller and clearly had no business picking a fight. *Must have been the scotch talking.* His narrow frame indicated he might suffer from being snapped in half if things had gone further south.

"Time to go home," Marty told the man, whose face was returning to its natural color from the ruddy hue it had been moments before.

He straightened his posture and moved his neck from side to side. "You got a good grip there, friend," he said to Marty.

"It's because I keep getting practice with you and your mouth," Marty replied. "Now go home and be a nuisance to Sally." He walked back to his place behind the bar, calling out to Jamie, "Three bar fights this week, and I haven't been punched once."

Marty's presence was one of her favorite things about working and living in the loft of Hemingway's Pier. A man who'd caused plenty of trouble on his own in his younger days, he had found his role as the elder statesman of alcohol-fueled brawls and ridiculous arguments. He had somehow become the voice of reason.

The world made no sense.

Cookie wedged his elbow into Jamie's side. "So you want to call your dad back so it's not hanging over your head? I'll tell Renata that we'll stop by the restaurant tomorrow morning. She's working the early shift."

"That works," she said. "I think I'll take this opportunity to examine the inside of my eyelids."

"Still not sleeping well?" Cookie asked. "More nightmares?"

She shrugged. "Sometimes. All that surveillance work we did hasn't helped, either. I can't turn my brain off."

"Try to get some sleep," he said. "We'll see Renata tomorrow and go from there."

Jamie hugged her friend goodbye and watched him leave Hemingway's. Her thoughts turned to Renata's sister, and those thoughts traveled to her niece, Kristen. Jamie reminded herself that Leah was a different person from a different family, and that alone was an advantage Kristen had never had.

CHAPTER THREE

Jamie pulled into the parking lot of San Juan's to discover the restaurant's drive-through was five cars deep and threatening to spill into the street. That happened most days, as the restaurant was known by locals and tourists alike as one of the best places for quality Mexican food on a budget. At times, Jamie wished the place weren't so popular, but she knew the family who owned it, and they worked nonstop to make it an island favorite. She couldn't begrudge them success simply because she didn't like crowds—or people in general.

She found a parking space in the back by the dumpster and turned off the ignition then checked her phone. Cookie had already claimed a table inside.

Jamie glanced at the battered red newspaper kiosk in front of the restaurant and noted that a new edition was out. Port Alene had only one weekly paper in print, although it was updated more often online. Her mind wandered back to a brief moment in her childhood, when her father would read the paper at a rickety kitchen table, circling what she thought were help-wanted ads, but that later turned out to be his method of spotting potential marks. Years later, she would realize what he'd been doing, her once-happy memory of remembering her family as remotely normal for a moment sullied by the reality that her father was scamming people even while eating breakfast.

Still, Jamie enjoyed having a copy of the *Port Alene Searcher* at the table. In addition to supporting a local business, she had become friendly with the paper's managing editor, Pepper Collins, who was a treasure trove of useful information about the town and its history. Few people knew more crazy stories about island life than Pepper, who managed to make the paper's police blotter some of the most entertaining reading around.

Jamie dug in her bag for quarters and retrieved a paper. She tucked it under her arm and opened the restaurant door, only to be greeted by a blast of artificially warm air and a loud mashup of conversations mixed with sounds of dishes and silverware scraping against ceramic.

She needed coffee.

Cookie waved an arm in the air to get her attention. He'd found a corner booth. Jamie slid into the seat opposite him, taking note of the two mugs in front of him.

"Bless you," Jamie said, reaching for a mug and taking a sip. "I take it that this is Renata's station?"

"Good detective work," Cookie said with a wink. "I waited until she had a spot free. It's busy today."

"What the hell's going on?" Jamie said, glancing around the restaurant at the crowd.

"I think there's a local music festival this weekend," Cookie said with an authority that made Jamie laugh. "And it's Sunday. Last meal before checkout time."

He had become an increasingly social creature of late, and Jamie joked that she thought his biological clock was ticking, causing him to go out into the wild in search of female companionship. In truth, Cookie was only in his midthirties and, in another unfair twist in the universe, could sire children well past the age of collecting Social Security. Jamie was thankful that she had no maternal instincts to battle. She was two years older than him, something he loved to remind her of on the regular.

Looking through the crowd, Jamie spotted Renata, who was busy chatting up some snowbirds. Balancing four plates on her arms, she cut between the tables with the grace of a dancer. She'd been at that gig a long time, from what Jamie remembered about Renata's past comments about having waited tables since high school. It was an underappreciated skill, and Renata was the best, sensing when a tea glass had tipped just below the acceptable volume and bringing out food while it was still piping hot. And if she was having a tough day, the customer would never know it. Renata was all smiles and pleasant small talk.

After placing her plates with customers, she made her way over to Jamie and Cookie's table, order pad in hand.

Jamie held up her coffee cup. "Thanks for this."

"Of course," Renata said. "I know how grumpy you get when you haven't had your coffee." She winked at Cookie.

Jamie couldn't help but notice the playful chemistry between them, although Renata wasn't his type, seemingly emotionally mature and responsible. Cookie had a weakness for lovely, temperamental women.

"You got a minute to talk? I know it's crazy busy." Jamie needed the caffeine because that day was going to be a long one.

Renata checked over her shoulder. "How about I get your order in, and then maybe I can steal a few minutes? It's busier than usual. A bunch of people came in for the music festival."

Cookie smiled widely, and Jamie ignored him.

"See? I told you," he said.

"Uh-huh."

"You want to do the special?"

Jamie nodded. "Sounds perfect."

Renata turned on her heels and left, disappearing into the crowd and back to the kitchen. Jamie watched her for a moment as Cookie sat silently with his coffee.

"I hope she comes back soon," he said, glancing into his mug. "I got zero sleep last night."

"Everything okay?" Jamie asked. "I'm usually the one with the sleep issues."

He nodded. "Yeah, for the most part. You know how my Uncle Albert is. He always texts me after I'm in bed, and even if I have my phone on silent, he keeps calling me if I don't answer. He's like a vampire, up all night and sleeping all day. The night shift is going to be the death of him."

"Because it's hard on his health?"

"Because I'm going to kill him," Cookie replied. "He's got to get a girlfriend or a dog or something else to entertain him. He's making me nuts. I'm like his security blanket."

"It's because you're the only person who always answers the phone. Make him wait a bit."

Cookie waved a hand in the air. "No, no. He'd just show up at my house. He's stubborn like that. And you know he's not known for his impulse control."

Jamie had to laugh. Cookie's Uncle Albert was a very sweet man in his midfifties, a gifted grill master and equally talented contractor whose billing rates were as generous as Jamie and Cookie's. He had a heart bigger than his income, which had once resulted in him offering rounds for the bar patrons "on him," which turned into Cookie covering the check.

"Well, it's easy to see why he caught up that time when the Cowboys finally made it to the playoffs," she said. "Probably never see that again."

"It took me weeks to pay off that tab. So glad Marty cut me a break on the total."

Jamie sipped from her cup. "And you got your mom's bathroom remodeled at cost."

Cookie grinned. "I think he learned his lesson after that one. You know how picky my mom is."

Jamie noticed her coffee cup lacked liquid caffeine, and Renata arrived with her coffeepot in hand.

"How do you do that?" Jamie asked.

"Just have a sixth sense about these things." When Cookie held up his mug to be topped off also, Renata obliged. "Going to drop this off, and I have a fifteen-minute break, so we can talk." Renata handed her coffeepot to another waitress then returned to their booth, choosing to slide in next to Jamie. To be fair, she had more room on her side. She sat for a moment, inhaled, then began. "First of all, thank you for answering my text."

"Are you kidding?" Cookie said. "Of course. We go way back."

"Something I'm just learning," Jamie said.

Renata glanced down at her hands before making eye contact. "Hey, I hear things went bad with Liana." She then added, "Not surprised it didn't work out, honestly."

Cookie remained tight-lipped.

Renata continued. "She's a lot. I know. A wonderful friend, but she goes from zero to a hundred like—" She snapped her fingers.

He nodded. "She's really nice. Just not for me."

"That's what I gathered. She's still mad at you, by the way."

Cookie sat back in the booth, his hands in his lap. "I tried to end it nicely. In person. But she wasn't too interested in what I had to say. And making a scene at I'd Tapas That was pretty embarrassing. I love that food truck, and now I can never go back." Cookie looked like he was blushing. "Anyway," he said, changing the subject, "let's talk about Leah."

Renata took a deep breath before speaking. "So as I said in my text, I'm worried."

"What's your relationship like?" Jamie asked.

She turned to Jamie. "Leah's four years younger than me. I'm the bossy big sister."

Jamie held up a hand in shared confession. "Same. Drove my little sister nuts."

"That's our job." Renata took in a deep breath then exhaled with force. She drummed her hands on the table.

"And you think something happened to her?" Jamie asked.

Renata reached up and touched her eye, a small tear threatening to form in the corner. She blinked it away and took a breath. "Boundaries are tough with her. When we were little, my mom would draw a line, and she'd dangle her toe over the edge with a smile on her face." She wiped her hand on her apron. "If you push Leah, she pulls away. That's just how she is."

"Is there anything you know about her life that would cause concern? A relationship? Some personal or work issue?"

She shrugged. "Leah would say no. She usually keeps her troubles to herself, but I know she left Austin last month and came here looking for 'a fresh start.' I told her she could stay with me, but she said she needed her own space." Renata rolled her eyes.

"And she stayed where?" Cookie leaned forward slightly.

"She found a roommate online." She pulled a piece of paper from her apron and handed it to Cookie. "Michael Ferguson. She said he was nice, the rent was cheap. She said she wasn't planning on staying in Texas long term. She wanted to move out of the state, try something new." Renata cradled her head in her hands. "I should have insisted she stay with me."

"Okay, so talk me through what happened. When was the last time you saw her?"

Renata lifted her head back up, straightened in her seat, and sighed. She wiped her eye with the heel of one hand. "The day before Halloween. Wednesday. I texted her later to ask if she was going to come with us to take my girls, Sophie and Clara, trick-or-treating, and she never responded. That's not like her."

"How old are your girls?" Jamie asked.

"Sophie is ten, and Clara is seven." She smiled.

"So she's a good aunt?"

Renata nodded. "Yes, she is. I can't say that she's always reliable, but when she bails on us, she at least sends a text. She doesn't leave my girls hanging like that. She at least apologizes for not showing up if she can't make it."

"What happened next?"

"I waited a couple of days, figured she was busy, and then I went by her apartment. Michael said he hadn't seen her since Wednesday either."

Jamie closed her eyes and did the math in her head. The current day was November tenth. Eleven days had passed.

Cookie leaned forward, his arms crossed on the table. "You said you went to the PAPD?"

"Yes, I talked to a Detective Herrera."

"He's a good man," Jamie said, with Cookie nodding in agreement. "And what did he say?"

"He was sympathetic but also said that adults are allowed to disappear. It's not against the law. Her car is gone, her purse and phone are gone, and so they said it doesn't look like there was any foul play."

Jamie glanced around the restaurant and noticed it starting to clear out, the prime meal rush ending. "Is it possible that he's right? That maybe she just needs a break from something she just doesn't want to discuss?"

"Maybe, but why can't she just text me and tell me she needs some space?"

Jamie had no answer, but she did have a buzzing phone in her pocket. She ignored it, focusing her attention on Renata and the quietly brewing panic the woman was struggling to suppress. She looked at Cookie, who tapped his hand on the table quietly, as though he were mulling something over.

"We can stop by her apartment and also talk to Detective Herrera. And we'll take it from there."

Renata leaned forward and hesitated for a moment before speaking. "If you find something... that looks bad... please don't go to the police. She got into some trouble when she was younger, and I don't want to make things worse for her. She went off the rails a bit when my mom passed. She's an adult. She doesn't owe me check-ins or explanations about how she spends her time." Renata reached up and touched the corner of her eye to keep a tear at bay. "I just want to make sure she's okay, but I have this knot in my stomach that won't go away."

"I'm really sorry about your mom," Cookie said. "I'm sorry I never had the chance to talk about it all after she passed."

Renata nodded. "It's okay. It took me a long time to be able to talk about it. I just threw myself into work and keeping busy."

Jamie exchanged a glance with Cookie. "We'll handle your case with discretion. I promise."

Renata said, "I know I said I didn't have the money to pay for your time, but I can get a loan—"

"No, no, that's not necessary." Cookie waved his hand. "Let us do a little poking around, and we'll take it from there, okay? And if you hear from her, let us know."

"Can you send us your text messages and anything else you can remember?" Jamie put a hand awkwardly on Renata's forearm then removed it. Affection was not her first language. "We'll let you know when we get done at her place."

Renata nodded and stood up to return to her shift. She returned with two matching plates of huevos rancheros con bacon. When they were done, Cookie and Jamie left the restaurant, and only a few tables were still occupied. The diner noise had quieted to a small tinkle of plates and glasses mixed with conversation.

Jamie opened her car door, and Cookie stood waiting for her to unlock his side. "Good start is to reach out to Herrera next?" he asked.

"Maybe he can tell us something Renata doesn't know." Jamie leaned against her Tahoe and checked her phone—more messages from her father.

"It's been two years since you've seen your dad, Jamie. Maybe you should call him back."

"Can we just focus on this case?"

He smiled at her. "Fine, but tomorrow?" He waved at her cell. "You handle that."

Jamie slipped her cell into her back pocket. "Deal. Since it's Sunday, I'm guessing that Detective Herrera isn't in his office, but I'll see if we can drop by tomorrow morning." She turned to glance back at San Juan's. "I'm going to go in and get us some tacos for later. It didn't feel right to ask for another order after that conversation."

"Tacos are my love language," Cookie said.

"I know" was her reply.

Cookie turned to walk to his truck. "So... meet you at Hemingway's for a data-trolling session?"

Jamie gave him a thumbs-up and slipped into the driver's seat. Her mind continued to turn over the details Renata had shared about Leah. The case served as an effective distraction from the thought of talking to Alex. She couldn't trust him. He'd shown her that, yet he was reaching out. Maybe...

She shut down that thought. Believing he had any sincere motive always ended badly. Maya Angelou's words echoed in her mind: "When someone shows you who they are, believe them the first time."

CHAPTER FOUR

Jamie pulled into Hemingway's parking lot and glanced over at Cookie's parked truck. She spotted him with his attention squarely on his cell phone. She claimed an open spot next to the vehicle and cut her engine, and Cookie turned toward her. The phone disappeared, and he stepped out of the truck.

"We need to start riding together more often," he said. "Gas prices are up again, and this beauty doesn't get the best mileage."

Jamie retrieved the brown paper San Juan bag that held two bean-and-cheese burritos with extra green sauce on the side. She'd taken the liberty of ordering one for herself even though she wasn't hungry yet. Just the smell of San Juan's was enough to break her resolve. She figured she would need the snack later, and she needed a change from Marty's bar food. San Juan's was also a lot cheaper. A dollar went further there than it did at Marty's place, not that she begrudged him in any way. He had to make a living. Plus, the rent he charged her for the loft was clearly in the category of a family rate. Marty had said he would only let a handful of people live above his place anyway, and she was proud to have made his short list.

"You got everything?" she asked Cookie, who was busy gathering his backpack and his super-sized to-go iced tea out of Jamie's Tahoe. She watched him as he searched the floor to make sure he hadn't left anything.

"Ooh, there's my beanie," Cookie said, taking the black knitted cap and putting it atop his head, completely hiding his hair.

"You look like you're about ready to rob a bank," Jamie joked.

"I know," he smiled. "It's my favorite beanie. I thought I lost it, but it was crammed underneath the seat in my truck."

Jamie held up the paper bag. "Glad you found it. Now, let's get going. I don't want to stand here in the parking lot, freezing my ass off." She turned her face away from the frigid wind.

Cookie left the cap on his head despite Jamie's playful prodding and slung his backpack over his shoulder. He slammed the truck door and followed Jamie through the back entrance of Hemingway's and up the stairs to her loft.

Once inside, the pair placed their bags on the floor by their office table, which doubled as Jamie's dining room table except for the fact she didn't have a dining room, so it was really just an office table where she also ate takeout while she worked. It resided in the middle of her loft, a catchall for various items including a deck of cards, miscellaneous electronics cables, and a stack of papers destined never to see the inside of a file folder.

Her bulldog, Deuce, stumbled out of his dog bed to greet her, his snout sniffing at the paper bag in her hand. She dropped it on the table and bent down to pet him.

"Nice to see you too," she said, giving him a good rub under the neck. His attention remained on the bag.

"Nope. I fed you already."

Deuce snorted and immediately went to Cookie, who also showed him some love.

"Sorry, buddy. I hear you're on a diet. No tacos for you."

One more snort, and he returned to his dog bed, his backside now giving the duo his version of the cold shoulder.

"Deuce is salty today," Cookie noted.

"He's not happy with the new diet."

"Clearly."

"First things first," Jamie said. "We need to split some of the background work. You want to take Michael, and I'll take Leah?"

Cookie dropped his brown lunch bag on the table and sat down. He pulled his laptop out of his backpack, followed by two Hawaiian shirts, which he folded neatly and placed back inside his backpack. Jamie shook her head at the sight.

"What?" he asked. "Sometimes I need a fresh one. These long days wilt my flowers, and right now, it's too damn cold to wear them anyway." He smiled at her and said, "Yes, I'll handle Michael and do some background checks and preliminary calls. Let's see what comes up."

Jamie pulled her laptop from a kitchen drawer, her standard makeshift hiding spot for it when she didn't have it on her person. Her cabinets were filled with items that didn't belong in a kitchen. She did own a few mismatched forks and spoons, dishes, and coffee mugs, along with a single skillet, rarely used except for cooking eggs. So the drawers were perfect for storing other important items such as office supplies, tools, extra T-shirts... and dog snacks.

As she sat down next to Cookie, she glanced at his laptop and saw he was already online and logged into SkipTrackCentral, a database they often relied upon for preliminary background checks. In short order, Cookie pulled a listing of possible Michael Ferguson files.

Jamie returned her attention to her own laptop. "Anything good yet?"

He shook his head. "Not yet. Still trying to compile. The good news is that there aren't a ton of Michael Fergusons in the listing, so I just need to narrow down the age range." He squinted at the screen as he scrolled down. "Guessing our guy isn't eighty-four years old."

"If he is, I want his moisturizer because he looks fantastic for an octogenarian."

Cookie's stocky fingers danced across the computer keyboard, and the screen refreshed to reveal new information. "Okay, I think we have our guy. Got his basics and his work history." Cookie skimmed the page, scrolling down. "Doesn't seem like he holds a job for all that long. This one looks like the longest stretch. He had a few retail jobs in Austin and around San Marcos before coming south. Nothing standing out."

"Maybe just restless?"

"Or running from something?"

"Who knows? Retail jobs aren't known for their long-term stability."

Cookie nodded. "Could be said about a lot of jobs these days." He continued typing. "I'll check to see if he has a record."

Jamie started off simply with a search of Leah Sandoval with the keywords "missing," "disappeared," and "Foster Bluffs." She then searched for any online social media accounts.

Nothing.

"That can't be right," Jamie muttered to herself.

"What?" Cookie asked, his gaze still focused on his computer screen, one hand reaching into his brown paper bag for his after-lunch snack.

"Already, Cookie?"

"What?" he asked over the crinkling of the aluminum foil wrapped around his bean-and-cheese burrito. "I need to eat it before it gets cold." He took a bite and smiled big for her. After chewing for a moment, he asked, "What can't be right?"

"Well, I've only done a basic search, but I'm not seeing anything for Leah Sandoval on social media. I mean, there are a few other Leah Sandoval accounts, but I can tell from the photos that they aren't right." She leaned in closer. "Except for one..." She clicked on an account that had a photo of the beach as the profile photo, a woman standing in the corner, back turned to the camera.

"Maybe this one is it," she said, clicking on the account. "We might have something..."

"Except..."

"Except that it's a private account."

"Can't send a connect request if she hasn't been online since she disappeared. She'd either not see it if she's in trouble or would be suspicious if she was trying to stay off the grid."

Cookie polished off the first burrito in short order as he worked. He wiped his lips then said, "I'm still amazed by how many people put all kinds of stuff on FriendConnect. I mean, people trying to hide still putting photos up. Blows. My. Mind."

Social media had proven a tiny treasure trove for private investigators. Even those who paid in cash and used burner cell phones would still, on many occasions, check in online with friends and blow their covers. The biggest hindrance to hiding long term was the reality that people were creatures of habit, and all but a rare few were unable to stay completely isolated for longer than a couple of weeks. It began to wear on the psyche. Even those more motivated to remain anonymous still required occasional contact with the outside world. That understanding guided Jamie's work. She knew time could work in her favor in longer-term skips because, at some point, the skip would reach out to someone, somewhere, and leave a trace.

She just had to know where to look.

Cookie continued typing. "Okay, here we go. Looks like our friend Michael has had a couple of minor brushes with the law: drunk and disorderly, two counts with a month in between, and..."

"And what?"

Cookie continued reading. "It looks like he had an argument with a past girlfriend or maybe wife. It says 'domestic disturbance' here."

"Well, that could be any kind of relationship, right? Domestic can mean any family member—spouse, aunt, whatever."

"Yes, of course," Cookie said. "I'll make a couple of calls and see if we can get more information before contacting him for an interview."

Afternoon turned to dinnertime, and the sun retreated to night-fall. "I really hate it getting dark so early. Still not used to it," Jamie said as she closed her laptop. "You want to go walk him with me before you go home?"

Cookie nodded, tied up his work, and slipped his laptop back into his backpack before standing up.

Jamie clapped her hands at Deuce to wake him from his slumber. "C'mon, boy. Time to go."

Deuce popped out of his bed, his sausage body wiggling in readiness. They gathered their things, with Jamie holding Deuce to keep him from going down the stairs solo. With his thick middle and low proximity to the ground, being carried was better for his joints.

"He's so spoiled. You know that, right?" Cookie gave his favorite pet a rub behind the ear.

The downstairs fed into a back hallway leading into Hemingway's, and Jamie spotted Marty behind the bar, prepping for the dinner crowd. He waved at them as they passed.

"You need to leave him here?" Marty asked. "I'm sure he could make some tips while you're gone."

Jamie shook her head as she placed him on the ground. "Maybe later. Going to take him out with us for a bit, and then I'll be back. He'll be ready to work the dinner rush."

Jamie walked toward her Tahoe and stopped short before opening the door. She pointed at a familiar black dually. Alastair Finn had just stepped out and was walking toward them.

"What the hell is he doing here?" Jamie asked.

Alastair smiled as though he hadn't noticed the cold welcome. That was one of fifty things that annoyed Jamie about him, even though their paths had just crossed for only the second time. He walked to the front door, taking note of Deuce, who stood waiting to go inside the car.

"Who's this little guy?" he asked, bending down to pet Deuce.

"Don't touch my dog," she replied. "He doesn't like people he doesn't know."

Deuce didn't seem to get the memo because he rubbed against Alastair's legs, searching for more affection—or French fries. Deuce could be bought with most fried food. Jamie ignored her pooch's temporary lapse in judgment and opened the door to put him in the back seat to take him to a nearby park for an evening stroll.

"What are you doing here?" she asked.

"Ask your partner," he said. "This used to be one of my dad's favorite places. Stopped by to get one of Marty's famous burgers for him for dinner."

"Marty mentioned your dad was sick," she said. "I'm sorry about that."

He shrugged. "Life's tough, right?" He turned to Cookie. "How's your mom?"

Cookie's expression softened. "She's good, thanks." He then told Jamie, "Let's go."

She nodded and said nothing more, slipping into the driver's seat and closing the door as she watched Alastair Finn go inside Hemingway's Pier. The idea of him in her home base made her skin itch. *Who is he to just start showing up and claiming my domain as his own?*

Cookie tapped her on the shoulder. "He can't feel your death stare. And even if he could, it would make him happy. We don't want him happy. We want him gone."

"So he knows your mom?"

"Kind of. I mean, Port A is a small town. Even your archnemesis might like your family. It's rude not to ask about them."

Jamie glared one final time. The fact that she couldn't burn a hole in the back of Alastair's head with her angry gaze didn't deter her.

"He gets a point for politeness, but he needs to find a new haunt."

"I know you think of Hemingway's as your home, but there's a lot of history here from before your time. You're still a newbie by Port A standards. Alastair's dad and Marty are friends from way back. His dad is good people. And yes, the dude's an asshole, but he's good at his job, and we need to keep our eyes on him, so maybe Marty can pick up some intel for us."

For the first time since she'd claimed Port Alene as her home, Jamie considered the vast history preceding her planting roots. She felt a pang of shame at the arrogance of such a position and, at the same time, frustration that Alastair Finn had the true right of calling the island town home. She was still a guest, earning her keep, earning her way.

It stung.

Cookie climbed into the passenger seat, and the two left to take Deuce on his early-evening jaunt. Deuce was good for them in more ways than could be counted. Becoming consumed by cases was all too easy, consumed by the unknowns of their skips, by the work itself. Deuce reminded her—reminded them both—to take a beat now and then. Stepping away often brought insight once they stepped back into a job.

"I don't like him... in there." When Deuce snorted in the back seat, Jamie reached behind to pat him on the back. "And don't you go acting nice to him, either. Next time, more teeth, less rubbing."

Jamie pulled onto the road and looked at Hemingway's Pier in her rearview mirror. Bad enough that Alastair Finn had taken her last job—he'd also laid claim to her safe harbor.

But she had larger concerns at the moment. Renata's little sister was out in the wind, and Jamie, reminded of the time her niece had disappeared, knew she couldn't simply turn her back on the case.

She would deal with Alastair later.

One crisis at a time.

CHAPTER FIVE

The Port Alene Police Department building was a well-groomed but unassuming space, a small brick rectangle with a Farley boat planter placed by the sidewalk. Farley boats provided an important part of Port Alene history, having helped fishermen and anglers who hoped to navigate the Gulf Coast's sometimes difficult waters. Jamie always smiled when she saw a Farley boat planter in town. The last count she had was ninety-two spotted in the area. Despite the care that the PAPD building had been shown in its groomed yard and clean walk space, the structure also displayed faded signage and weathered spots, a reminder of island weather coupled with an up-keep budget the size of a thimble. The concrete parking lot showed its age. Long snaking lines of asphalt filler created a road map of repairs. Jamie knew Detective Herrera often handled some of the maintenance himself.

Jamie stepped out of her vehicle and waited for Cookie, who'd been completely glued to his phone on the entire drive over. She'd almost forgotten he was in the car, which was a very unusual experience. He was normally the one to provide comic relief, adjusting her radio in order to find the most annoying music. But not that day. Cookie was *persona ocupada*. She waited for Deuce to hoist himself out of the backseat, which he did almost completely unassisted. She attached a leash to his collar, and he snorted his disapproval.

"Hey, you coming, or are you going to keep texting your girlfriend?" she joked, standing with the driver's-side door open.

He glanced up at her long enough to offer a quick side-eye and paused his texting marathon to hold a finger up to signal a moment. Thankfully, he had offered his forefinger and not the other one.

She resisted an urge to goad him further. He was clearly in the middle of some sort of drama, possibly with his uncle, and she only hoped it wasn't something that would translate into their doing more pro bono work. They couldn't afford it. Marty would have them washing dishes for a year if they didn't pay down some of their tab soon.

After what seemed like forever—but turned out to be only two minutes when she checked her watch—Cookie stepped out of the car and closed the door.

Jamie decided to tuck her sarcasm in her back pocket for a moment. "Everything okay? You completely failed to entertain me on our drive over here."

Cookie shrugged his substantial shoulders. "Sorry about being delinquent in my duties. We've got some family drama happening, and I'm trying to be Switzerland." He glanced at his cell phone, his lips pressed tightly together.

"How's that working?"

"Apparently, I suck at diplomacy when it comes to my family. Now my mom and my aunt are both pissed at me." He tucked his cell phone into his back pocket. "Okay, enough of this mess."

He waved a hand toward the walkway, and Jamie made her way to the front door with Deuce leading them. She opened the door to find Annette, Detective Herrera's assistant, at her desk. She was the gatekeeper and a damned good one. Fortunately, she had a soft spot for Deuce. They all did.

Annette had a name twenty years too old for her. She was maybe in her midthirties, and her full-sleeve tattoo on her right arm was on display in a simple navy sleeveless wrap dress. She was beautiful in a gloriously unconventional way—her skin showed its love of the island sun and wind, and her eyes crinkled at the edges when she smiled. Her dark hair showcased a bright-fuchsia streak winding its way through her ponytail. She was behind her computer, typing something that kept her fingers busy for a bit before she looked up to address Cookie and Jamie. She tilted her head to greet Deuce first.

"How are you doing?" Annette asked, pushing herself back to greet Deuce with a pat. "I'm guessing you're looking for David?"

"Yes. Is he in?"

She replied, "Unofficially, yes. Let me go back and see if he's available. He's been on the phone all morning."

Jamie nodded and waited patiently, glancing over at Cookie, who seemed to be resisting the urge to pull his phone from his back pocket again. She could hear the vibrations from all the texts blowing up his phone.

"Don't answer it," Jamie cautioned him. "Nothing good can come from stepping in the middle of two women arguing, and you need to put your full attention here."

"You're right," he replied. "I know. You're right."

She looked at her partner and could see that whatever that argument was about, it was getting to him. His mother and his aunt were the two most important women in his life. Jamie joked that she was in third place after those two, but it was a distant third. She would take the bronze. At least she was on the podium.

Cookie shifted his weight from one leg to the other, the vibration of his cell phone causing him distress.

Jamie held out a hand. "Give it here."

"Why?"

"Because they're lighting you up like a Christmas tree. I can see it on your face. You're clenching your jaw so tight it's going to snap." She wiggled her fingers at him. "Hand. It. Over."

Cookie begrudgingly followed her order, placing his cell phone facedown on her outstretched hand.

Without glancing at it, she tucked it into her handbag. "You aren't missing anything. The feud will wait for your return."

While Jamie sat down in a metal folding chair in a modest waiting area, Cookie eyed four other empty chairs but remained standing. Deuce quickly assumed the napping position.

Annette returned from the hallway where Detective Herrera's office was located. She returned to her desk and said, "He's free now. Technically, this is his day off, but you know... He can't help himself."

Jamie nodded to Cookie, and the two walked down the hallway to Herrera's office. The door featured a central glass pane with his name etched in white letters on the front, and she could see him at his desk. He looked up from his laptop and waved them in.

"How are you, David?" Jamie asked. "I hear you're working on your day off."

He stood up from his chair and nodded. "Yeah. Two drunk guys hurt themselves drag racing grocery carts at the Sip N Save. I'm behind on my paperwork." He reached over to pet Deuce.

Bow to the furry king of Port Alene.

"Not sure if you heard, but we returned Marian to Sandy's Shell Shop," Jamie said.

Detective Herrera tossed his pen onto the desk, smiling as he looked down. "Glad to hear she's back. Sandy called it in like usual, but we don't bother with the formal paperwork anymore. Marian always seems to find her way home."

Herrera shook Cookie's and Jamie's hands then gestured to the seats across from his desk. "Please. Make yourself as comfortable as possible in my cheap chairs."

Herrera's office was all business and very spare—metal desk, basic wooden bookshelf half filled with reference books with a layer of dust that suggested they hadn't been useful for some time, and a few photos of Port Alene on the wall, likely taken by a family member or local artist searching for display space. If Herrera had a family, nobody would know it from stepping into his office. Jamie didn't know much about his personal life, and she felt that was deliberate.

"How can I help you?" the detective asked. He leaned forward, his fingers interlaced, hands resting on the desk. He seemed weighed down by something he likely couldn't share. The bags under his eyes added age to his fortysomething features.

"We wanted to talk to you about Leah Sandoval."

Herrera nodded. "Yes. Her sister came and filed a missing person report. Do you know her?"

Cookie shifted in his seat and straightened his posture. The chair was not made for a man of his stature. He grimaced as he moved, the metal creaking as he adjusted. "She's a family friend. Renata came to us because she said she was told that there wasn't much that could be done. She seemed to feel that you believed there wasn't much of a case."

Detective Herrera sat back in his chair, arms crossed over his chest. "You two know enough about missing person cases to under-stand our situation. There isn't any evidence to support the idea that Leah is under duress or missing due to another's actions. Her car is gone, along with her cell phone and her wallet. No one saw or heard anything unusual at her apartment complex, and there's zero talk about any type of confrontation. And she's not a kid. She's twenty-five."

"What kind of car does she drive?" Jamie asked.

Herrera checked his notes. "A black El Camino."

"Very cool. Also a pretty recognizable body style," she said. "It's a car you'd notice." She thought for a moment. "Did you talk to Leah's roommate, Michael?"

Herrera's lips tightened at the question.

"Sorry," Jamie said. "Of course you did."

"I did, and he also let me look around the apartment. She did leave some things, so it's hard to know if she packed an overnight bag. So maybe she left for some reason and plans on coming back."

Jamie glanced at Cookie, who offered her a "he's right" look supported by a shrug. Maybe Renata was an overprotective sister unable to control her younger charge. Jamie considered having to tell Renata that maybe, just maybe, Leah took off for a bit without feeling the need to explain her actions. Still, Jamie knew the feeling—the idea that this time was different. She wouldn't close the door on that instinct just yet.

"You know I have to dig a little, given our history," Jamie said.

"Of course." He leaned forward slightly in his chair. "I would expect no less."

"Was there anything unusual or anything that stuck out to you? Even something small?" Jamie asked.

Detective Herrera pushed back in his chair a bit, rocking as he considered the question. "There were a couple of very small things, but nothing I would say indicates this to be a missing person case."

"Like what?" Cookie asked.

"Well, it looks like she left stuff in her bathroom. You know—toiletries, toothbrush, makeup. I'd consider this a possible check in the missing column, but I have sisters. They had multiple makeup bags, and that stuff was spread all over the bathroom and their bedrooms. They could have packed half of it up, and I'd never have noticed. So that one could go either way."

Jamie eschewed cosmetics for the simple fact that she had good skin and little patience for anything more than mascara and sunscreen. It just seemed like such a hassle, and she preferred spending that time on other pursuits. Like chasing sleep. Or chasing people.

"Okay, that's fair," Jamie said. "Anything else?"

"Michael didn't have an alibi we could confirm because he said he was home alone the last night she was supposedly seen. He told

Renata that he came home after work, ate dinner, and watched TV all night. Couldn't find any witnesses in his apartment complex who said they remembered seeing him come home when he said he did."

Jamie knew the difficulty that could pose. Many alibis were difficult to prove, especially when someone claimed to have simply spent an evening at home. In most situations, Jamie herself would have trouble proving her own alibi since she often did that exact thing when she was off a job. Her social life consisted of binge-watching a comedy with Deuce, who made for a lousy character witness. And he had bad taste in male friends as of late.

"Nothing else?" Cookie asked.

Herrera leaned forward and thumbed through some files in a plastic divider on his desk. He sorted through them until he found one and opened it for review. He scanned the few brief pages inside and said, "There's one more thing, but again, not sure it means anything, considering the other things we know."

"We'll take anything we can get."

"Michael did say that she seemed more anxious than usual the last day he saw her." He read from his files. "She was on her phone a lot, distracted, and in a bad mood." Michael had said he didn't know her well enough to know what normal behavior looked like. He also added that she was a woman and that "women are moody and won't tell you why because you're supposed to know these things."

Cookie smiled at Herrera's recitation of his notes.

"Not a word," Jamie cautioned her partner. "Not. A. Word."

Herrera closed his file and returned it to the stack on his desk. "So, ignoring the debate about how women deal with frustration, her behavior could indicate an issue, but put together with everything else we know, the evidence currently points to her leaving on her own."

Jamie and Cookie sat quietly with the information Herrera had offered. After several moments, Jamie stood up. Cookie took note and followed suit.

"Thanks for taking the time," Jamie said. "We're going to look into a few more things, and then we'll meet again with Renata."

"I hope things work out."

Detective Herrera knew better than most people how certain missing person cases impacted Jamie. He'd traveled that road with her when he helped her search for her niece, Kristen, and that shared experience had forged a bond both strong and unspoken. When they crossed paths for a case or just in town, they never spoke of it, but it was always there between them, this thread of trauma forever connecting them.

Jamie extended her hand to Herrera, then Cookie did the same. Deuce, sensing food would not be part of this meeting, stood up and pulled toward the office door. After a nod and polite wave to Annette, the trio were out the door with little more than what they'd had when they arrived. Still, it seemed quite possible that Leah had simply left of her own accord and would be back after she'd dealt with whatever drama she'd hoped to escape when she left Austin.

Cookie held his hand out. "Meeting's over. Give me my phone back. I need to make sure no felonies transpired between my family members while we were in there."

"Maybe don't check? Plausible deniability?"

Cookie cracked a smile. "I wish."

Jamie dug in her bag and handed him his phone. "If it makes you feel any better, your family's definition of drama is so... basic. Entertaining but basic."

"Speaking of family, did you call your dad back?"

Jamie shook her head, looking off toward the ground. "It's on my list today."

"Maybe he's got good news." Cookie's expression told her he didn't believe a word of it.

"No, he doesn't call unless he wants something big. He uses Grace for everything else."

Grace was Jamie's younger sister, the favored sibling in their family, mostly for her willingness to continue assisting in their con jobs. Her skills were impressive, Jamie would admit, but she wasted them on all the wrong people.

"Maybe I'll meet her one day."

"You better hope not. She'll take you for everything you've got."

"I'm not that stupid, Jamie."

She patted him on the shoulder. "It's not that, friend. She's just that good." Jamie nodded toward the car. "C'mon. We have one more stop before checking in with Renata."

"Right."

CHAPTER SIX

Port Alene continued to betray visitors with her frigid temperatures and winds so harsh that even the tallest palm trees seemed eager to retreat. Jamie shuddered as she stepped out of her Tahoe and waited on Cookie, who was digging in his backpack for who-knew-what. As he leaned forward in the passenger seat, his favorite black beanie strained to stay on his head, the seams stretched to the point of slipping. She shook her head and smiled, knowing the current weather was testing the limits of his normally sunny outlook.

She tapped on the hood and was met with a grimace and a hand gesture that could have been interpreted in any number of ways. She grinned and turned her back to him and waited for him to leave the warm cab of her vehicle. When he emerged, he frowned at the wind hitting his face.

"When is this going to end?" Cookie pulled at his hoodie and straightened his beanie.

"I had no idea you were so fragile." Jamie stood with her hands on her hips, bag hanging from the strap on her shoulder, and waited for his retort. "But I hear you. My blood is too thin for this cold."

"Hey, global warming is real, and it's now made its way to us."

Jamie nodded, thinking, *This is no time to poke the bear.* "This looks like the right building. Number 505 should be over there," she said, pointing toward the apartment complex on her left. "You think he's here?"

Cookie shrugged. "If he's here, I hope he likes surprises."

"Surprises are for birthday parties," Jamie said, staring at the building. She hated nothing more than being caught off guard.

"But in our line of work, one of the best advantages we have." Cookie pulled a hand from the warmth of his pocket long enough to gesture toward the apartment complex across from them.

Jamie tilted her head downward to keep her face from meeting the cold wind head on. She shivered as it traveled past her neck, blowing her ponytail to the side. "Last one on the right."

"Oh good, first floor. If we were higher up, there could be ice on the stairs, and I could slip and die, leaving you without a partner." Cookie grinned as he said it although Jamie knew he hated stairs in all forms.

"It's a good thing Bobby Z broke your fall during that scuffle."

Jamie's reference to Cookie's struggle with a skip who grabbed him and pulled him down a flight of stairs earned her a grimace. To be fair, the guy was close to the same size, and all the padding between them no doubt protected them from breaking any bones. Still, Cookie complained of a tricky knee after that day although Jamie suspected that was merely a way to avoid running unless a heated pursuit was involved. He was known to be faster in the water than on land. His scuba diving skills were well known at the local dive club.

They arrived and stood at the front door. Jamie knocked and waited to hear something inside, a rustling of activity or movement. She could hear what sounded like a television but nothing else.

A second knock.

She heard a thump followed by a few choice profanities. After several seconds, the door opened to reveal a twentysomething man who'd clearly been woken from a nap. He squinted at them as if his eyes were still adjusting to daylight.

"Yeah?" was all he offered.

Jamie started by saying, "Are you Michael Ferguson?"

The guy met her question with a squint. "Yeah. Why?"

"We're friends of Leah's sister, Renata, and we wanted to talk to you for a minute. Can we come in?"

Michael glanced over his shoulder, the door cracked only enough to reveal his body. "She hasn't been back, so I don't know what to tell you." He kept the front door fairly close to him, but Jamie could smell stale cigarette smoke from where she stood.

"I know. We just have a few questions, and then we'll get out of your way." Jamie wanted to slap him into consciousness but thought better of it. Having him a bit off-balance might prove useful. Maybe he'd say something he wouldn't otherwise share.

He looked at Cookie, who took the prolonged stare as an invitation.

"I'm her partner" was all he said.

He opened the door wider. "Okay, yeah, come in." He turned his back on them to clear some clothes and a pizza box off a nearby love seat. Jamie took note of the blanket on the couch, further confirming her suspicion of their interrupting some solid afternoon slumber. She glanced around the room, careful not to stare too long or appear to be making judgments, but her eyes lingered on the piles of takeout boxes and plates in the nearby kitchen. Michael noticed her gaze.

"Sorry. Cleaning lady has the week off. I wasn't expecting company."

"No problem. We didn't mean to wake you."

"That obvious, huh?" He scratched his forehead then smoothed his dirty blond hair with a hand. "I'm working nights now, and it sucks. I have to sleep whenever I can."

"What do you do?" asked Cookie, who'd settled back into the faded love seat.

Jamie felt the cushions shift and straightened her posture.

"I do night security for a construction company. Usually have to just hang out in a trailer and walk the property to keep people from stealing equipment or vandalizing the area. It's not hard. It's just boring as hell, and it screws up my schedule." He scratched his head once more. "I feel like a damned vampire."

Jamie knew the feeling. She would charge extra for all-night surveillance or even hire a friend, James Brown—no, not that one—to do the work instead. It was worth it to not have to pull multiple all-nighters.

"How long have you had this job?" Jamie leaned forward, her forearms resting on her legs, her posture struggling to counterbalance Cookie's. "Is security what you normally do?"

He shook his head. "No. I've done different construction jobs. I'm a little good at a lot of things, so I can usually pick up work most of the time."

"Do you work alone at night?"

He nodded. "Most of the time. Sometimes, a manager will come and check on me, but it's just to make sure I'm not sleeping when I shouldn't be."

Cookie asked, "You have a weapon with you when you work?"

Michael's posture changed, stiffening.

Cookie added, "I mean, do they expect you to sit out there all night without any way to defend yourself?"

The last thing they needed was Michael going on the defensive. The clarification worked. He relaxed his shoulders and nodded.

"I have a concealed carry license. A little security never hurt."

Jamie nodded. "I bet. Imagine it's a little creepy being out there alone." She then glanced down the hallway. "We don't want to keep you, but we just wanted to talk to you about the last time you saw Leah, what you know of her. And maybe we can take a quick look at her room."

Michael's gaze followed Jamie's toward the bedrooms. "I guess so. I still feel like she might come back. She left some stuff here."

"So you saw her last... when?" Jamie discreetly pulled her notebook from her bag, taking extra effort to not call attention to it.

Michael sat for a few seconds in silence, his head tilted as he looked up toward a beer poster taped to the wall. "It was the thirtieth, I'm pretty sure. Day before Halloween. But I saw her in the morning. Around nine."

"How did she seem?"

"I mean, I don't know her that well. She was only here a few weeks. Definitely not a morning person. And she hated that I didn't have a coffee maker. She would always go out for some."

"Where?"

"The local Shop-n-Save on Fielding. She'd run over there and get coffee and bring it back."

"Anything else?" Cookie had scooted forward on the couch determined to swallow them both whole. "Did she mention anyone or say anything about friends or work?"

"She didn't really talk too much, and we were on opposite schedules. I heard her talk to her sister sometimes. I think she was looking for cleaning jobs because I remember her asking about it." He gestured around the living room with a sweep of his arm. "Clearly never hired her."

Jamie tapped on her knee with her pen, wrote a few notes, then stood.

Cookie sank deeper into the couch then hoisted himself out of the cushion hole. "So which room was hers?"

He pointed down the hallway. "The one on the right. I haven't been in there since her sister came by. I don't think she likes me."

"What makes you say that?"

He shrugged. "She was pretty angry at me for not knowing where she went. Maybe she thinks I'm not telling her everything, but I don't know Leah very well. She paid her rent to me for the month in cash, and we only talked now and then."

"Well, she's worried, that's all." Jamie nodded.

She walked down the hallway with Cookie right behind her. She took a quick survey of the room. The space was sparse. A full-sized bed and box spring along the back wall, along with a small bookshelf and a battered chest of drawers, were the only furnishings in the room. Nothing had been hung on the walls to offset the worn brown carpet. The comforter on the bed was folded halfway as if tossed off when Leah got out of bed. Jamie opened the drawers, searching around the clothes, which already appeared shuffled and rifled through, not placed neatly inside but a jumble of fabric in each one. Marlboro Light 100 filters were crammed into a circular plastic tray.

Nothing seemed out of the ordinary, other than the fact that Leah hadn't had the time or the care to decorate the room, an indication that it was indeed a brief stop on her path to somewhere else.

The bathroom offered no clues other than her toothbrush and makeup, still on the small single-sink countertop. The first glance didn't seem to show she'd intended to leave for good—maybe just a brief trip to see an old boyfriend or someone Renata didn't approve of. *Hard to say.*

After a few moments of giving the room his own once-over, Cookie shrugged and stepped back out. Jamie did the same. They walked to the living room and saw Michael reaching for a pack of cigarettes and a set of matches in a shiny black cover with gold foil. He bent the cover backward to light the match against the sandpaper strip and dropped them on the counter.

Jamie picked them up. "Vince's Comedy Club? This place any good?"

"No idea," Michael said. "I just found them here. I guess Leah left them."

Jamie resisted the impulse to reach over and tap him on the back of the head. Most people didn't realize they knew more about a person or a situation than they realized, and this was a prime example. Michael claimed not to know anything about Leah and where she spent her time other than coffee runs, but maybe she hung out at a comedy club. Maybe she knew people there. Jamie gave her partner a small nod.

"Okay, Michael. Thanks." Cookie took a business card out of his back pocket and handed it to him. "Call us if you think of anything else. Like the comedy club or something."

Still crickets. Maybe he'd been smoking something stronger.

Once the door closed behind them and they were out of earshot, Cookie asked, "You believe him?"

"Seems pretty straight up. Clueless, tired, whatever, but at least we have a little something. The place doesn't look like he tried to clean something up after the sign of a struggle. Her room tells me she could have just left for a while. We have no idea if she took clothes or other stuff with her. Car's gone, and no hits on that from local PD. Phone's gone."

"Maybe she just left and didn't want to tell Renata why."

They had reached Jamie's Tahoe, and she opened the door. "Maybe. But we should check one more place." She started the engine. "You like comedy?"

CHAPTER SEVEN

Corpus Christi was often called the Sparkling City by the Sea. While the majority of the city's miles were made of water, at the moment, they were made mostly of traffic. The vehicles on SPID, South Padre Island Drive, ran three lanes each way with enough cars to offer a steady stream of brake lights for viewing pleasure. The exit ramps reminded Jamie of cannon shots, with trucks pulling boats and trailers darting off the main road at high speed as though they were lapping in the Indy 500.

"I'm just waiting for one of these trucks to jackknife a trailer, switching lanes like that," Jamie complained, her eyes shifting from her rearview mirror to her side mirror as she switched lanes. "This isn't Charlotte, people. Slow down."

Cookie's head bobbed to the music on the radio. It had a dance beat, catchy but slightly annoying. Jamie worried the earworm would be stuck in her brain for the next three days. Cookie looked out his side window and tapped on the glass. "All the places on restaurant row are looking nice and busy. Good for the economy."

"I'm sure the mayor will be glad to hear that you approve of his economic initiatives to get more people to eat out. Where is this place again?" Jamie asked Cookie, who was still swaying to the music. "Did you put the place on the GPS?"

"Yeah, I did." He glanced at the directions on his phone. "Three more miles and then exit."

"Got it," Jamie said. "What's the name of the place again? Vince's..."

"Vince's Comedy Club."

"I hope Vince is hilarious."

"Hard to say," Cookie said. "Their FriendConnect page only has about five likes per post. You'd think that being funny would get you a bigger online audience."

"Well, maybe they're just funny in person. You know how some people are funny one way but not another?" Jamie wondered why she was suddenly trying to defend the funny or unfunny nature of people she'd never met. Maybe that was because she had the kind of sense of humor only a select few would appreciate. Jagged sarcasm was often an acquired taste.

With a wave of his hand, Cookie prompted Jamie to exit, and she followed his instructions. They had their own shorthand for almost every situation and had been together long enough that they finished each other's sentences. Marty had joked that they were like an old married couple but without the romance. Jamie smiled when he said it. She wouldn't admit it, but she had come to rely on Cookie as her family, the ridiculous younger brother she'd always wanted but didn't get. Her only brother, on a scale of one to ten, ranked a negative million.

Even Cookie wouldn't dispute that.

Jamie continued on the access road, and as she drove, the lighting and buildings were fewer and farther between. The buildings went from nicely lit and fairly well kept to weatherworn and neglected, as if they were aging as she traveled down the road. "I can't wait to see the kind of crowd Vince attracts."

Cookie surveyed the area and nodded. "I never come down this way. No reason." He pointed at a strip center and said, "Turn here."

Jamie turned her Tahoe into a parking lot loosely patterned with cars, the dim lighting leaving a great deal to be desired. The concrete was cracked and the faded guidelines barely visible. She'd walked in such conditions alone plenty of times, but she wouldn't recommend it. She stretched her neck to read the signs for the businesses. A barber shop looked decent and fairly well kept. The sign was aging, but it was clean and had a couple of potted plants and a striped barber pole out front. The place next door didn't seem to warrant the same care. It had a generic sign stating Nails and Waxing and gave little confidence that the business would be good at either one. Vince's Comedy Club was on the far-left corner, with the sign missing the *l* in Club, so it was really Vince's Comedy Cub.

Tonight's feature includes hilarious bears? Jamie thought.

Maybe a dozen cars, perhaps a few more, were parked in the general area in front of Vince's. One outdoor lamp flickered on and off, offering a glimmer of hope that one wouldn't get mugged on the way to one's car once the show was over. Two men stood outside, both wearing baseball caps and both smoking, as if conspiring on their latest set. *Do improv performers wear baseball caps?* Jamie had no idea.

A woman exited the front door with a cell phone attached to her ear, easily visible with her chestnut hair pulled back in a ponytail. She had a black waitress apron tied around her waist, creating a divider between her neon-orange T-shirt and her jeans. She walked away from the two smokers and continued toward the barber shop's front door, where she sat down on the bench outside.

Jamie watched the woman on the phone. "Time for a drink."

Cookie nodded and said, "Let's go inside and see what this place is all about. I could use a good laugh."

Jamie and Cookie walked through the parking lot to the glass front door for Vince's and pulled it open. The two men nodded at them as they passed through the entrance, friendly enough, both taking long drags from their cigarettes. Cookie gave the guy the half nod that was common among the men she knew.

She shook her head at him.

"What?" she said.

"You know what." She mimicked his half nod.

Cookie threw one back at her and pinched her arm. "Quit giving me a hard time. All the cool dudes do it."

"What about the cool chicks? They do it too?"

"Yes, and it's clear you aren't in the cool club because you have no clue."

Jamie swatted Cookie on the shoulder as they stepped side by side into the entryway. A young woman, maybe midtwenties, with auburn hair pulled back in a ponytail, looked up at them through green hipster glasses. Her smile reminded Jamie of those forced smiles she'd served up during elementary school class pictures—in the years she was in school when they were taken. Sometimes a small con job took priority.

"Cover's ten bucks. Grab an open table," she said, pointing toward the half-empty seating area behind her. She held her hand out as Cookie reached into his back pocket for his wallet. He dropped a twenty in her palm and gave her the half nod.

The woman cracked a genuine grin, taking Cookie's cash and placing it in a cash box behind her podium. Jamie walked ahead of Cookie to survey the seating options. Jamie pointed at a round four-top behind two bald guys drinking cheap beer.

"That looks good. Far enough away from the stage if the act stinks but close enough to hear them if they're funny."

They made their way to the table, weaving down aisles positioned haphazardly on the main floor. The club had the proper amount of dinginess and lousy lighting, punctuated by the scent of stale beer.

Cookie and Jamie took their seats just in time to watch three men get up on stage. One started clucking like a chicken while the other two danced around him. Not one chuckle in the room so far. Not even a pity laugh. Even the drunk guys in the corner failed to represent. Jamie figured it was a bad sign when even drunks didn't think someone was worth the hassle to heckle.

A waitress walked up to their table—neon shirt, jeans—the woman who'd been on the phone outside. "Can I take your order?" she asked. "We've got some specials on draft if you're interested."

"Two Shiners, please," Jamie said.

"We don't have it on draft. Bottles okay?"

Cookie nodded. The waitress turned and walked to the back bar to order her drinks. She returned a few moments later with the beers. The house wasn't really packed, so keeping up with the patrons' orders didn't seem to be much of a challenge.

She placed the bottles on the table without the benefit of coasters, which wasn't much of an affront since the tables looked like they'd been pulled from a recycling bin. The laminate surface on theirs was peeling around the edges and bubbled in several places.

"That'll be eight bucks," she said, standing at attention with her tray table resting on her hip.

Jamie reached for her bag at the same time Cookie went for his wallet. "I got this one," she said and handed the woman a ten. "Keep the change."

"Thanks."

As the woman turned to leave, Jamie asked, "Hey, can you help us with something?"

She turned back to them. "Sure."

"We're looking for a friend, and we heard she was here recently," Jamie said.

She tipped her head down, folding her tray underneath her arm. "I just started working here last month, so I'm not sure I can help. This place has a pretty high turnover. Tips aren't great."

"Not surprised." Jamie pointed lamely toward the act still dying on stage. "I'm sure you get more tips if you can get them to quit their set early."

"It's not this bad all the time. You picked the wrong night to be here. Mondays generally suck. Our weekend nights are the headliners. These amateur nights are really just a bunch of office warriors and dentists living out a lifelong dream to try improv."

"Glad you said it and not me," Cookie chimed in. "I really should ask for my cover charge back."

"Good luck with that," she quipped. "The owner would arm wrestle a child for a quarter in the parking lot."

"Tight with money, eh?" Cookie replied.

"Like a rubber band. And the tips here are fine on the weekends if you can get the best shift, but during the week, I should just stay home. And my name is Penny, so he has fun with that."

Jamie held her phone up to show Penny a photo of Leah and her sister. The waitress glanced at the act on the stage—still bombing. She reached for the phone and looked at the photo. "She looks familiar, but it was dark. She seemed a little distracted. If it was her, I just chatted her up a bit, mostly small talk."

"Did she have any tattoos or anything you'd remember?"

She stood still for a moment. "Not that I remember." She handed the phone back to Jamie. "And I'm not sure the person I saw was your friend." She shrugged. "Wish I could help you more, but there's not much to it." She pointed at another waitress. "Maybe ask Manda? She's been here a while. She might know more."

Penny waited until Manda looked in her direction and waved her over.

Manda walked toward them, her blond hair pulled into a high messy bun. She tucked a pen into the apron wrapped around her waist, an order book peeking up from one of the pockets.

"What's going on?"

"These two are looking for a friend of theirs and think she was here before."

Jamie took the prompt from Penny and held her cell phone up with the image of Leah filling the screen. Then she studied Penny, who walked away from their table toward the next set of patrons waiting for a drink. She glanced at Cookie then back at Penny and again at Cookie.

After Manda stared at the photo for a second, she returned the phone to Jamie. "Yeah, she's been here a couple of times with some guy."

"What can you tell me about him?" Jamie asked.

"Stocky guy, muscular. Had a tattoo down one side of his arm of a spider web with small skulls on it. That was memorable. Really short hair, a little longer on top. Jeans. He came in and just waited by the front door. She left her table and walked over to him. They left together. She seemed... a little uptight."

"Uptight being with him?"

"Hard to explain. She wasn't into the comedy."

Jamie wondered how many people in the room at that moment felt that same way. If people came here to relax and laugh, Vince's Comedy Club had its work cut out for it.

"Do you remember when?" Cookie asked.

Manda glanced up toward the ceiling, her lips pressed together. After a moment of contemplation, she said, "Pretty sure it was before Halloween. I only remember that because I had to work that entire week to cover for a girl out sick."

Jamie slipped her fingers into her back pocket and retrieved a slightly wrinkled business card. "Please give me a call if you remember anything else or if you see either one of them back here."

Manda glanced at the card, held it up between her fingers, and placed it in her apron. "Will do." She stole a glance at the main room. "I'd better get back to my five paying customers."

"Thanks, Manda," Cookie said.

Manda left to tend to her other tables. Jamie figured it was time for them to leave.

Jamie raised a finger to her eyebrow and pressed at her temple. A headache was forming in her eye socket. She wondered if she was allergic to bad comedy. She then flicked her wrist and pointed at Cookie's beer bottle. "Finish that up. You've got a good two bucks' worth left inside. Don't waste it." She checked her watch. "I need to relieve Marty of his dogsitting duty."

"You know, he really should use some of the tips he makes off Deuce to offset your tab. The dog's gold."

She smiled. "I'll work that in when my lease is up for renewal."

Cookie tilted the bottle back until all the amber liquid had disappeared. He plopped it down and wiped his hands on his cargo shorts. "Might have spilled a little." He then stood, and they waited together for another moment to see if the comedy had improved since they'd last tuned in.

Nope.

"It takes a lot of guts to put yourself up there for people to judge," Cookie said. "I'd never do it, and I'm way funnier than those clowns."

Jamie wondered how the place stayed afloat with such limited patronage. *Probably drugs or money laundering. Kidding. Or not.*

"Let's go," Jamie said. "This place is depressing."

"Guess that's not a good endorsement for a comedy club, is it?" Cookie replied. "I've been in a better mood leaving a funeral."

"They're probably not going to put that on a bumper sticker."

Jamie reached for the door, but Cookie moved ahead of her to prop the glass door open, a film of fog forming on the glass with the humidity hitting the barrier. He craned his arm forward and leaned back, making space for her to go through.

"Your mama taught you good manners. You know that?"

The parking lot looked every bit as sad and desolate as it had when they'd walked in. Few people were clamoring to spend a night at Vince's Comedy Club. Dental office openings had better attendance.

Cookie offered, "The guy she left with? Maybe someone she knew? Doesn't sound like a bad date since she left with him."

"Haven't you ever had a really bad date and wanted to make a run for it?"

Cookie smiled at his partner. "You know me. It takes a while for me to uncover the crazy. They all start out nice enough."

Jamie tried to make sense of what the waitress had told them. Leah may or may not have shown up alone at Vince's Comedy Club and then left with a mystery man, either willingly or not.

"So what's next?" Cookie asked.

"We've got our missing sister in a dead-end comedy club with a guy, and she doesn't seem to be happy about any of it."

"It doesn't make any sense."

A small knot formed in Jamie's gut. She didn't know if they'd found a dead end or a new lead, but she knew she wouldn't stop until she got some answers.

CHAPTER EIGHT

Coming from Vince's Not So Funny Comedy Club to Hemingway's was an experience in contrasts. At ten o'clock on a Monday night, Marty's place, from the looks of the parking lot, had a solid crowd. Jamie and Cookie walked into the bar to find Marty busy serving patrons and Deuce snoozing on the floor in the corner.

Jamie decided to let Deuce be for the moment. After all, an evening of being fed and adored by Marty's patrons had surely been exhausting. She and Cookie found two open spots at the bar by the television and claimed the stools. Only moments passed before Marty placed two beers in front of them. Jamie glanced up to see the local news anchor discussing a missing person case—the second wife of a well-heeled real estate mogul named Edward Van Zant. The female reporter, blond bob grazing the collar of a black peacoat, clutched a microphone in her gloved hands as she spoke directly to the camera, her expression serious as she used the historic Franklin Hotel in Austin for her backdrop.

Cookie pointed at the screen. "Husband did it."

"Husband paid someone to do it," Jamie countered. She took a sip of her beer. "Just wait, there's going to be so much stuff coming out about her, him, them. All the dirty laundry is going to start showing up on the media clothesline."

"I don't think I'd like to be famous, but I'd settle for rich and anonymous."

"Rich and anonymous is definitely the way to go," Jamie said. "All the money, none of the drama. Just us living on a private island, drinking beer and watching the seagulls."

"Don't you think you'd get bored after a while?" Cookie said. "I mean, I know I'm pretty good at relaxing, but I think you're too high strung for that life. You still don't know how to live on island time."

"Because island time is so slow," Jamie joked. "I mean, it makes your granddad look like a track star. Takes forever to get anything done."

"Or maybe it's a lesson to teach you that most things aren't as urgent as you think they are. People always in a hurry for what? Not much. Plus, island time is perfect for doing surveillance. I mean, it's so boring, but it's good training for the work."

"I'd much rather chase people than do surveillance," Jamie said. "Except for the running. Not a big fan of the running."

"Ditto."

Cookie signaled to Marty for a second round of beers, and Marty obliged after making a set of margaritas for three women at the end of the bar. From the looks of them, they could be related—sisters or cousins—all three with bleached-blond hairstyles from the eighties, brightly patterned blouses, skirts, and cowboy boots. One wore tooled teal boots with brightly colored leaves at the toe. They were truly wearable art.

"What are the Swansons up to tonight?" Cookie asked. "Big night out at Hemingway's?" He glanced over toward the women, prompting Marty to do the same.

"Oh, I think one of them just finished another closing out at Pelican Moorings," Marty said. "They're just burning through a bit of that commission by spending it here, which is fine with me. Shop local—support your bartender." He winked at Jamie.

"These women all fall for your bullshit, don't they?" Jamie joked. "That seaman vibe, the gray beard and matching flowing hair." She waved a hand up and down in front of him. "They buy all of it, hook, line, and sinker. Forgive the fishing pun, but it fits."

"I do okay," Marty said. "But you know me. Not built for a long-term relationship."

"I hear that," Jamie replied. "I don't want to be around anyone for more than, like, two hours. Three if he's really good looking, maybe four if the dude reads."

"You want to know an interesting fact about those women over there?" Cookie asked. "Some local lore you may have never heard?"

"Hit me." Jamie glanced again at the television screen. It was a local car commercial, easily one of the worst she'd ever seen. The projected background of the mountains made absolutely no sense since the dealership was in the valley, and the sound quality was so bad that it traveled above the chatter of the bar crowd.

"Those ladies are considered some of the most ruthless real estate agents in South Texas."

"Really? In the savage business insides of Port Alene?" Jamie laughed at the idea of it, as they looked like they might run a successful souvenir shop.

"Oh yeah. Don't let their looks fool you. Plenty of men over the years have tried to land one of them, and from what I heard, they made a pact in their twenties to never marry. They were going to put all their effort into their businesses instead."

Jamie liked the women more and more. "So none of them are married? Even now?"

Cookie shook his head. He nodded toward the trio. "The one on the end? Mary? She got close once, but rumor is the other two ran him off. Don't know what they did to him, but he dropped her like third-period French."

"Hmm," Jamie said. "Cheers to them, then." She held up her glass to Cookie, who gave her a clink and a drink. "Maybe we should do that—make a pact to stay single and build an empire?"

Cookie shook his head. "Umm... no. Mrs. Hinojosa numbers one, two, and three are all out there. And running an empire sounds damned exhausting."

"Well, I imagine other people would run it for you, and you could just take the missus out on the private jet."

"Sounds like a lot of maintenance."

"The jet or the wife?"

"Both. Besides, I trust people about as much as you do. If I have a lot of money, I'm micromanaging the shit out of it." He looked at her. "Oh, lord. We're going to be together forever, aren't we?"

Jamie winked at him. "Only if you're lucky."

"Did you call your dad yet?"

She grimaced at her friend. "Way to kill the vibe." She nodded. "I sent Alex a text," she said, clarifying the man's name. "So you can stop nagging me about it."

"I nag because I care."

"I know you do," Jamie said. She looked around Hemingway's, taking in the comfort of her local hangout. "It's really important for me to keep my distance with him. You know that. I can't keep getting dragged into their drama. It messes with me."

"I get it. But maybe this will be the time when you can handle whatever it is and then just move on for a while. At least you won't have the unknown hanging over your head the entire time."

She knew her partner was right, but she also understood her family in a way he never would. His mom, his family, always had his best interests at heart. Alex and Stella Rush were a powerful couple. Not in the sense of extensive criminal reach or influence. In that regard, they were still somewhat small-time cons working a regular hustle. But they were powerful in the way that all parents are powerful, even long after childhood is in the rearview mirror and one can view them with adult eyes and experience. Jamie could never completely cut off her family for the simple reason that, in her grown-up, guarded heart, she still wanted one—wanted them to be one.

And they would use that against her.

She would keep Alex at a distance, no matter how hard he tried to pull her in. She had no choice. She couldn't afford whatever price she would pay by being back in their fold.

CHAPTER NINE

Jamie awoke to the sound of a knock at her door. She lay in bed, groaning at the unexpected call. She glanced over at the clock on her bedside table, the numbers 8:32 mostly visible from behind the book resting in front of the device. She craned her head up to check on Deuce, who was as interested in getting out of bed as she was, his snoring uninterrupted by the bang on the door.

"Let me in," Cookie said from the other side. "I've got tacos."

"Use your key," Jamie called. "I'm not getting out of this bed."

The lock moved, the sound of the key finding its way until the door opened. Cookie was freshly showered, his hair still partially wet, and his Hawaiian shirt of choice, burgundy with yellow flowers, looked to have made contact with an iron, although it peeked from beneath a heather-gray zip jacket. He seemed unusually chipper, although San Juan's breakfast tacos did have such an impact on people. They were magical in a way impossible to explain.

"I got you two bacon and egg, plus one bean and cheese for later," Cookie offered.

Deuce perked up to the scent of the food contained in the small brown paper bag Cookie dangled in his hand.

He looked down at the pup. "Don't worry. I got you one too."

"Please tell me it isn't bean and cheese," Jamie pleaded. "The gas he lets off after is enough to force me out of my loft all day."

"You know I wouldn't do that to you," Cookie said, a smile on his lips.

"You do that on the regular, Cookie."

"Oh, right," he replied. "I didn't do that to you today. Bacon, potato, and cheese today."

Jamie, sitting upright in her bed, reached for a ponytail holder from her bedside table to tame her morning hair. "Let me brush my teeth really quick, and I'll be out in a sec. Can you put some coffee on?"

Cookie nodded, his attention fully on unwrapping Deuce's breakfast taco, taking a moment to pull the tortilla into small pieces, and placing it in his dog dish in the kitchen. Jamie lumbered out of bed, still dressed in an oversized Santana T-shirt. She stood slowly and stretched, releasing a yawn so wide she felt her jaw crack.

Cookie let loose a laugh. "You're a real mess in the morning, you know that?"

"Hey, if I came to your house while you were still in bed, I have a feeling you'd be less than runway ready yourself."

"Are you kidding? I woke up like this," he joked, gesturing at his shirt.

Jamie grimaced at her friend, leaving him to handle coffee duty while she pulled herself together. She closed the bathroom door behind her and surveyed her face. *Definitely not a beauty first thing out of bed*, she decided. She'd been told she had great skin, which was surprising due to the amount of sun she'd taken in the last few years, even with sunscreen. Her face rarely saw the touch of any makeup, save for specific jobs that required her to become someone else, although she did love a little mascara. Still, small laugh lines seemed more evident as of late, and she wondered if, at almost thirty-seven, her face would start showing more of her secrets. She still considered herself young—the thirties were supposed to be some of the best years of a woman's life—but she wondered if that required said woman to know more about what she planned on doing with the rest of it for it to apply. She had few goals for her life outside of choosing which jobs to take each month to make ends meet. Deciding between living in the moment or an aimless existence could go either way.

Jamie exited the bathroom, her hair tied back in a ponytail and her eyes better able to focus on the breakfast Cookie had laid out. He sat at her dining/work table with two cups of coffee in mismatched mugs, the scent of steaming-hot caffeine mixing with the breakfast tacos. Her appetite was fully awakened. She had to appreciate her friend. He knew the way to her heart was through her stomach, just like his.

Jamie slipped into the seat beside Cookie, the chair creaking. "Maybe I should cut back on the breakfast tacos," she joked. "Don't want to break the chair."

"Yeah, you might be breaking one twenty by now," Cookie dead-panned. "I'm like a jealous girlfriend. You eat whatever you want, and you still have those chicken legs." He slid the two foil-wrapped tor-tillas filled with San Juan goodness her way, along with a tiny cup of roasted salsa verde. "Here, eat your breakfast tacos before they get cold. I got extra verde in case you want to blow your sinuses out."

Jamie unrolled the tortillas and poured the salsa in a long line atop the bacon and eggs. She took a bite and washed it down with her coffee. "I really needed this," she said. "Thanks."

"Of course." Cookie had made quick work of his first one and was quickly finishing his second, his coffee barely touched. "Still surprised that someone Leah's age doesn't have any social media," he said, chewing and swallowing as he spoke.

Jamie wiped her hands with a napkin then used it to clean a spot on the table where stray drops of salsa verde had escaped from her breakfast. "Not really. Think about it. There are a couple of reasons why people aren't online. Some are introverts, some are rebelling against FOMO and being 'on' all the time, and some are hiding something. Which one do you think Leah is?"

Cookie considered her analysis. "Well, I was thinking introvert before last night, and maybe she still is. Or she has reason to stay low. We think she was at Vince's Comedy Club. She knew the guy, it seems. Maybe she's just someone who lives her life in person."

"That's pretty rare."

"It shouldn't be."

"Agreed."

Cookie reached for the wrappers and gathered them up to place them inside the paper bag. He crushed it into a ball then tossed it into the open trash can by the wall.

"If I had a quarter for every time I made that shot..."

"You'd have enough for a beer downstairs."

He pointed at her phone on the table. "Let's divide up the labor and see what pops up."

Cookie typed feverishly, his substantial fingers working his laptop keyboard. Jamie resisted the urge to look at his screen. Instead, she checked her email on her phone to see if anything new had come in from Leah's roommate or other people she had contacted. No updates on that front, but she did get some other news.

"Hey, we received payment on the McKinley case. Finally."

Cookie nodded, his attention still on his own laptop. "Only took them three months, but hey, they paid, so I guess we can't complain."

"What a mess, right? I hate doing cheats and divorce cases. Makes me wonder how anyone ever stays married. Or wants to get married."

Cookie stopped typing, his expression solemn. "Jamie Rush. You do not want to be alone forever, do you? One of those women hanging out at the bar late at night, reliving your glory years when you used to chase cases and do dangerous stuff." He tilted his head. "You know I'm going to find my soul mate, preferably one with a very large trust fund and nice parents, and I won't be able to take care of you forever."

Jamie leaned back in her chair and crossed her arms. "I'm not going to be hanging out in bars like some sad sack. I'm going to be at home with my five bulldogs and ten cats, watching bad TV and eating entire boxes of frozen Thin Mints. I think it's a lovely way to spend my later years, don't you?"

Cookie grinned at his friend. "You could go outside and yell at teenagers to get off your lawn. You know, for fun."

"I like it. That sounds like a good time." She leaned to the side and rested her head on his shoulder for a second. "I think we should just be old and unmarried together. We can gamble at Erin's place and run the tables."

Cookie rubbed Jamie's head, messing up her ponytail. "You can be my Plan B. If I'm not married in twenty years, you get to be my backup wife."

"Deal."

Jamie had just returned her attention to her phone when it pinged with a text from a number she didn't recognize.

"Oh, here we go," she said.

"*Qué?*"

"It's from Manda from last night. It says, 'Just realized I remembered something. The guy your friend was with was wearing a memorial shirt. It said, "Justice for Layla Ramirez." Remembered it because the case was on the news a couple of years ago. Hope that helps.'"

"Layla Ramirez? Why does that sound familiar?" Cookie started typing, putting Layla's name in his search bar. "I feel like I should know this."

Jamie scooted her chair closer to Cookie and craned her neck to read the search results. The page reloaded with several links leading with Layla's name. Cookie double-clicked to open the top match.

A photo of an attractive young woman in her early twenties popped up on the screen. She wore a navy V-neck T-shirt and a smile. The headline read, "Corpus Woman Gunned Down by Boyfriend."

Cookie scrolled down, Layla's photo disappearing from the screen as the first paragraphs of the article came into view. Jamie and Cookie read silently together, with Cookie scrolling farther for the rest of the story.

"I remember this," Cookie said. "Her family was in the press, really unhappy because her boyfriend had been violent in the past and more should have been done to protect her. I saw them on TV. Heartbreaking what happened to that family."

The story was coming back to her—the young girl's face, the parents' outcry for justice. And then, like so many similar cases, it seemed to fade into the background, lost in the news cycle of bringing the latest horrific injustice to public attention.

"She looks like she could still be in high school, that young face," Jamie observed, with the photo of Layla on the screen again. "It says she was twenty, but she sure doesn't look it."

Cookie nodded, saying nothing.

Jamie's thoughts turned to her niece, Kristen, and she noted that their ages weren't too far apart. Cookie looked at Jamie, studying her face.

"You okay?"

Jamie swallowed hard, but the lump in her throat remained. "It's just a shame these women can't get the help they need." She cleared her throat. "The help they deserve." Jamie'd had a friend once who hid her most private burdens from her, the bruises carefully covered with makeup and long sleeves. Jamie had tried to get her to open up, to confide in her, but it never happened. Her work took her to a new town, as it often did in those days, and they'd lost touch. She wondered what had happened to Darla—if she'd ever gotten out, if another friend had been able to reach her in a way Jamie hadn't. That was one of the most difficult parts of her nomadic calling—every now and then, she wanted to plant roots but couldn't, if not for the town, then for a few people in it.

Cookie's fingers navigated his laptop keyboard, the screen refreshing search results for Layla Ramirez. He scanned each article, looking for information or photos that would prove helpful. After a few more clicks, he came across a memorial page. On the front page were several photos of family and friends gathering for a memorial on the second anniversary of her death.

Jamie returned to leaning over Cookie's shoulder, studying the photos from the event. Reaching over to scroll down, she got the side-eye from Cookie. He hated it when she took over his tech. She glanced at the URL then typed it into her phone.

"Just trying to help," she explained. Jamie scrolled through the website in search of photos from the most recent memorial. She selected a few that included men who might fit the description of the man Manda saw, copied them, and pasted them into a message to Manda.

"Do any of these men look familiar?" she asked in her text.

A couple of minutes passed before she received a response: "Second photo. Guy on the left."

Jamie zoomed in closer on the image and spotted a hint of the tattoo Manda had described before. It was a match. She leaned over again to check Cookie's screen. She pointed at the man Manda had identified. The names of the victim's family were included in the caption below.

"Looks like his name is Ronnie Arroyo," he said.

Jamie nodded, reaching for her coffee cup. "Maybe we'll get lucky." She took a sip. "How about you? What do you think?"

"I think we're going to need to find Ronnie Arroyo, and I think he's not the kind of guy who likes small talk."

"We still have Michael's domestic disturbance issue that we need to follow up," Jamie said. "Talk to the other side just to make sure he isn't involved somehow."

"He didn't seem like the type to put his hands on anyone."

"Those are the worst ones."

Cookie closed his laptop and tucked it into his backpack. He pointed at Deuce. "Is he covered while we go out?"

Jamie finished the last of her coffee and put the mug in her sink. "Maggie is coming to take him out for the day. A little beach time, about four minutes of chasing seagulls and sandpipers before he gets tired. He's got a big day ahead."

"So do we," Cookie said. "But Deuce is going to have way more fun."

Jamie was willing to trade fun for answers. She wasn't good at fun anyway—not built for it. She wanted to know where Leah was, if she was safe, and if she was missing because she wanted to be gone. A closed case was more satisfying than any day on the beach. She wasn't sure what that said about her, but she hoped it meant she was the right person for the job.

CHAPTER TEN

Port Alene remained in the thirties during the day, throwing in twenty-mile-an-hour winds for good measure. The local weatherman proclaimed numerous records were being broken with the winter temperatures, with Mother Nature's edge taking a deeper bite into the local landscape. The palm trees seemed as out of place as if they'd been searching for Margaritaville but accidentally ended up in Maine.

Jamie reached for her heavy jacket, now in regular rotation, and traded her ball cap for a beanie. She'd even purchased a dog sweater for Deuce, extra large. Yes, she'd become a woman who dressed her dog in clothes. She thought he looked adorable. Deuce's glare told her he disagreed. She couldn't let Cookie see him that way. She would never hear the end of it.

She wondered how long her town would keep its community embraced in ice. She shivered as she stepped outside, pulling her beanie down lower on her forehead, her chin tilted down to shield her face from the wind.

After she took Deuce for his morning walk, Maggie, her dogsitter, had come to pick him up for a day of adventures. Deuce barely glanced back when Maggie arrived, leaving Jamie to wonder if she was an absentee dog parent, with all the surveillance work she'd been doing. Then she reminded herself that Deuce loved anyone who would take him to the beach and feed him treats. He was simple and easy that way, like some men Jamie knew.

It's not a low blow if it's true.

Cookie met Jamie outside Hemingway's Pier, his car in his regular place. He always placed a parking cone in the space when he wasn't there, and Jamie often took the cone and moved it around the parking lot for fun. He probably suspected she was behind the gag but never called her out on it. He just smiled and shook his head, returning it to its proper place.

"We can take your truck this time if you'd like. We already ate breakfast, so no risk to that luxe leather package."

Cookie walked toward Jamie, who was standing next to her car. "Let's not ruin a good thing by switching vehicles. Besides, I just got my interior detailed."

Cookie drove a King Ranch F-150 and loved that truck more than he loved most people. He'd bought it used, got it for a steal when it was headed for the repo lot. Jamie suspected he'd become addicted to supple leather seats.

"You sure you don't want to drive this time?" Jamie asked.

Cookie wrinkled his lip at her. "This is *not* a road trip or surveillance vehicle. This baby is all short drives and dates. No sand, no dirt."

"Cookie, it's a King Ranch model. You know, after the vaqueros and the cattle land? Your truck was made for all that fun, dirty stuff."

He waved off her analysis of his vehicle. "We're taking the Tahoe like we always do because it's nice and broken in and it has such a good close ratio for cases."

Jamie smiled at him and nodded in an exaggerated fashion. "You're full of crap, but you're also right."

She opened her tote and double-checked that she had everything she needed. Behind the driver's seat, Jamie kept a canvas bag with water bottles, a large bag of Doritos, and a package of Thin Mints. She had a weakness for cute Girl Scouts selling sugar. She placed her cell in the hands-free stand on her dash and entered Claire Reynolds's last known address in Monroe as the GPS destination.

"So half hour or so ETA?" Cookie asked between sips from his coffee cup.

"You just finish your coffee so you can get to working while I'm driving. I'll take care of getting us to Monroe."

Monroe was a small, sleepy town known for little more than being close to a naval air station and a strip center. It was an older area, not shown much love by developers or investors. The homes were dated, and many of the roads were in dire need of repairs beyond the basic tar patching that pebbled the streets. Jamie never had much cause to visit Monroe. The place simply wasn't interesting enough to warrant her attention.

"You know, I once dated a girl from Monroe," Cookie offered.

"Really? How on earth did you meet a girl from Monroe?"

"Met her at a bar in Corpus. She was nice enough, but..."

"Boring?" Jamie asked.

"Like watching grass grow. I think she must have been born there, because her idea of excitement was going to put gas in her car."

Jamie drove to Highway 361 and followed it out of town through Corpus Christi. As much as she liked Corpus, she hated the traffic. Although the city had never really taken off the way San Antonio, Austin, and Houston had, the place retained a promise of untapped potential. It was like a less-favored sibling in Texas, its valuable assets sometimes overlooked.

"Have you found anything else about Michael that could be useful?" Jamie asked Cookie, who'd been sitting with his laptop resting on his legs, the technology jostling around due to the bumps in the road. "You aren't on one of those dating websites again, are you?"

Cookie glanced her way then returned his attention to his laptop. "Oh ye of little faith." He added, "I did find the profile of this cute little brunette..."

Jamie reached over and punched her friend in the arm. "Focus."

"I'm kidding!" Cookie said. "Sheesh." He tapped on the keyboard and used a forefinger to skate along the touchpad. "Michael seems like a pretty straight-up guy. I did find that he's involved with an online forum for fantasy football. Can't say he seemed like the type."

"That sounds almost as boring as living in Monroe," Jamie said. "Lots of people are into fantasy football, I guess, although I have no idea why. I'd rather just bet on the actual teams."

"You're no fun."

"So I've been told." Jamie waved her hand at Cookie. "You find anything interesting?"

"He seems to have a lot of side conversations."

"A female person?" Jamie's voice lifted at the suggestion.

"Well, one is texasfantasybabe2120, so I'm guessing it's a woman, although in this day and age, it could just as easily be some old dude living in his mom's basement. Hard to say."

"Okay, so he's got rapport with some hot chick who's into fantasy football. Texasfantasybabe is a catfish. It's a fifty-year-old dude."

"You're so jaded," Cookie replied. "But in our line of work? Fair."

"I guess it could be just two people into football, flirting online," she said, not believing a word in that sentence.

Jamie knew exactly what Cookie meant. It could be an innocent conversation. Part of studying subjects involved following instincts. Sometimes, those instincts led places that made no sense on the surface, but with some persistence and digging, puzzle pieces would begin to fit together. Jamie had spent countless hours studying online conversations between people, learning to spot hidden meanings in comments and discerning how a conversation topic could be used as cover for something more nefarious.

They were ten minutes away from Monroe. The scenic appeal had lessened substantially as they traveled closer to their destination. The area leading to Monroe began to reflect the town. Fewer trees were in sight, and the landscape flattened, a building here or there peppering the landscape. They passed a defunct bowling alley, half the letters missing on the front sign and weeds growing tall around the concrete base of the building.

"Let's hope Claire is home and also willing to talk to us about her incident with Michael."

Jamie took note of the homes as she pulled into the neighborhood—single-story brown-brick structures coupled with weathered wood, with no real front porches or decorations. Curb appeal sufficed by way of actually having a curb. When Jamie came upon the home's address, she parked a couple of houses back and took a moment to survey it—unremarkable, like the others, though the lawn was trimmed and neat.

Jamie reached for her bag and pulled out her notebook. She thumbed through her notes to recall which questions she wanted to ask and in what order. She took a couple of minutes in silence to gather her thoughts, and Cookie, knowing her well, avoided tossing sarcastic comments her way. Although it didn't seem like it, Cookie did know when to hold his tongue. His superpowers included reading a room and responding, although he also enjoyed tossing a good sarcastic comment Jamie's way as often as possible.

"So you want to lead on this one?" Cookie asked. "I figure it's best to have you be the face of the conversation since I'm, you know..."

"A large man with a ridiculous Hawaiian shirt peeking out of his hoodie? You think she won't take us seriously?"

"I told you. My Hawaiian shirts are sad. Had to wear them somehow."

Jamie tucked her notebook and phone into her tote and stepped out of her vehicle. Cookie did the same, taking time to straighten the creases in his shirt created by his seatbelt. He reached into his shirt pocket and pulled out an aluminum tin of mints. He popped one into his mouth then extended them to Jamie.

"That pico de gallo just stays, you know what I mean?"

She did. She reached for two mints then signaled to Cookie. "Ready?"

He nodded and said nothing more, instead following her to the front door of the address they had for Claire Reynolds. Jamie walked lightly up the concrete stairs, taking note of the cracking ends. The harsh gaze of summers there could break just about anything—and anyone, given the right circumstances.

The door was fashioned of plain wood, with no windows or side panels to give a peek into the house. Jamie knocked on the door. Cookie remained at the foot of the steps, as the two of them on the small porch would feel like too much of an intrusion.

Jamie knocked a second time and heard the lock turn on the other side. The door opened, and Jamie wasn't sure what she was expecting, but she was pretty sure that woman wasn't it. She was taller than Jamie by several inches, maybe five foot ten, with short, spiky blond hair and muscles that would make most men jealous. She wore square, red-rimmed glasses, a T-shirt with some obscure band reference, and a gorgeous tattoo of a magnolia on her forearm.

And no smile.

"What do you want?" she asked Jamie, her thin lips tight again as soon as she finished speaking.

Jamie glanced at Cookie, who looked down at his feet in a lame effort to hide the grin on his face. He always enjoyed seeing her thrown off her game.

"Yes, I'm looking for Claire Reynolds. Is she home?"

"Yeah, I'm Claire. What do you want? And if you're selling anything, you damn well better get off my front porch. I knew I should've gotten one of those No Solicitation signs."

"Can we speak for a few minutes? I'm here about Michael Ferguson."

Her expression softened. "What about him?"

"Michael's roommate may be missing, and I understand you and Michael had some sort of issue a few years ago?"

Claire gave Jamie the once-over then peeked around to survey Cookie. "Who's the hottie?"

Cookie blushed at the flirt.

She let him squirm a moment before answering. "That's my partner, Cookie."

Claire shrugged. "Sure, c'mon in, but only for a few minutes. I have to get to work soon."

"Thanks," Jamie said and motioned for Cookie to come up behind her.

They walked inside the small home and found it, too, was a substantial contradiction to Claire's physical appearance. The tan checkered couch had two matching recliners, a small coffee table with a lace doily covering the surface, and end tables to match. On a corner bookshelf stood a tall cabinet with enough glass figurines to keep a person dusting tchotchkes for the better part of an afternoon. More glass figurines and dainty teapots and mugs served as decor in the living room and nearby dining room.

"This is my grandmother's place," Claire said, explaining her surroundings. "I moved in to take care of her."

"Ah, now it makes sense," Jamie said. "You didn't look like the figurine-collecting type. No offense."

"None taken, trust me." Claire gestured toward the chairs. "Have a seat."

Cookie and Jamie each claimed a recliner, while Claire sat across from them solo on the couch. She leaned back, crossing her legs and sinking into the cushion behind her.

"Thanks for taking a minute, Claire," Jamie said. "We just wanted to talk to you about Michael and what you know about him. Through our background check, we found that there was a domestic disturbance that included your name."

"Yeah, hell of a night, that one," Claire said, taking off her glasses for a moment to rub an eye with a thumb.

Cookie sat straight up in his chair. "So what can you tell us? And, more important, what can you tell us about Michael? How well do you know him?"

"Well, I haven't seen Michael in a couple of years, and we don't keep in touch. He was friends with a guy I was dating at the time, and that's how we knew each other."

Jamie rubbed her hands together for a moment then returned them to her lap. She wanted to reach for her notepad to take notes but thought better of it. She didn't want Claire to stop talking.

"So what happened that night? Were you in any danger?"

"From Michael? Oh, not even," Claire replied. " Have you seen him? I mean, it wasn't like what you may be thinking." She sat more upright and leaned forward on her elbows. "We were at my boyfriend's apartment complex, and we had a pretty good party go-ing."

"So did your boyfriend and Michael get in a fight?" Jamie asked.

Claire shook her head, her spiky hair not shifting an inch with the movement. She straightened her glasses. "So, a neighbor and I got in a fight, and Michael jumped in the middle to break it up. His elbow caught me in the eye and gave me a shiner, but it was com-pletely accidental. We were all pretty drunk and obnoxious. I yelled at him and told them it was his fault because I was pissed at him for jumping in the middle of my business."

"Oh" was all Cookie offered.

"Not my best showing as a friend, I know," she replied.

"So did Michael drink a lot?"

She nodded her head. "Oh, yeah. He never missed a party. He had a real problem for a couple of years. Spun out, from what I remember Eric telling me..."

"Eric?" Cookie asked.

"My ex," Claire explained. "I thought I'd heard he was going to check into some rehab or something. He could be a pretty angry drunk, I'll say that. I mean, I was never scared of him, not really. He wasn't violent, not from what I remember, but he did break some stuff."

Jamie asked, "Can you tell me where to find Eric?"

Claire bowed her head. "Eric died last year. He was drunk, fell asleep, and drove into a ditch off Old Chapman Ranch. Stupid bastard."

"I'm sorry to hear that," Cookie said.

"Yeah, that was a real wake-up call. I've been sober ever since. No alcohol, not even on New Year's Eve. We were all out of control back then. Guess it's good that me and Michael were able to turn it around. Eric's rock bottom didn't give him a chance to do the same." Claire glanced at her watch. "Don't mean to be rude, but I've got to get to work."

Jamie and Cookie stood up in unison, and Jamie extended her hand. "Thanks for talking to us, Claire. It helps."

"Sure, no problem. I hope everything works out with Michael's roommate."

"Me too," Jamie said. "Me too."

Cookie and Jamie returned to her SUV. She started the engine and waited for him to get himself sorted in the passenger seat. He reached inside his pocket and grabbed another mint.

"So that was... unexpected," Cookie said. "I thought we were walking into a traditional domestic disturbance case, and it turned out to be a drunk rager with Michael breaking up the fight instead and taking the fall for it." He shook his head. "You just never know."

Jamie smiled at her friend. "Well, I can't say I'm unhappy that it turned out different than we thought. I'm also glad to hear that Michael isn't an abusive bastard."

"You know what this means, though?" Cookie asked as they drove out of Monroe and back toward the island.

"It means that we can cross Michael off the list, but where does that leave us?"

"It's time to see if we can find Ronnie Arroyo."

"So, we've taken off one lead and added a different one?"

"Looks that way."

CHAPTER ELEVEN

Jamie and Cookie sat in line, awaiting their turn to load onto the ferry. The off-season for summer tourists had come, so the line comprised only a few vehicles in the queue. Jamie peeked her head out her window to check how many ferryboats were in operation. Four total were there, although only two were running back and forth at that particular moment. The line lead, wearing a reflective vest over his T-shirt and jeans, adjusted his baseball hat as the wind tipped at it. His shoulder-length hair, wavy and tangled, was light brown like his beard, and he waved the line of cars through while also pushing his hair off to the side. Jamie thought the man could use some ponytail holders on his wrist, the way she always kept one on hand.

Jamie followed the line lead's signal and followed the white Dodge Charger ahead of her, taking her slot on the right side of the ferry, angling her tires close to the rounded metal guides running along the edge of the boat. Another ferry worker carried a wheel chock and stopped, placing it ahead of Jamie's tires. She could never quite see how they secured the weight by the tire because her front bumper concealed her view, but she always trusted that they knew what they were doing and would remove it properly before she drove off after reaching the other side of the bay. The worker held his hand up in the air, made a fist and turned it side to side, indicating that she needed to cut her engine. She did so but rolled down Cookie's window first. Normally, like Deuce, he liked to stick his head out the window to enjoy the bay breeze as the ferry crossed the water, but the icy winds slapped at his skin, and Cookie quickly reached for the control to put the glass barrier partway up.

"You think Ronnie Arroyo is going to appreciate this surprise visit?"

"Not likely," Cookie replied.

The boat's engine idled up, a low roar, and the sound of churning water mixed with that of the mechanism. Jamie closed her eyes for a moment, listening to the sounds of the ferry transporting them across, and she inhaled deeply. That was as close to meditating as she would ever come, but something about the ferry calmed her, centered her. She only wished its journey took a bit longer to complete.

"Still no dolphins," Cookie complained. "I think they know when I'm on board."

A few scant minutes later, the ferry arrived on the other side, a duplicate crew awaiting their arrival and taking their places at the head of the ferryboat. Jamie watched as the worker reached down for the wheel chock, pulled it back, and signaled her to start her engine. She did so and waited her turn to drive across the metal step to solid ground. The line was orderly, as ferry passengers had no other choice but to comply succinctly, and the single-lane road soon split into two lanes, with Jamie staying on the left and hitting the gas the moment she had the opportunity to pass the Toyota next to her. Nothing against the Camry, but those folks were clearly in no hurry.

The sun shone brighter in the afternoon. Partly cloudy skies had given way to blue, and the heat intensified a bit as the rays were given their freedom.

"So how do we handle approaching Ronnie?" Cookie asked, his face turned toward the window, his short hair mussed by the wind cutting through the window.

Jamie had considered that question. "I'm guessing that we should catch him before he goes to lunch unless he's an early bird. And his boss said he was working today, so we'll at least get a crack at him.

Maybe just go slow and ask him a few questions. Get a read on his personality first, you know?"

Jamie had spent time in Rockville Heights over the past year. Two cases led her to the shady sibling of Port Alene. It had its lovely areas as well, but Jamie's work rarely took her to any of those locations. That was the nature of her work.

Jamie continued to follow her GPS's instructions, turning left down a road that opened up after passing several portable metal buildings. They were in different states of health—some were newer models, the metal clean and reflecting light from the sun, while others were sullied with rust and wear, the pattern revealing no rhyme or reason. Another two miles and three more turns led Jamie to IslandCraft RV & Marine. The shop's sign was large, the paint in various states of translucence from being exposed to the elements, but the sign's state projected a sense of credibility rather than a lack of attention. As they walked toward the main building, Jamie surveyed the business. Two large metal buildings were there, with boats lined up in an ordered way in an open work area, as if they were waiting to launch—except for being stuck on land.

"Should we go inside to the main office?" Cookie asked, glancing around the property. The hood on his sweatshirt blew in the wind, pushing his collar up like a bad Elvis impersonation. After Jamie walked closer to correct the issue, he said, "Thanks. Don't want to embarrass you in public."

"Since when?" she deadpanned.

As they continued walking, Jamie picked up the pace and made her way toward two men standing by a boat being loaded onto a trailer. Cookie kept pace alongside her.

"Excuse me," she said, singling out the friendlier-looking man of the duo.

He was tall and lanky, easily six feet, wearing a tattered flannel shirt with a black SkullCrusher T-shirt underneath. His hair was long but thinning, his hairline clearly on the retreat.

"I'm looking for Ronnie Arroyo," she said. "Is he in today?"

The man looked at his workmate, who offered nothing more than a shrug, then said, "I think I saw him earlier in the back. Maybe check the second line? He was working on a Gelcoat repair."

Jamie gave her thanks and signaled to Cookie, and the two made their way toward Ronnie's location. As they moved closer to the work yard around back, Jamie saw a solitary man kneeling while applying blue tape to the side of a fishing boat. He looked up from his work as Jamie came closer to him.

"You looking for the manager? He's in the boathouse office in the front." He signaled in the opposite direction.

Jamie shook her head. "You Ronnie Arroyo?"

The man glanced toward the ground then back up to her. He stood up, his full size proving him larger than Cookie. "Who's asking?"

She held her hand out. "My name is Jamie Rush. I'm working on a case where I think you might have some information that could help."

He reluctantly shook her hand and looked at Cookie. "Who are you?"

"I'm Cookie. Her partner."

"Nice name."

Jamie could tell by the look on Cookie's face that he didn't care for the new guy.

The man nodded. "What can I do for you?" He stood with his arms crossed across his large chest, his expression giving nothing but slight irritation that his work was being interrupted. Jamie took note of the recognizable tattoo.

"We understand that you were seen with a woman named Leah Sandoval. Leah was recently reported missing by her sister."

His eyes flashed a hint of recognition then quickly returned to his stoic expression. Jamie had wanted to hit him hard early, given his demeanor, hoping to throw something his way that might put him off balance, if even for a moment.

He shook his head. "Where was I supposedly seen with this woman?"

"At Vince's Comedy Club," Cookie replied. He and Ronnie had an attitude standoff of epic proportions happening, with Jamie serving as mediator.

"Never heard of the place," Ronnie said. "Do I look like the kind of guy who goes and listens to people who think they're funny? And pay for it?"

Jamie appreciated his sarcasm as she, too, considered herself a connoisseur of the art form, but his stonewalling proved frustrating.

"We have an eyewitness," Jamie said.

"Eyewitnesses are notoriously unreliable. Just ask anyone in law enforcement," Ronnie stated with some authority.

Jamie had mixed feelings on the topic. Eyewitness accounts were critical in finding skips and closing cases but, in court, could prove problematic, as the human memory often proved fallible.

"Well, you must have a doppelgänger, because our contact swears you left with this woman." Cookie kept the staring contest alive, never looking away, even as Ronnie's expression turned more aggressive.

"That's a big word."

"Big guy, big word. So you denying it?"

"Damn right," Ronnie said with some conviction. "I don't go into Corpus unless I absolutely have to. Not my favorite place."

"Okay," Jamie said. "If you say so."

Ronnie reached down for the roll of gaffer tape and knelt down by his work project. "Now, if you don't mind, this job has a deadline, and I have to get it done."

"Thanks for your time," Jamie said before turning to leave.

Cookie stood for a moment, staring at Ronnie and saying nothing. She cocked her chin at her friend and signaled him to leave. He took her cue.

As they walked away out of earshot, Jamie asked, "Did you catch that?"

He nodded. "We never told him the comedy club was in Corpus."

"He was there. The question now is why?"

"I don't know, but we're going to find out."

CHAPTER TWELVE

Jamie stepped inside Hemingway's, her eyes adjusting to the lower-light atmosphere Marty adored. "Makes me look younger," he would joke, as if being mistaken for sixty instead of seventy was some huge dating advantage. Maybe it was. She had no idea. The man could go on a different date every night for a year if he wanted. He had a solid crowd that night, possibly because construction had started on a recent condo development, and many of the subs and contractors needed a place to gather. Cookie decided to call it a night. He needed to check on some family drama before going back to his apartment. Jamie glanced at the crowd. Some of the faces seemed familiar to her, but no one she'd call a friend—except one.

Erin Clay sat at the far end of the bar, catching Jamie's eye and waving her over. Jamie gave her a half nod, Cookie style, and immediately felt like a moron. As she neared Erin's stool, she spotted Deuce on the floor next to her, an empty bowl by his snout.

"Hitting the drafts too hard, I see," Jamie said, her head tilted toward Deuce, as she hugged her friend.

"He just can't handle the jalapeño poppers the way he used to," Erin said with a smile. Erin's long blond hair, straightened to perfection, was pulled into a tight ponytail, and she wore a black button-down shirt, jeans, and low heels. Erin had Manhattan style but had somehow found her home in Port Alene. She could make a trash bag look fashionable. Jamie waited for Marty's glance then signaled for a beer, also pointing to Erin, who was nursing her signature Malbec. Marty only carried it for her—secret menu.

"You just wanted to hang out with your friends in low places tonight?" Jamie reached for a barstool and pulled it to the opposite side of Erin, making sure not to wake Deuce from his fried-food stupor.

"I haven't seen you much since the Cowboys keep losing," she joked. "I miss you… and your bets."

"You should lean hard on your winter Texans from the northeast. They're crushing it again, as usual."

Marty arrived with draft Shiner Light Blonde and a second glass of wine. "You need to drink faster now that she's here," he told Erin.

"Put it on my tab?" Jamie asked him.

"Already done."

She turned her attention to her friend. "Okay, seriously, what's up? I'm current on my owe, right? I didn't rack up some extra debt by betting in my sleep. I can't be held accountable for any sleep betting."

She shook her head. "Nothing like that." She reached for her wine glass. "My dad called."

Erin's dad, whom Jamie knew, was very influential in the Vegas betting industry. You didn't want to be on Daddy Clay's radar for any reason. Many times, he'd tried to get Erin to close down her small-time snowbird-centric betting business to work alongside him in Vegas. From the outside, Erin fit the role perfectly—blond, thin, gorgeous, smart—but she wasn't nearly mean enough.

"How is he?"

"He's great. Making a fortune. Scaring people. The usual."

"You never got bullied in high school, did you?"

"Untouchable."

"He still trying to get you to move?"

"Yes, but he also asked me to talk to you."

Jamie wrinkled her brow and tilted her head. "Why?"

She traced the top of her wine glass with her finger. "Your dad called him."

She took a long drink from her draft. "Please tell me that my dad doesn't owe your dad money. Shit's going to get really complicated between us if that's the problem."

Erin smiled and put her hand on Jamie's shoulder. "No, no, love, nothing like that. He asked my dad to get me to tell you to call your father because you're ignoring his calls."

Jamie bowed her head and tapped on the bar in a mock banging motion.

"This is embarrassing. Tell your dad I'm sorry. He shouldn't be wasting his time with my family's bullshit."

"Well, he's had a front-row seat to your family's bullshit from back in the day, so it's okay. He gets it." She winked at Jamie. "And he'd never lend money to your dad. He knows it would ruin our relationship because..."

"Yeah, he'd get stiffed, and my dad would disappear and—"

Erin snorted at Jamie's joke. "We're two sick women, you know that?"

"Yes, and that's why I love you."

Jamie signaled to Marty for a second beer. She glanced at Erin's wine and noticed she still had a full glass waiting for her.

Jamie tried to downplay how angry she was at her father for reaching out to Papa Clay, but her insides burned from embarrassment. She still felt that familiar burn of hot shame even though Papa Clay would never say a single word. He treated her like family, which made her own family reaching out to him even more painful. That was a precious boundary crossed.

"Please tell your dad that I'll call Alex tomorrow once I've had some sleep and I'm less pissed off than I am now."

"You know, it's been a couple of years since—"

Jamie cut her off. "It's still his fault."

Jamie held Erin's stare, and she knew her friend understood when to back off. She'd seen, more than anyone, what Jamie's parents' life choices had done to the people around them. She still carried emotional shrapnel from her youth from trying to protect Grace, from trying to take her education as a kid constantly on the run and parlay it into something useful.

Erin deftly changed the subject, turning to stories of her favorite seniors, who were back for their winter adventures and gambling their fortunes on games large and small. "Mr. Vasquez keeps asking if you're going to stop by for a visit. I think he's interested in you being Mrs. Vasquez number five."

"Do I want to know what happened to one through four?"

"I'm guessing they're all around somewhere. His taste skews about forty years younger than himself, so you're right in the pocket."

Jamie laughed at the idea. "He's a smooth talker—all the bragging about his office-supply empire in Michigan. Very tempting."

As the friends continued laughing, the opening front door caught Jamie's eye. She recognized the man coming in, who smiled at her. She returned the smile through pressed lips.

"Damn," Jamie said.

"Who's that?" Erin asked, her smile nudging at Jamie. "He's kind of cute—tall, dark, and brooding."

"If you're attracted to jerks who steal your jobs, he's a perfect fit."

Erin opened her mouth to respond, but Alastair Finn had made his way over, propping one forearm on the bar, his other arm waving for Marty's attention.

"We keep running into each other," Finn said, his smile wider after reading the annoyance on Jamie's face.

"That's because you keep coming into my bar."

Erin extended her hand. "Hi, I'm Erin. And you are…"

"Alastair Finn," he responded, taking her hand and shaking it. "Just felt like getting out and having a beer. It's been a long time since

I've been back. Faces have changed some," he said, nodding at the crowd near the pool tables. "Maybe I'll see if I can pick up a game later."

"There are lots of other places in town for you to hang out," Jamie said. "I mean, Alibi Alley seems more your style."

Alibi Alley, an off-main street lined with dive bars frequented by questionable people doing questionable things, was named for its easy access to people who would claim they were having a beer with an alleged guilty party during the time an affair/car theft/break-in had occurred. Twenty bucks could cover a multitude of sins on that block.

"Nah. My dad and Marty go way back, and he likes me to bring him food from here."

"So you came here to get food for your dad? Again? Really?"

"And a beer. Or two. For me. He's sleeping now anyway. He's up half the night and gets hungry really late."

Recalling that the man's dad was sick, Jamie softened her stance. "I'm sorry."

"He's doing okay," Alastair replied. "Besides, I get the chance to grace you with my presence."

Jamie found Alastair's smug smile about as appealing as a stomach bug. She turned to Erin. "So, Alastair works for Big Louie." She then turned back to Alastair. "Erin's dad would eat Big Louie for a snack."

Alastair seemed impressed by the claim. "Really?"

Erin held her hand up. "I don't want to brag, but..."

"You done stealing my business?" Jamie could barely stand the look of his smug face.

Alastair shook his head. "Nope. I like seeing you angry."

He then walked to the opposite side of the bar in a second attempt to get Marty's attention. Jamie fumed as she watched him chat up two locals about something or other.

"What am I going to do about that guy?" Jamie said. "He's costing me money, and he's annoying. Don't like him."

"I think you do." Erin jabbed her friend in the side.

"Oh, no. I mean, I know my taste in the past has been less than aces, but that one?" She glanced his way. "Not a chance. I'd rather gargle a pound of tacks."

Jamie wasn't sure Erin was convinced, but she wasn't going to waste another moment on it. She doubted the seeds of annoyance would bloom into a flower of affection. He threatened her livelihood, and there wasn't a damn thing sexy about it.

Jamie intentionally turned her back to Alastair, who took the hint. After giving Erin the full rundown of what had happened with Finn and her last job, she gave her friend a hug then woke Deuce from his bar slumber.

Jamie walked Deuce toward the hallway to her loft, with no way to avoid Alastair, who stood in the way, talking to another patron. Alastair reached down for Deuce, who immediately went to him for the cheap attention. The dog had no loyalty. None at all.

"Quit touching my dog," she told Alastair.

"He likes me."

"He doesn't know you yet."

She made a clicking noise, and Deuce followed her down the hallway back to the stairs. She picked him up to carry him. "You and I are going to have to talk about your choice in friends," she told him.

He snorted and rubbed his face in her shirt. She couldn't stay mad at him for long, and they both knew it.

Once upstairs, she closed the door behind her, desperate to wash the day away—Alastair, her father, Leah's case, all of it. She wanted to clear her mind of all the things she couldn't control but was expected to conquer. She reached for a bottle of Irish whiskey, given to her as partial payment on a job last month, and imagined herself in Dublin, at the famous Dead Rabbit bar, instead of drinking alone at Hemingway's with a new nemesis crowding her territory and a dangerous father who refused to leave her alone. She decided at that moment, the next time she was ready to start over, she would research her Irish roots.

Would tomorrow be too soon?

CHAPTER THIRTEEN

J amie had always known the day would come.

She knew her father would call her one day, asking once again for her help. In the deepest corner of her heart, she still worried about turning her back on her family completely, lest she be in a position to provide safety during a dangerous time.

And her parents were addicted to dangerous times. It was their love language.

The call Alex Rush had placed to Erin's father was the last straw. She would hear him out, say no to whatever he was asking for—most likely money or something of value—then wish him well and change her number.

His first request involved asking for a ride. She made him promise that she wouldn't be walking into anything sketchy. She agreed, primarily because a talk in the car seemed less personal than meeting in a bar or restaurant and having to look each other in the eye. At least she could drive, keeping her eyes ahead, which meant she couldn't read him, but he wouldn't be able to read her either.

Jamie pulled into the parking lot of Snarky's Spirits & Beer on Highway 361 at the corner where Port Alene and Mustang Island met. She sent a one-word text to him: *Here.*

She held her breath as she waited for him to emerge from the brightly lit shop, its rows of liquor on display from the outside for shoppers to see. Finally, she spotted him walking toward the glass doors in a brown leather jacket and jeans, his dark hair longer than she'd remembered but still neatly trimmed about the collar. He was still handsome by almost any standard, and he knew it. As the door opened, he spotted her and briefly held a hand up in a weak wave of recognition. He reached for the passenger door and pulled on it, but it remained locked.

Jamie pretended she'd forgotten to unlock it, but in truth, she'd been debating leaving him in the parking lot and never looking back. She knew the wave of nerves pulsing through her would never settle until the two had finally said all they needed to say. Then she would never have to say another word, ever again.

Letting her father into her Tahoe felt like Alex was getting a foothold into her life. Jamie didn't want him to get comfortable, to assume her willingness to hear him out meant anything more than simply listening to his request. As he slipped into the passenger seat, shifting his weight to put on his seat belt, Jamie couldn't help but feel a small resentment at him occupying space that normally belonged to Cookie. She took a deep breath, her mind focused on slowing her heartbeat, which was so loud that she wondered if it would drown out her father's words.

"Okay, you've got ten minutes to fill me in."

"Nice to see you too, kid." Alex buckled his seat belt.

Jamie refused any eye contact. She left the parking lot and turned right onto the access road back to the overpass. While part of her wanted to drive through Port Alene, she had no interest in tainting her safe place with his presence—even if that meant a tour of the main roads. She wanted to protect the town, and herself, from even a whiff of his existence. So instead, she doubled back and traveled away from Port Alene toward Northland, a small neighboring community with an array of attractive vacation homes well above both of their budgets. As she turned right into the entrance, Alex took note of the two-story homes nestled on the bay, touting boats with private docks.

"I'd always hoped to live in a place like this one day," Alex said, pointing out the rolled-down window.

Humidity laced itself through the car's interior, blowing Jamie's ponytail to the side and leaving a salty residue on her skin.

"You hate the water" was her reply. "You don't even know how to swim."

Alex glanced over at her. She looked straight ahead as she drove, resisting any eye contact. He returned his attention to the row of houses on the bay.

"I like the water," he said. "I'm just not interested in getting wet."

"Because you can't swim."

"Point taken."

"Can we just get on with this?" Jamie asked, already weary from the false banter where their conversation should be. "Why are you here? Why do you keep calling me?"

Alex sighed in that way that she knew meant he was going to give her information in small portions. Like always, she would need to push him.

He rubbed his thigh with the palm of his hand, his eyes on the motion. "Well, your mom and I have a situation."

She glanced his way before returning her eyes back to the road. "I figured as much. You don't call unless you have no other option."

"That's not true," he said though his expression told her she was right.

"Alex, just spit it out. How bad is it?"

Alex looked out the window as though searching for the right string of words to put together to soften the blow. "It's a big problem." He turned toward her, his mood serious, another look Jamie knew. "Your mom and I need to leave the country."

Jamie tightened her grip on the wheel and slowed her breath so that she wouldn't lose her temper. That was a plot twist she hadn't expected.

Calm, calm, she told herself. "Okay, so you and Mom are going to run, and you're going to buy a place... where?"

Alex shook his head. "We're thinking of heading to Belize. Maybe settling in Belmopan."

Jamie took in his comment with hesitation. On the one hand, she wanted him—them—out of her life. They'd done nothing but use her and turn their backs on her when she needed them. And she was going to get her wish.

She wondered if that was what she really wanted.

She reminded herself that she was mourning only the idea of losing an imaginary family—the kind she longed for—and not for the actual family she had. She'd been given a losing hand in that regard. *Better to fold. Let them go.*

"Belize sounds like a good plan. I'm sure Mom would love it." She glanced at him for a moment before returning her attention to the road. "How soon are you thinking about leaving?" Jamie wondered if her father was telling her the truth about Belize or if he had a different destination in mind and was feeding her false information to keep her out of the loop. Unlike past situations, lying to her would be beneficial in that case—plausible deniability and all that, not that she felt he had her best interests at heart. Alex Rush was a man who prided himself on being the smartest man in the smoke-filled room. He sometimes overestimated his abilities but was also skilled at getting out of trouble.

Jamie turned onto Suncatcher Drive and was greeted with a row of enviable homes, a combination of Mediterranean and traditional beach with a few craftsman in between. Those were custom homes where the acre lots alone fetched more funds than almost any island locals could afford—correction: any honest-living island locals. She glanced at Alex, his attention on the homes as she slowly passed, and she could feel the envy emanating from his pores.

"Thinking of getting one of these in Belmopan?"

"Yes, but maybe not so close together," he said. "These people, in their seven-figure homes, don't have any privacy. I don't want people watching me in the kitchen."

"Well, you know the water lots are a premium, so if you want lots of land, try East Texas. You can find places where you won't see people for miles around."

"Nah, you know your mother. She'd go nuts without some city life, people. We're not built for that."

"But you think you're built for Belize?"

Jamie continued driving, and for a minute, the two sat silently, allowing the space between them to settle. She knew better than to rush to fill it with words—that behavior showed weakness. She let him take the next step.

"I don't know if we're built for it, but we don't have much choice," Alex explained. "We've got a good contact there once we get settled, and it's far enough away that we don't think these people will come for us there."

Jamie turned to look at him, her eyes on him before returning to the road. "Just what the hell did you two do?"

Alex straightened in his seat and adjusted the belt running diagonally across his chest. Jamie continued driving, her eyes forward and not meeting his. He reached into his pocket for a cigarette.

"Nope. Not smoking in my car."

Alex shook his head at his daughter's rebuke, but the rectangular pack of tobacco remained in his shirt pocket. He patted his pocket for a moment, as if touching the tobacco would provide the same calm as smoking it. He rolled up his window. Jamie had no interest in granting him a single comfort.

"You know how I've always wanted to find that one big score? You know, so we can stop this life and just take a breath for a while?" He waited for an answer from Jamie but received only a slight nod.

"I found one in Dallas. I did a little favor for someone up there, and he set Mom and me up with a business guy who needed some help."

"Who is this fabulous job hunter?" Jamie asked.

"I don't know if I should say..."

"What if something goes down and I need to get more involved?" Jamie asked. "Not that I want any part of it. You two really need to handle this mess on your own, but..."

"His name's Rookie Rayburn. He's a connector of sorts. Like a middleman who puts employees and... uh... businesses together."

"Like a headhunter for illegal businesses?" Jamie asked. "Sounds promising."

"Just like that," Alex said. "He gets a small cut for making the introduction if they take us on, and they did, and it was good for a solid six months."

"What were you doing?" Jamie asked. She should have kept her mouth shut. The less she knew, the better. Still, if something went sideways, she should have the truth in her pocket. Jamie turned left onto another road and continued her slow, scenic tour of the neighborhood while her father unloaded his nefarious dealings.

"Terry needed a footman and a bookkeeper, and we were the perfect pair for him. We pitched how he could trust us because we're married, worked well together—"

"Terry who?" Jamie asked.

"Terry Stokes. He owns a club, a dry cleaner, and a couple other businesses. Self-made guy, don't-mess-with-him kind of guy, and..."

"You messed with him?"

"We didn't see it that way," Alex explained. "We just needed to put aside some cash so we could invest in our gig later. Your mom has this technique for skimming that's really solid. She's used it before with smaller jobs, and it's foolproof. Except this time..."

"It wasn't."

Alex tilted his head slightly, the tension in his jaw visible. "Nope."

"Terry found out?"

"This guy's really well connected. He's got some placement in local government, people on the street, solid. We had his trust, or so we thought, so we figured small slivers of deposits wouldn't be noted. He's got so much money going through these small businesses. It was a blur of green." He waved his hand at the neighborhood outside the car window. "He could buy a whole street of these fancy homes."

"But he's looking for you now? Wants his money back?"

Alex nodded, reaching to run a hand through his hair, a nervous gesture more than anything. "Rookie gave me a heads-up but said he couldn't cover for me. We've been hiding out ever since. Terry's got connections everywhere. I can't trust anyone in my circle. Too risky…"

"So you came to me as the last resort."

"You're also one of the best—"

"Don't waste your breath. I get it." Jamie sighed and went for a second loop around the neighborhood, as their talk was going to take longer than expected. "Have you ever considered that your confidence is really just misguided arrogance? That you finally just got in over your head?"

Alex quickly dropped his charisma and replaced it with stoicism. "We got greedy. It happens. But don't you dare question my abilities or my resolve. You have no idea what I've done the last few years."

Jamie knew her father had moved into more dangerous emotional territory—like a switch had been flipped. "I hope the money was worth it," she said.

"Ask me that from Belize," Alex said. "We cleared mid-sixes. It was too good to leave on the table."

"You didn't think Terry would miss that?"

Half a million and some change was worth crossing borders to get back. Alex's confidence was puzzling and dangerous, but it had served him well up to that point.

"The way Mom handles the books? She's a master."

Jamie stifled a sigh and asked, "So what happened?"

"Terry's daughter, Cathy, is a real eagle, never liked your mom from the beginning, always poking around. She would ask questions about regular takes, moves, where stuff was going. Cathy started snooping, and..."

"Wow," Jamie said. "So did Mom ever think that maybe doing the job straight would have been better since Cathy had a thing for her?"

"Women don't like your mom. You know that."

Jamie had to admit that her mother was still gorgeous, as though being old enough to be a grandmother simply didn't translate on her features. She worked hard at it, though. That much, Jamie knew. The woman never ate dessert, even on her birthday, and spent more money on skin care and minor procedures than some Hollywood housewives. Her beauty was not only an asset but also her greatest weapon. Stella Rush was sharp and resourceful and had a mind for numbers. All those assets, she enjoyed hiding behind her external attributes. Like Jamie, she enjoyed being underestimated. It was a rare trait they had in common.

"Stella was never much of a girl's girl, that's for sure," Jamie noted.

Her mother was definitely one to enchant men and intimidate women, and she was fine with it. In fact, she thrived on it. Few things made Stella feel more powerful than letting a woman know that her husband wasn't immune to her charm.

"Okay, so you've got yourself in trouble, you're sitting on some cash, and you need... what?"

Alex ran a hand through his hair and shifted in his seat. He looked Jamie right in the eye. "We need your help to get to Belize."

Jamie scoffed at the idea. "I'm not United Airlines, conman edition. What do you think I'm going to do?"

"I just need a connection, Jamie. I can't go to Frankie anymore for credentials because he knows too much about our past work. If Terry's crew got hold of him, he'd sing like a canary. Like I said, I can't use my resources. I wouldn't have enough time to get out."

"People are not resources," Jamie corrected. "They're people." She shook her head. "So you're fine putting me in danger because you're in so deep that you're cornered." She looked out the driver's window and took a few deep breaths. She'd rather eat glass than allow her father to see her hurt. She didn't want him to have that power over her anymore, yet he still did.

Dammit, DNA.

Alex reached for Jamie, making her retreat against the driver's side door. "It's not like that, honey. I don't want to put you in a bad way by telling you more than you need to know, although I know you can handle yourself. I've seen you keep quiet in some pretty tough situations."

"Tough situations you put me in," she added. "Like this one."

"This is how we make a living, Jamie. It's dangerous."

Jamie scoffed at the notion that his life of crime was similar to something like Pacific crab fishing or firefighting or some other dangerous but honorable profession.

"Tough situations? It's a dangerous living? Can you hear yourself?" Anger bubbled in her chest, tightening in her lungs. She choked it down. "Do you know that I still go to bed at night with a ditch bag under my bed because I'm still afraid that Norman is going to find me?"

Alex flinched when Norman's name left her lips. Norman had the face of a librarian and a heart colder than an Alaskan winter. His slight build and nondescript face gained him entry to almost anywhere, the idea of him as a physical threat about as likely as a herd of unicorns flying through a bedroom window.

But through the window he came, a man so dangerous he was known by only a benign first name.

Long ago, Alex had crossed someone so terribly that Norman was sent to settle the score. Stella's insistence that Jamie keep a switchblade under her pillow had bought them just enough time. She still kept the knife in her bag, not only for defense, but as a reminder that most people couldn't be trusted.

"Your mom and I both still feel terrible about that... event," Alex said, sidestepping the trauma he'd unleashed on his eldest. "But Norman moved on. He's working on the East Coast, from what I hear."

Jamie never used her channels to inquire about Norman for fear any questions might put her back on his radar. On those rare nights Jamie's slumber was trampled by nightmares, Norman's face was the one in the darkness, tucked in the dark corners of her mind.

"I was eighteen, Alex, and I'm still terrified. Every now and then, I think I see him in a crowd..."

Alex reached for Jamie, making her pull her shoulder back in response. "Look, I know I'm not going to be father of the year..."

"You haven't been a father at all." Jamie took a deep breath and steadied her anger. She couldn't let him push her buttons. *Calm, detached.*

To that day, her parents refused any discussion that included Norman's name.

"All I need is for you to help us get a new identity," Alex explained, diverting attention from Jamie's deepest cut. "Driver's licenses and passports but not social media. Documents only. I don't care what it costs. They need to be top notch, and I know you. I know you're not going to risk anyone with second-rate goods."

Jamie knew he was flattering her only because he needed something. Used to that kind of negotiation, she considered his request.

"You realize if I put you in touch with my contact, that means I have to vouch for you, and I'm not sure I want to do that. I'm not interested in risking that relationship on you and Mom. I don't have the confidence that you won't screw him or screw me somehow. And trust me, this guy isn't someone you want angry. He will find you."

Alex sat quietly, his fingers to his lips, as he stared out the window. Jamie turned her attention to her window, and they sat, father and daughter, backs toward one another, attention past the glass. A small part of her wanted to make it better. That was the little girl in her still, wanting her father's approval, his attention, his favor. She reminded herself that she wasn't a little girl anymore, and his past behavior had been far from fatherly. He put himself and Stella above all others, even their own children. That had been a lesson she needed to learn over and over again.

Especially now.

Alex turned toward her and sighed. "Your mom told me to not even come to you. She didn't want to ask for help, and I didn't either. We have no choice. We need to get out. This is our shot to start over, but we need to be far enough out of Terry's reach. He's not going to go out of country to pursue us, but he'll track us across the states. He's rolling in cash. He's not worried about what we took. He just needs us to pay here to teach others a lesson about not screwing him over."

"And if I help you, then what?" Jamie stared at her father, her gaze narrowing and dark.

"You won't have our murders on your conscience," he joked.

Jamie had to smile a bit. That was actually the biggest motivator for her to help them. She didn't want to get pulled into their mess, but if something happened to them, she knew she would never forgive herself. And Grace would certainly never talk to her again.

She would lose what little family she had left.

"I'll get in touch with my guy and see what he can do."

"Thanks, Jamie," Alex said. His face registered relief, which pissed her off a little, making her think she should've made him work harder. "It means a lot to your mom and me."

"Well, I'm not doing it for you two. I'm doing it for my own conscience." Jamie turned and left the neighborhood, a parade of beach homes in her rearview mirror. "What's your time frame?"

"As soon as possible," Alex said. "Terry's crew is looking for us, so we're on the move a lot right now."

"If I agree, it's only because I expect you to go for good. That's the deal. We do this my way. I'll tell you how it's going to be done, and you're going to follow my rules exactly, or I cut you loose, and you're on your own."

"It's a deal. We'll do it your way."

"I can't believe we're working together again," Jamie whispered under her breath.

"Just like old times."

He said it like it was a good thing.

CHAPTER FOURTEEN

Nightlife in Port Alene wasn't much to brag about during the off-season. Live music was harder to come by because the Winter Texans wanted to be in bed by nine and the crowds of drunk college students thinned to a small pack who had flunked out the previous semester. Still, the town's local crowd knew how to mix things up. They had ample opportunities to get in a little trouble if one knew where to go.

But Jamie wasn't looking for trouble. She was looking to get paid for the next job.

Jamie didn't care much for rowdy nights, but she knew one of her skips enjoyed letting loose after payday. And she'd gotten word that Bobby Battula had made plans to celebrate being flush by dropping some dollars at Tank's Tavern. Bobby liked to flash his cash for the brief time it was under his control before an evening of bad decisions reversed his fortune. Jamie had heard that Bobby was also into people other than just her client, so she needed to get to him first.

The item in question on the Battula job was easy to spot. It was a Ford Mustang Bullitt in dark highland green. Launched by Ford to celebrate the fiftieth anniversary of the Steve McQueen film, it was designed specifically to pay homage to one of the greatest filmed car chases ever. That thing of beauty deserved better than to be driven by a guy like Bobby, who was flashy, sloppy, and lazy—his mother's words, not Jamie's.

Ouch.

Tank's Tavern was off the radar of Port Alene weekenders, hidden down a partially paved road with the absence of outdoor lighting designed to cover a multitude of sins. Tank's didn't even have a sign announcing its location. People had to know to take a right past the abandoned boat-storage building then another right at a small junkyard. Another mile down, and voila—time to hang out with like-minded friends in low places.

Jamie spotted the Bullitt parked in the back corner of the lot, away from other cars, although she was still admired by passersby making their way inside the bar. She pulled her Tahoe next to the prize, cut the engine, and checked her phone. Cookie was running late—he would meet her inside.

She shivered as she stepped outside, the biting wind whipping at her neck, her hair unable to shield her from the weather. She checked her watch. Just past ten. Two men were walking past and slowed when they got closer.

"Keep walking," she said, making direct eye contact with the bigger of the two.

He gave her an annoying half nod but kept his mouth shut, thankfully. She figured him to not be one quick on the pickup. She waited for them to go inside before she walked to the front door. She could hear an argument in the distance, two men yelling about someone's girlfriend, but it didn't seem to be traveling closer. They needed to keep that mess across the street.

Jamie opened the door halfway, enough to slip in and close it behind her. She had no intention of announcing herself with a huge blast of warm air, but she still drew looks. She didn't consider herself a stunner, but any halfway decent woman walking into the place solo had to be prepared to field unwanted up-and-down stares and requests for services she didn't offer, paid or otherwise.

She knew better than to linger, so she walked straight to the bar, choosing the least crowded section where she could signal the bartender. For a good minute, the man didn't look her way. He was busy with a row of shots and making sure people paid for them. She said nothing, waiting quietly until he moved to her side.

"What are you having?"

"A Jameson and a Shiner."

"Draft or bottle?"

"Draft if you keep your taps tight."

He smiled at her. "Drafts are solid here even if some of these clowns don't appreciate it." He turned his back to get the bottle and poured the shot. He put the beer next to her. "That's eleven."

She handed him a twenty, left three on the bar, and pocketed the six. As she pulled her hand from her back pocket, she glanced at the man standing next to her, largely because she could feel his breath on her. He had only a couple of inches on her, but he was built like a refrigerator. From his sloppy smile and glassy eyes, she could tell his buzz had taken hold—not drunk but well on his way.

"What's a pretty lady like you doing here alone?" The word "alone" had three syllables when he said it.

"I'm not alone." She reached for her Jameson and put the shot glass to her lips. She downed it and tapped the bar before leaving it. Then she picked up her beer and turned to walk away.

He grabbed her jacket sleeve, and when she jerked it away, some of the beer in her glass spilled onto her jeans.

"Sorry about that," he said, not looking the least bit sorry. "Let me help you clean that up." He reached toward her.

She stepped back. "Get your hands off me."

She kept his stare, his eyes glassier and his smile one that she was desperate to slap off his face, but she didn't want to waste good beer. She took another step back and felt the presence of someone behind her.

"Need some help?"

She knew that voice. She turned and looked at him.

"No thanks, Finn. I've got it."

He leaned around her and made sure his face was close to her unwelcome guest. "The lady said she doesn't want company, so unless you want mine, go do something else."

The man nodded, and it wasn't lost on her that Finn had a good six inches on the guy. His physical presence was something she envied. If only she could be six four and two hundred twenty pounds. Buzzed Man made himself scarce, and Alastair Finn took his place at the bar, waving his hand at the bartender to get his attention.

"Seriously, Jamie, what the hell are you doing here solo? This isn't the safest place for—"

"A woman?" She dared him to finish the sentence.

"I just mean, being here alone."

"I'm not alone."

He grinned at her. "Not now that you have me, but you shouldn't be—"

"I can take care of myself," Jamie said, brushing off his concern. "You'd be horrified at the places I've been to alone. But I'm not stupid."

"Remains to be seen, so far. I mean... this place?"

"Well, I have good reason."

Alastair raised an eyebrow. "Work, eh? Skip who likes cheap beer in a shitty shack?"

"Definitely not having this conversation with you."

In the corner of her eye, Jamie saw the front door of Tank's open, and Cookie appeared, filling the entire frame. He looked at her, then at Alastair, then back at her. She knew his "what the hell" face. She tilted her head slightly as he walked toward her.

"See you around, Finn," she said as she met Cookie halfway.

He remained at the bar, and although her back was to him, she could feel his gaze still on her. He enjoyed getting under her skin, and she hated that he knew how.

Jamie found an empty table, placing her partially spilled beer on the battered surface. She wiped the remnants of the amber liquid on her jeans. She couldn't imagine the bathrooms would offer anything other than additional health violations. She sat with her back against the wall then reached for the chair across and pulled it next to her for Cookie. She knew he'd want to have a better view of the place.

He placed his draft on the table and took a seat before surveying the place. "Actually, pretty busy tonight," he said, scanning the room from end to end. "I take it you noticed that we know a few of these guys."

She nodded. "Yep, but at least none of them are on our lineup. We just need the one."

"You sure Bobby's going to show?"

"I'm never sure, but I know he got paid, and his on-and-off-again girl kicked him out of their apartment because he was running around." Jamie drank some of her beer. "She also mentioned that he kept eating all her food. I think she was madder about the food than the cheating."

"So the girl's your source?"

Jamie nodded. "Don't get between a woman and her snacks."

Cookie held his glass up, and they toasted even though they had nothing to celebrate other than being able to drink on the job.

"What's the deal with Finn?" Jamie asked. "The man keeps getting in our space."

Cookie glanced over and studied the man, who was chatting up another woman next to him at the bar. "If he's back working, we're going to see him more. Which really sucks. We're going to need to stay on our toes." Cookie grimaced into his beer. "Alastair is very connected, and his having the weight of Big Louis behind him is a problem."

"I see what you did there," Jamie said, giving him an elbow to the side. She glanced Alastair's way but was sure to keep her attention on the room, searching for Bobby, but the front door hadn't opened in several minutes.

"You don't think he's here for Bobby, do you?" Cookie's face registered concern. The last thing they needed was Finn taking more money out of their anemic bank account.

"If Bobby's into Big Louie for something, then yeah, we're going to have a problem."

"You saw the car, right?"

Cookie gave a low whistle of admiration followed by a chef's kiss. "Gorgeous."

"Too new to hotwire, which is a bummer. We could take it while Bobby's inside getting loaded." She glanced around again. "Speaking of, his car is here, but I don't see him."

The idea that Alastair Finn would be chasing the same skips lingered between them as they took turns looking at each other then the room. They were good at being nonchalant, hanging out, drinking beer while taking in the details of the people around them. Another round later, they were still waiting for the guest of honor to arrive.

Then the door opened.

Bobby Battula walked in with two other guys, his face flush with the idea that he was going to blow through some cash that night.

Or at least, that's what he thinks.

Jamie and Cookie turned toward each other and began making fake small talk. She discussed the upcoming Cowboys/Packers game, making cracks about Dak Prescott and trying to get her partner to bust out a smile. She could tell from Bobby's loud voice over the distance that the first round of beers with his friends was on him. They were going to have to get to him before he burned through too much of his paycheck. They waited for him to sit at a table, and it didn't take long before the first round was nothing more than a memory.

"When do you want to go? After round two?"

Cookie watched the trio of men laughing at the table. They weren't louder than any other group in the bar, which made eavesdropping tough.

"Yeah, it's actually better if he gets a little more alcohol in him first. Slow his reflexes."

"Let's hope he orders some shots."

It was as if Jamie's wish had landed in Bobby's ears because that's exactly what he did.

The trio made the second round scarce, with an extra round of shots to boot. Jamie and Cookie surveyed them casually, their attention split between their skip and the people coming and going around their table. Waiting for a little bit of space would be best. A tight crowd emboldened by alcohol could go bad in a hurry.

Before Jamie could slide off her barstool, Alastair Finn suddenly appeared behind Bobby. He said something to the back of Bobby's head, and Bobby looked down, his expression morphing from smiling to stoic. The two men with him each took a tentative step backward, watching as Alastair kept a hand on Bobby's shoulder, guiding him to turn toward the door.

The pair cut a path through the bar and disappeared behind the entry.

Cookie shook his head. "No, we're not doing this again. I'm not losing another paycheck to Finn."

Jamie stood up and waved at her partner. "Let's go."

They made it to the parking lot and spotted Alastair towering over Battula toward the back of Tank's parking lot. Cookie's pace quickened, his substantial frame alerting Finn to the fact he now had competition for what Battula had in his pocket—the keys to the Bullitt.

Finn straightened up, and both men stood shoulders back, like two peacocks competing for the best flair. Battula was the unlikely prom queen with two unwanted suitors.

Jamie quickstepped between the two men. "Finn, that's a dirty move, and we all know it. If you think you're going to keep sweeping in and stealing our jobs, you're in for a rude awakening."

Finn seemed genuinely amused by Jamie's pronouncement. He suppressed a smile, which served as a red flag waving in Jamie's face. He shifted his weight, hands on his hips, and looked her squarely in the eyes.

"Here's the thing. Chances are, a lot of your skips are in debt to more than one person. You've just been lucky that you haven't had much competition lately. It's making you a little lazy, maybe?"

Cookie didn't take kindly to Finn's comment. "Just because you used to live here doesn't mean that you get to come back and pick up where you left off."

"Really? Cause it seems like it does, and having Louie Marchese as my client gives me a pretty big bat to swing."

"I'm pretty good with a bat too," Jamie quipped.

They walked to the prize in question. The Bullitt sat parked and ready for someone with better judgment than Bobby to take over. The group took a moment to silently acknowledge the car.

Bobby was cornered now, with Alastair on one side and Jamie and Cookie on the other. He was like a child asked to choose a favorite parent. Like any kid of divorce knows, there's no winning that one.

Alastair put a hand on Bobby's shoulder, and when he did, Bobby shrank by a solid inch.

"Bobby, Mr. Marchese is pretty angry right now, which is why I'm here. You're in deep, and this car is collateral."

"Funny, he used it as collateral with our client too," Jamie said.

"Maybe so, but which person is more likely to harm your physical health if you don't repay?"

That was a competitive advantage, albeit a morally repugnant one, that Jamie and Cookie couldn't claim. As soon as that reminder left Alistair's lips, Bobby fished in his front jeans pocket and pulled out the key fob for the Bullitt. Jamie considered grabbing it, but in doing so, she would also put Bobby in real harm's way. Her client had put zero bodies in the bay.

But Big Louie Marchese?

No telling.

She glanced at Cookie, who kept his focus on the asphalt parking lot, as if studying the small black pebbles would reveal an answer to how the hell they were going to get rid of this guy.

"The sting of defeat is a tough one," Alastair said, "although I don't experience it much."

He then clicked the fob on the Bullitt, opened the door, and squatted low to get inside. Watching him contort his lanky body inside the muscle car was a small victory. He groaned as he moved his legs.

"You're too old for that car," Jamie said right before he closed the door. His face told her the words landed, and she smiled at that tiny good fortune. It didn't last long. He pulled away, leaving Bobby, Jamie, and Alex behind—just like the Rutger case.

"This can't keep happening," Jamie said. "I don't know the answer yet, but we can't sit by and watch Alastair take money out of our pocket.

"We could start working for a dark overlord with a high body count." Cookie said. "I mean, that's his advantage, right?"

Jamie took a moment, hands on her hips, to collect herself. "C'mon, Cookie, I'll buy you a drink at Hemingway's." She turned to Bobby, who'd been quietly mourning the loss of his fine ride. "You're on your own."

Jamie wasn't willing to trade her morality for money, but she knew that, in her business, that meant she was vulnerable to those not bothered by such distinctions.

She needed to rid herself of Alastair Finn, but she didn't know how.

CHAPTER FIFTEEN

Jamie spent the morning on her laptop, chasing down possible leads on Leah, but came up short. Cookie had texted to let her know he was busy with tasks for his mom, and he would check in once he was "off her clock." The day had started with Jamie going from one frustration to the next. The thought of Alastair besting her a second time claimed valuable space in her head that she needed for more important things. And Alastair Finn was the least important thing in her universe.

Jamie decided a quick early-afternoon trip to the beach would be a much-needed break for both her and Deuce, who'd been spending way too much time hanging out in bars. She loaded Deuce up for a quick drive. The waters leading to the Gulf of Mexico were churning and choppy, a reflection of the unusual bitter weather blanketing the Island.

She stepped out of her car, her boots finding footing on the sand. Port Alene's harsh winter was continuing for yet another day, and Deuce was over it. After she picked him up from the floorboard and placed him on the shore, he shuffled his paws, kicking sand behind himself. He wore the disdain he felt for his red-checked doggie sweater all over his scrunched face and snorted several times to remind her of his opinion. He took off toward the dunes in search of sandpipers to chase, a task that would last for only about fifteen seconds. Deuce's endurance stretched about thirty feet.

While Deuce rolled in the sand in a futile effort to free himself of his sweater, Jamie reached into her back jeans pocket for her phone. She pulled up a phone number and stared at the screen.

She didn't want to make that call.

Conversations with Grace rarely went well.

Discussions with her baby sister were often fraught with drama and misunderstood signals. Grace could misread a restaurant menu and leave the place offended. Jamie, to her detriment, was always quick to be defensive, and she knew it. Still, Grace had always been coddled and handled with kid gloves. Her parents let her off the hook even when she was clearly wrong. Jamie used to think it was because Grace was her parents' favorite child, but with their willingness to leave the country, she felt her parents must not think much of either of them. Grace was simply easier to appease because she supported them regardless of their choices. She loved Grace and wanted to protect her, but Grace often felt Jamie was too harsh. They could come together in a moment, only to quickly push away at the first sign of tension.

Jamie held the phone to her ear and waited. She wished she'd worn gloves. The biting wind nipped at her knuckles, and she gripped the cell hard, turning her back against the wind. She watched Deuce making tracks back and forth on the same stretch of beach, where a few sandpipers teased him into thinking he had a chance of catching them.

"Hello." Grace's voice was monotone, almost annoyed, flat.

"Hello, yourself," Jamie replied. "How are you?"

She sighed into the phone, the kind of heavy sigh designed to encourage friends to ask further about one's well-being, to offer a "What's wrong?" as an invitation to lay bare all one's troubles.

"What's going on, Grace?"

"As if you care."

"Of course I care. I called you back, didn't I?"

"Yes, you did." Grace sighed into the phone. "I guess you know I'm calling about Mom and Dad."

Jamie wondered if Alex had actually told his youngest daughter the truth for once. Jamie had figured her parents wouldn't tell Grace anything until the last minute, but maybe she was wrong. Maybe they were up front with her. She figured it best to assume nothing and see what she knew first.

"When was the last time you talked to them?" Jamie tilted the phone away from her mouth and called for Deuce to come closer. He ignored her.

"Mom texted a few weeks ago. Said they were in between jobs. Nothing special."

"Did they say anything else?"

"Not really," Grace replied. You know how I get when they don't return my calls."

"Sometimes it's the nature of their work. It's not personal."

"They're my parents."

Still not personal, Jamie thought.

She switched topics. "You still in Key West with that guy?"

Silence.

"What was his name? Brett something?"

"Brad. His name is Brad, and no, we're not together. He decided a divorce was going to be too expensive, so he went back to his wife. But yes, still in Key West. He put me up in a place for another couple of months."

"Married guys are a risk, I guess."

"Did you call to judge my dating choices?"

It was Jamie's turn to sigh.

Grace knew the score when it came to her parents. They both did. They gave Grace the good jobs and the flush money, and Jamie served as last resort, which suited her fine. Jamie got the truth first because she could handle it. She'd proven herself many times in that regard. Grace would retreat faster than an introvert at a Toastmasters convention once a difficult conversation started. Jamie, on the other hand, was quick to take confrontation head-on.

But this time was different. Part of her wanted to prepare Grace for the blow she would feel once their parents left the country. She didn't know if they would prepare her or share their plans before leaving.

Jamie hated the idea of Grace being hurt so deeply, but with the hurt came knowledge, and with knowledge came the ability to protect herself. Jamie had learned that lesson long before.

"Have you worked with Alex on a job recently?"

"Why do you do that? He hates when you call him by his name."

"I know," Jamie answered without even a nod to the truth. She sighed into the phone. "Don't waste your time worrying, Grace."

Grace laughed into the phone. "I know you don't mind if they don't check in, but I do. What if something went sideways?"

Jamie reached down to pet Deuce before he left to once again roam the sands. "They usually have a Plan B or a way to reach out to you. But please let me know if you hear something."

"Will do."

"And Grace?" Jamie tilted her head toward the sky, the cold wind nipping at her cheeks. "I'm here if you need me. Understand? Always."

"I do, Jamie. Thanks."

The phone went dead, and Jamie looked at Deuce, with not a care in the world, sporting his adorable dog sweater speckled with sand. Her body had absorbed the chill from the wind, her heart wrapped in a coldness that made the winter air feel warm. She was keeping secrets from Grace and felt awful about it.

Jamie clicked her tongue at Deuce, calling him back. He chased two birds with little success then returned to her, stomping his pudgy feet and shaking his sausage body. She lifted him and put him in the back of the Tahoe. Her family would continue to smolder, little fires threatening to spread, but she had bigger concerns.

At a buzz in her pocket, she checked her phone.

"What's up, Erin?" She turned to check on her furry friend, who was busy rubbing sand all over the backseat.

"I think you need to come by my office."

"You got a job for me?" Jamie could use another paying gig, especially after having lost the last two.

"More like a lead. It has to do with Leah."

Finally. A bit of good news. "Sounds good. We'll be by in a bit."

Jamie then texted Cookie, who sent a reply expressing his gratitude for giving him an excuse to leave his mother's supervision of work on her back-deck repair. Jamie pulled out slowly, leaving the Gulf of Mexico in her rearview window. If only she could do the same with her family drama.

CHAPTER SIXTEEN

Jamie stood at the front steps of Senior Sands, waiting for Cookie to make his way from the parking lot. Deuce, upon seeing him walking toward them, pulled at his leash. Jamie let him go and watched him bound down the thankfully short concrete steps. Cookie bent down to give his buddy a pat and picked up the leash, taking his time going up the stairs.

"How's the deck repair?" Jamie asked.

"Driving me to drink, thanks."

Jamie took note of Cookie's attire. "How on earth did you find a Hawaiian-print sweatshirt?"

"You can find anything online. I can't believe I didn't do this sooner." He rubbed the front of the orange-printed fabric with affection.

The man needed help.

The trio stepped inside the front door, with Deuce in the lead. He liked to make an entrance. Jamie knew she ranked last with that crowd. She couldn't compete with a charming guy in a Hawaiian shirt and a lovable bulldog who would give affection to anyone with food. Jamie surveyed the lobby. Lots of seniors were holding clear plastic cups, chatting, laughing—happy hour.

The time was barely two in the afternoon.

An elderly man in a checkered golf shirt, matching sweater-vest, and pressed pants caught her attention. He rocked a styling fedora, which shouldn't have worked with the outfit but somehow did. He appeared to be very happy already. Happy hour might have pushed him over the edge.

"Make it a double," the man said, slapping the makeshift bar in the lobby. "I'm not driving, so I can live it up."

"Frankie, didn't you lose your license last year after you ran your Cadillac into the crabbing canal on Mustang Island?" The woman, Vivian McCormick, considered herself a Port Alene local in that she'd been vacationing in the town for a solid decade. She wore her senior street cred proudly in her attitude, as if it garnered her the authority to call out just about everybody else in the center.

The Winter Texans, like Jamie, seemed to become territorial quickly.

Erin was busy tending bar and just smiled at Frank as he surveyed her pouring abilities. She gave him a generous pour of tequila in his margarita. "Here you go, Mr. Waller. That should light you up like a Christmas event in Rockefeller Center."

"I love the holidays," he said, reaching for the plastic cup and holding it up in a mock toast. "Merry Christmas!"

"It's not even Thanksgiving yet," Vivian said, rolling her eyes at Frank's merriment. "You're going to need to cut him off soon."

Erin waved to Jamie, causing a slew of seniors to turn around and take note of the newest guests. A group of women made a beeline for Deuce, taking turns gushing over him and petting him as though he were a prized show dog. He pranced around, reveling in the attention as Cookie held his leash. He smiled at the whole performance.

Jamie stood behind Vivian and waited her turn for a drink. Vivian liked chardonnay, and a heavy pour at that. Erin poured her drink just shy of the point of kissing the top lip of the glass. Vivian, a woman who seemed rarely satisfied, seemed to be so for the moment. She turned and spotted the group of women fawning over Deuce and went to see what all the fuss was about.

"What do you recommend, bartender?" Jamie asked her friend, who was wiping down the small bar space in front of her, brushing salt and small spots of liquid with a gingham dishrag. Every element of Erin's life held a touch of class, right down to her housecleaning inventory.

"I make a mean margarita, but I know that's not your thing. I've got some Modelo in a bottle. Keep it for one of my regulars. How do you feel about that?"

"I think that sounds like a great idea," Jamie replied, glancing around behind her at the growing gathering of Erin's clients. "So, where's this lead you promised me?"

Erin straightened the plastic cups stacked to one side then poured herself a glass of Malbec.

"She's over by the adoring crowd worshipping your partner over there."

Jamie walked, beer in hand, over to Cookie. Deuce was too busy being adored to notice his owner's arrival. Cookie served up some side-eye.

"Thanks for getting me one," Cookie said, surveying her drink. "I see how much I mean to you."

"I thought I'd let you go get one yourself so you can take a break from basking in all the affection this little guy is getting," Jamie said, reaching for Cookie's hand to take over the leash. "Take your time. Maybe chat up some of those guys on the couch over there."

Cookie gave Jamie his charge then made himself scarce. Jamie took a sip of her beer and smiled at the ladies standing around Deuce.

One woman, bent over the bulldog to scratch his ear, returned to standing. "My back's going to give out if I stay there much longer," she said. "But he's just so adorable."

"Thank you," Jamie said. "He loves coming here and getting all this attention."

"Marilyn has the same problem," the woman said, joking, to the woman next to her. "Don't you, Marilyn?"

"I appreciate someone who appreciates me," she said. "How is that wrong?"

"Can't argue with that logic," Jamie said, taking a sip from her beer. "It's good to know your own worth."

"I guess I should have thought about that when I settled for my husband fifty years ago," the first woman said. "But it was comfortable, you know? Like your favorite slippers."

"Didn't want to be alone. I get it, Joyce."

"Of course, now that he's dead and I'm alone, I had no idea how great it would be. I wasted so much time!" Both ladies laughed at Joyce's joke—gallows humor on full display.

"So," Jamie said, trying to find the proper segue into the next topic, "what's going on here in Port Alene? Anything new and exciting?" She threw the bait for Vivian, who took it, as expected.

"Well, Tricky Dick's still has that fantastic buffet for six ninety-five. If you get there early enough, you can stock up on the coconut shrimp. Amazing."

The other women nodded in agreement. Jamie was grateful Marty wasn't there to hear the praise heaped on his competition, although she doubted he'd want any of those ladies darkening his door for dinner, no matter how much money they had.

Erin inserted herself into the conversation. "Didn't one of you notice someone driving a new car or something?" She turned to a woman standing to her left, small, wearing a matching coral twinset. "Was it you, Corrine?"

Corrine stepped forward a bit through the crowd, dropping a shoulder to cut between two other patrons. "Maybe?"

"Spill it, Corrine," Vivian prompted. "We've been pretty thin on gossip since Ellen ran off with that insurance guy last month."

Corrine wrinkled her nose at Vivian and turned her attention back to Erin, who signaled for her to continue.

"You know Yvonne? She's got a place in Gertrudis Pass, but her husband passed a while back, and she's been spending more time here on the island."

"Sweet lady," Erin said. "A real rocket when it comes to poker. Don't let that demure smile fool you. She'll rob you blind and smile on the way out the door with your money in her pocket."

Jamie nodded in approval. "Sounds like someone I'd like to hang out with."

"So she showed up yesterday in this car. Some sort of old half car, half pickup. Very not her style. She said someone she knew asked her to keep in in her garage, but she still hasn't come back for it. Said she felt like taking it out for a spin."

"An El Camino," Mr. Waller called out as he made quick work of the drink Erin had prepared him. "Black paint, kind of old looking, but a real looker, although Yvonne's not bad either."

Jamie stifled a smile. Mr. Waller was firing on all cylinders.

She asked, "Did she say anything else? The person's name?"

Corrine shook her head. "Only that this girl needed to take care of something and not to drive it."

"So Yvonne is joyriding in someone's car?" Vivian asked. "That's it? That doesn't sound so exciting. I was hoping for an affair, an argument in a restaurant, some sort of scandal."

"Sorry to disappoint, Vivian," Corrine popped off. "Maybe I could knock you out of your support soles. That could be exciting."

Damn. Corrine went from sweet senior to gangster in two flat.

"Remind me not to piss you off, Corrine," Jamie said, joking but also not.

Cookie stood to the side, sucking in his laughter, struggling to keep a straight face. He turned purple in the process.

Erin disappeared for a few minutes and returned with a piece of paper, which she handed to Jamie. "Here's Yvonne's info. Maybe you can go check on her for me?"

"Of course. Be happy to." Jamie glanced at Cookie, who was still struggling to keep a straight face as the group of happily mingling seniors waded through the awkwardness of Corrine's offer to rearrange Vivian's face.

Jamie and Cookie hustled themselves away from the Deuce Appreciation Society with a promise to Erin that they would let her know if anything came of a visit with Yvonne.

"It could be nothing," Jamie said. "It could be any girl."

"Maybe," Cookie replied. "Grandmas drive boosted El Caminos all the time, right?"

CHAPTER SEVENTEEN

Fresh on the heels of the new lead from Erin's senior set, Jamie and Cookie decided to go straight to Yvonne's place. They walked to Cookie's truck, where he reached inside the cab for his backpack, a jacket, and his sunglasses. The combination of the Hawaiian sweatshirt and the sunglasses was simply too much to leave alone.

"I don't even know what to say about this," Jamie said, making a circular motion with her hands in front of his chest.

"You can say I'm amazing and leave it at that."

Jamie got Deuce settled in the back and Cookie in the passenger seat. The dash clock said it was four o'clock. They had only a couple more hours of daylight and didn't want to show up at Yvonne's unannounced after dark.

From the information Erin had provided, Yvonne lived in Gertrudis Pass, a small town nestled between Port Alene and Foster Bluffs. It was an often-overlooked area, its small population in steady decline as more people chose to live in Foster Bluffs or Corpus Christi. Gertrudis Pass, with its small-town center with half-empty brick buildings, was a place one might choose for the cheap cost of living while still being close to the larger neighboring towns. That was a solemn reminder that the once-vital small town, like so many in the state, had fallen on hard times.

"This town makes me sad," Jamie said as they passed a run-down strip center.

The windows were fogged from age and decades of harsh sun, highlighting empty spaces rather than clothing displays and other small-town enticements. A standalone café appeared to be open, a smattering of cars parked in the lot.

"Well, that's a good sign," Cookie said, pointing at the café as they drove past. "That place has some business. Might be the only place in town, but it's something."

"Maybe, but I think I'll wait to get back to Port A for dinner."

"No doubt."

Jamie pulled up to the address Erin had provided for Yvonne. It was a modest, single-story ranch house with a two-car garage. Weeds peeked out of the cracked sidewalk, but in the winter months, that hardly mattered. The front porch was clean, with two small metal chairs with faded floral cushions. The lots were of a decent size, about an acre or two, depending, and the house had no neighbors directly close by. It wasn't isolated, exactly, but was reminiscent of old small towns where houses were scattered at odd distances throughout a neighborhood. A walk to a neighbor's house would require a bit of dedication, especially in that weather.

Jamie knocked on the front door. Cookie stood next to her, an unusually wide smile on his face. He had his jacket over the Hawaiian sweatshirt in an effort to tone down the look. He didn't want Yvonne thinking they were going to force her to attend a luau, although given her joyriding nature, she might like the idea.

"What is that thing you're doing with your lips?" she asked.

"I don't want to scare the lady, so this is my friendly grin."

"Dial it down a notch, or she won't answer the door."

Cookie grimaced at her at the exact moment the door lock turned. They both straightened their posture as if preparing to meet a teacher.

The door opened to reveal a petite woman, five foot three, with short curly gray hair and ornate readers hanging around her neck.

Her blouse and pants were a tribute to orange Creamsicles, and she wore white support trainers. She would have loved Cookie's sweatshirt.

"Honey, are you lost?" She smiled at Jamie.

"I don't think so."

"Oh," she said, looking at Cookie and offering him a smile. "I don't get much company. Even people selling stuff door to door skip this neighborhood."

"Don't worry—no sales calls. Are you Yvonne?"

She nodded. "Yes, I am. Is everything okay? Bernie isn't in jail again, is he?"

"Bernie?"

"My grandson. He's got a problem with sticky fingers."

Jamie glanced down for a moment to stifle a grin. "No, ma'am. We're not here about Bernie. I'm sure he's fine." Jamie wasn't sure at all, given his grandma had just thrown him under the bus.

Cookie jumped in. "Erin from Senior Sands gave us your information."

"Oh," she said. "I'm uh... current on my account."

Jamie smiled. "Oh, it's nothing like that. She's a friend." She pointed toward the garage. "We were actually interested in the car you drove yesterday."

"Car? What car?" Yvonne wasn't skilled at playing dumb. She glanced over her shoulder and then back at her guests.

We're actually here about the El Camino," Jamie explained. "We've been hired to help find a woman's sister, and we think that car might help us."

"Oh," she said, bunching her fists by her sides. "I knew I shouldn't take it out. But my car needs a new battery, and I really didn't want to miss happy hour. Erin's happy hour is very popular, and as you can see..."

"Not so happy here?" Cookie asked.

"What do you think?" Yvonne grimaced as she glanced at her surroundings. Jamie liked her immediately.

"So maybe taking it out was a good thing," Jamie offered, hoping to assuage the woman's guilt.

Yvonne grinned wide. "She's a beauty."

"Can you show it to me?"

She shrugged her shoulders. "Sure."

"You said you shouldn't have taken it out?"

"It's not mine. I was told not to drive it."

"Why not? It sounds like a cool car." Cookie had an affection for El Caminos dating back to when he was a kid. That was another story for another time.

"It really is," Yvonne said. "I need a little booster pillow in the driver's seat, but it sure is fun. Feels sturdy, like people should get out of your way." She looked down at her feet. "Wouldn't mind keeping it if she decides she doesn't want it anymore."

"So why aren't you supposed to drive it?" Jamie asked.

"I'm not sure if I should say. I don't want to get anyone in trouble."

"Oh, of course," Jamie said. "It's nothing like that. A friend of ours asked us to help find her sister, and she also drove an El Camino."

"Well, I don't think she's missing. She just asked if she could store her car in my garage for a bit. Offered me free housecleaning sessions when she gets back." She reached for her glasses and touched them. "Funny, though. I haven't heard from her since. I thought she was just on a trip. I hope she's okay."

"What's her name?" Cookie asked.

"Leah. She's lovely. Very sweet young lady."

Jamie and Cookie exchanged a glance.

"Can we take a look inside your garage?"

CHAPTER EIGHTEEN

Jamie reached for the lever of Yvonne's garage door, but Cookie stepped in and held an arm out.

"Allow me," he said, giving Jamie a small nudge out of the way.

Before Cookie could bend down to lift the door, Yvonne waved him off. "There's a button right here," she said, pressing it. "I'd never get out of the house if I had to lift that thing up every day."

The garage door opened, jerking and creaking.

"This place is a long-term rental, by the way. Guess I should call a handyman to fix that."

As the door retreated into its slot atop the garage ceiling, Jamie's eyes landed on the El Camino in all its shapely glory. The car wasn't a shiny showpiece—basic black, tinted windows that suffered from heat bubbles at the edges, a little battered on the back end. The car had stories, possibly told over a beer for maximum effect.

At the sight of this stroke of Chevrolet's genius, Cookie's eyes lit up like those of a kid who'd been told he had his choice of any toy in the store. "Brings me back to my childhood," he said, a forlorn look of affection on his face.

Jamie put a hand on his shoulder. "You're going to have to get one of your own. This one belongs to someone. Someone we need to find." She turned to Yvonne. "We don't want to keep you, but I'd like to take a look in the car if that's okay. You can go back inside, and we'll let you know when we're done."

Yvonne hesitated. "I hope this is okay. Leah told me to just keep it here. I'm sure she had no idea I was going to take it out. She's not in trouble, is she?"

Jamie glanced over at Cookie then said, "We hope not. That's why her sister hired us. We just want to make sure she's okay."

Yvonne's hands went to her mouth, her eyes widening. "I had no idea. I thought she just needed to go somewhere for a while."

"And maybe she did," Cookie said. "We don't want to jump to any conclusions. Do you have a number for her?"

Yvonne replied, "I can give you the number I used to call for her to come over for housecleaning if that helps."

"That would be great, thank you."

Yvonne disappeared inside her house and returned with a set of keys and a scrap of paper, which she handed to Jamie.

"Thank you so much."

Yvonne nodded. "I hope everything works out." She looked at Cookie. "Nice to meet you," she said before returning inside her home.

Cookie and Jamie stood in front of the El Camino, arms crossed as they studied the vehicle.

"What do you think?" Cookie asked.

"It's a pretty distinct car, right? I mean, it's not a Toyota that just blends into traffic in a nondescript way. So if she's hiding, she's going to need to get a different car." Jamie checked the file on her phone. "This one's license plate is different."

"So she swapped it to keep from being found in a BOLO? More evidence that she's hiding?"

"That's the million-dollar question," Jamie said. "Was she planning something that went wrong? Was she taken before doing something she needed to do but was able to hide the car first? Was the car supposed to hide her intentions, or is there a reason she needs this specific car hidden?"

"Let's take a look," Cookie said, stepping toward the car. He held out a hand out for the keys, which Jamie reluctantly dropped to him.

"No drag racing, okay?"

She took the passenger's side door and slipped into that seat while Cookie moved into the driver's. Cookie rested his hands on the wheel, possibly imagining himself cruising down SPID through Corpus Christi on a Saturday night. Jamie reached for the glove box, which gave her a fair fight before relenting and opening for her examination. She found little of interest aside from a tire pressure gauge, two pairs of cheap sunglasses, and a few receipts. One in particular caught her attention.

"Check this out," Jamie said, leaning toward Cookie and interrupting his driving fantasy. "It's for a coffee shop in Austin."

"Not much of a lead. We know she left Austin, and let's face it, it could be some random place she stopped."

"Maybe," Jamie said. "Or it could be her regular place. Maybe close to where she was living, something we don't know yet, right?"

"Right. Renata said she'd never been to her place in Austin and didn't know the address, which, with cell phones, doesn't seem like a big deal these days."

Because the seating was one long bench, the car had no center console to search for extra tidbits or clues. Instead, Jamie reached underneath, her hand rooting aimlessly for anything that might make contact with her fingers. Having no luck, she slipped out of the seat and onto her knees, crouching to inspect visually.

Nada.

So they had a car that Leah had wanted to hide. The car was somewhat recognizable, but then again, in Texas, the style was still a niche fan favorite. Jamie got out and looked into the back of the El Camino, which was empty save for a few leaves and small branches, possibly from hauling brush or some other outdoor endeavor. Cookie joined her as she studied the long back opening.

"Nothing here," she said.

Cookie smiled, reaching up to his chin. He examined the back end of the vehicle and lowered the tailgate. The bed resembled a truck's but attached to the body of a car instead. He hoisted his sizable frame into the vehicle and moved to the left wheel well.

"My uncle's El Camino had a smuggler's box built underneath," he explained as his hands ran around a lined groove. "I think there might be one inside here, but I might need some tools to open it." He tilted his head toward Yvonne's front door. "Pretty sure she doesn't have any tools outside of a screwdriver in the kitchen drawer."

"We really should take the car so it doesn't cause any issues for Yvonne," Jamie said. "You think she'd be okay with that?"

"Renata hired us to find her sister, and it looks like this is her car," Cookie said. "I agree that taking it from Yvonne would be safer for her anyway."

"Maybe we should find a place to store it so it's not in plain view," Jamie said. "Hemingway's won't work."

"Erin still has that office building, right?" Cookie asked.

Jamie nodded. "Wouldn't be the first time we've hidden some questionable contraband in there."

"Actually, we didn't hide anything there. We just found it later. Speaking legally." Cookie was very quick to remind his partner that their past ventures related to that past thing at Erin's building had always been honorable even if they walked a fine line of legality.

Cookie slid off and secured the back, keeping the keys in his possession. "Let's let Yvonne know we're going to borrow the car for a bit."

"I take it you want to drive it?"

Cookie nodded with enthusiasm.

"Okay. We'll just take it in and then come back here. Let's wait to tell Renata anything until we know more. No point in worrying her."

Cookie smiled as he returned to the driver's seat. As Jamie watched the El Camino retreat from the garage, she wondered if the vehicle still had something to offer about Leah's location and reason for disappearing.

Fingers crossed, she thought.

CHAPTER NINETEEN

In her SUV, Jamie followed Cookie as he pulled the El Camino into the back garage of Erin's office building. Erin had purchased it from a past client who was in deep and had used it as partial collateral. She had entertained ideas of how to best use it for the benefit of the community while also earning enough to cover the maintenance and property taxes. She had yet to come up with a solution, so it sat waiting for the occasional opportunity to provide shelter to Erin's friends in tricky situations.

Cookie stepped out of the El Camino and greeted Erin. "You like?"

She nodded. "Very cool," she said, turning to see Jamie getting out of her vehicle. She walked over to join the pair and give Jamie a quick hug.

"Thanks for letting us park here for a bit while we search the car."

"No problem," Erin said, studying the vehicle. I'm digging this car. So this belongs to your missing person?"

"Missing or hiding out—not sure yet," Jamie replied.

"Bold choice in vehicles," she said. "I like it."

"No offense, but I think you're more BMW than El Camino," Jamie said.

"Not on the inside" was her reply.

"I can see that," Jamie said. "It's got the benefit of a coupe in the front and a truck bed in the back. I mean, it's the best of both worlds."

Meanwhile, Cookie had circled the car twice, lightly banging on a few areas.

"Careful, Cookie," Jamie cautioned. "We need to get this car back to her, and I'm not paying for any damage."

"There's already a small dent here," Cookie noted, pointing at the front panel on the driver's side. He reached over and ran his hand across a small indentation in the metal. "You know what they say about women drivers..." He threw her a smile along with the jab.

"Yeah, that we're better than men because we can stop and ask for directions."

"Touché." Cookie returned his attention to the car, giving it one more look before reaching for his toolbox and placing it in the back bed. He then hoisted himself into the back and positioned his body in an awkward sitting position, not ideal for a man built like a linebacker. He grunted as he tried to get more comfortable.

"Let me help," Jamie said, springing easily into the back. The ease with which she landed next to him brought a grimace from her partner.

"Okay, Tinkerbell, quit showing off."

"I'm not showing off," she countered, "and you would look completely ridiculous doing the same thing, even in your best Hawaiian shirt."

Jamie studied the bed and reached toward a corner by the back left wheel well. The bed seemed fairly new, weathered but certainly not circa 1967 like the car itself. The metal bed's grooves, rows of raised lines punctuated by dips between, camouflaged a small seam, an opening. Cookie leaned forward to study a perpendicular gap in the metal running from one side of the cab to the other, right behind the cab window. He signaled toward the cab.

"Hop back down and check the glove compartment, will you?"

"For what?"

"Looking for a remote," he replied. "I don't want to bust this open with tools and damage it if I don't have to."

Jamie slid off the back and leaned over in the coupe to open the glove box a second time. She discovered nothing new: the same original car manual, some napkins, and an emergency window-breaking tool.

"Nothing so far," she called. "Gimme a minute." Jamie ran her hands underneath both seats, picking up nothing but dust bunnies and a few straw wrappers. She then inserted her hand into the fold of the passenger seat and ran it from one side to the other.

Bingo.

Her hand stumbled on a small plastic square. She pulled it out. It was a simple remote with two buttons. She went to the back of the coupe's truck bed, hopped up inside, and handed it to Cookie.

"Is this what you're looking for?"

Cookie smiled and pressed the button, and when he did, the panel responded with the hum of an automated lift. The hatch door was now partway open, at an angle, revealing a secret storage compartment running along the width of the truck behind the coupe cab.

"Leah—or someone—installed an actuator controlled by this remote to hide this space. My uncle did something similar. Smuggler's box."

"What did he want to hide?" Jamie asked. "And you have a lot of uncles."

"Never asked, and yes, I do. A lot of people just use a smuggler's box to keep valuable tools secure without needing to add a camper top, which would completely ruin the look of this fine vehicle."

"Like putting training wheels on a Harley?"

"Exactly."

The compartment revealed a painter's tarp. Jamie pulled it back and, in one corner, found a nondescript black duffel bag.

"You want me to open it?" Jamie asked. "Make sure there's nothing scary inside?"

"Don't be silly," Cookie said. "There's no dead-body smell. Nothing to be scared of."

Erin had stood by quietly, watching her friend finesse secrets from the El Camino. She took a step closer. "You sure you want to do this? Once you open it, you can't go back."

Jamie said, "I know. But it's most likely just clothes or some personal belongings she didn't want stolen. No formal trunk in this car, so..." She didn't believe a word she was saying.

She reached for the duffel bag and unzipped it.

Definitely not clothes.

She widened the bag's opening to reveal neatly wrapped bricks of cash, a mix of hundreds, fifties, and twenties. Erin leaned in closer to the El Camino for a look.

"Uh, that's a problem," Erin said.

Cookie whistled low. "Definitely a problem."

"Damn." Jamie resisted the urge to touch the money and instead zipped the bag closed. "So maybe Leah isn't as innocent as Renata thinks she is."

"A common misconception amongst sisters," Erin said. "She's the youngest, right? The youngest can do no wrong."

"Trust me, I know," Jamie replied.

"Sounds like you've got to work out some childhood stuff," Cookie joked. "But you're right. The baby of the family gets away with everything."

"But now we might be in possession of a car with some contraband, and you know what?"

"What?"

"She's going to want this back—or whoever it belongs to."

Erin added, "For her own safety, she may need to get it back."

"You think she's a courier?"

"She's not cleaning houses for that coin. I'm going to guess that the money belongs to someone else, and she's either working a job, or she took it."

Jamie said, "I have the number she gave Yvonne for housecleaning. It's the same one Renata has, so it won't do us any good. The number goes straight to voice mail, and we can't track the location."

"Yeah, I guess you don't need to use a burner cell to take appointments for housecleaning jobs."

"So now what?" Erin asked. "What if she goes back to Yvonne and finds the car missing?"

Jamie replied, "That's not what I'm worried about. What I'm worried about is what if there's some reason she can't get back to the car? She's not responding to anyone—no online contact, nothing."

That was the fact that concerned Jamie the most. *It's one thing if Leah chooses not to respond, but what if she can't?* As Cookie studied Jamie's face, she could feel him reading her mind.

"Don't think like that," he said. "We've got work to do."

CHAPTER TWENTY

After taking Cookie back to pick up his truck from Erin's, Jamie continued home to Hemingway's after the long night. On the way, she'd received a text from Renata, asking to meet. She called Cookie to let him know to come over. Her evening apparently wasn't over yet.

Just past ten o'clock, Jamie pulled into Hemingway's Pier. Renata stood in the parking lot, leaning against her navy Toyota Corolla, a cigarette to her lips. She seemed smaller in that space, unlike when her large personality brought so many regular patrons into San Juan's. Her normal bright smile and high energy were absent as she watched Jamie claim a parking space.

"Where's Cookie?" Renata asked as Jamie stepped out of her Tahoe. She tossed her cigarette onto the ground and stubbed it out in the gravel with her shoe.

"He's carefully ironing his Hawaiian shirt collection so they'll be ready when the weather warms up again." Jamie smiled at Renata, whose face displayed the struggle of appearing to be fine. "What's wrong? Aside from the obvious."

Renata shivered, and Jamie was unsure if that was from the uncharacteristically freezing wind or simply a ripple of the current state of affairs. "I had a visitor today at work."

"Really? Someone you know?"

She shook her head. "He's looking for Leah."

Jamie nodded toward the door. "Let's go inside. It's too damn cold out here." She gestured to Renata to step ahead of her. "I can wait on you for a change."

They stepped inside the warm retreat of Hemingway's.

"It's been a long time since I've been here," Renata said. "Still mostly locals?"

Jamie nodded. "Just the way Marty likes it."

When they stepped inside, the place was moderately full, with some familiar faces. Behind the bar, Marty nodded to her as she signaled toward her back table. They slid into Jamie's downstairs "office," which was really just a corner booth shielded from other tables, a bit more private than the other seating in the place. A waitress soon brought a pot of tea and two mugs.

"Pretty impressive," Renata said. "I never figured this place to be a tea house."

Jamie sat upright and postured. "This is my doing, actually. I like Earl Grey, and Marty never carried it. It's now part of my rental agreement for my loft—tea included as long as I buy it and put it in the kitchen."

Renata brought her cup to her lips, closing her eyes for a moment as she took a sip. "My nerves needed this." She looked at Jamie. "I probably really needed tequila, but I have a shift in the morning."

"So tell me about this man." Jamie reached for her notepad and pen as Renata continued drinking her tea. "When did he come in? What does he look like?"

Renata glanced over her shoulder before speaking. "White guy, black hair, short. Stocky guy—he didn't look too tall, but he was sitting down at a table. He had some sort of a dragon-style tattoo down the side of his neck. But it was his eyes that did it." She shuddered again. "He wanted me to know he was watching me. I could feel his stare every time I turned my back."

"Did he say anything?"

"He told me that I needed to tell Leah to get in touch with Ormond or there would be trouble."

Jamie continued taking notes. "Did he say how to get in touch?"

Renata finished her tea and reached for the pot for a second cup. "No. I think he just assumed that she knew."

"Have you ever heard of him?"

"No, never. She never mentioned him when she was living in Austin, but then again, she's pretty quiet about her personal life." She shrugged. "I've been accused of smothering and giving unwanted advice."

"Same," Jamie replied. "I still give it because I actually do know everything."

Renata nodded at the shared sister experience. "Really hoping that he doesn't come back again," she said. "But now I'm more worried than ever. Maybe Leah's gotten tangled up in something. She's always been a risk taker. Doesn't want advice from her *hermana mayor*. Says I already act like an old lady." She took a sip of her tea. "Maybe she's right."

Jamie reached for Renata's hand. "I know it's tempting to let your mind go to the worst-case scenario, but all it's going to do is keep you up at night. You've said that she's not the kind of sister who keeps in close touch, so maybe there's another explanation."

Renata seemed skeptical. "Do you really think so?"

No.

In light of Renata's visitor, Jamie felt it best to update her on what they'd found. Jamie explained their progress on Leah's case, finding her car at Yvonne's, and the money inside the smuggler's box.

"Damn it, Leah," Renata muttered. "What are you into now?"

Jamie replied, "I just know it's best not to jump to conclusions, but yes, the Ormond thing and the car kick the situation up a notch. Don't worry. Cookie's on his way, and we'll get right on it. And maybe stay somewhere else if you don't feel comfortable being at home. We don't know what we're dealing with yet."

Renata stood to leave. "Thanks, Jamie. I'll think about it." She said, "I'll at least have my girls stay with their dad for a while. To be safe."

As Renata walked out the door, Cookie arrived. The two greeted each other at the door before Cookie made his way to their booth. He sat down opposite her, taking note of the teapot.

"Where are the scones? Did you give the queen my best?"

Jamie wrinkled her nose at her friend. "Yes, and she's quite disappointed that you stood her up." She then gave Cookie the scoop on Renata's uninvited guest. "I don't have Ormond's last name, but we can still try to do some digging."

"Did you tell Renata about the El Camino and the cash?"

Jamie nodded. "Yep. She's up to date. She's going to have her kids stay with their dad."

"Good call."

Cookie immediately reached inside his backpack to retrieve his laptop. He then waved to Kay, a waitress with a soft spot for his Hawaiian flair. She came to the table and took his order for chicken strips and fries. Jamie held up her hand to signal two orders.

"We just blew through dinner. I'm starving," she said, "and I don't want to share my fries."

"Ditto."

Jamie excused herself to retrieve her own work gear from her loft upstairs, first stopping to greet Deuce, who was happily basking in the attention of local patrons. She reached down and gave his jowls a rub. "Feel free to keep spoiling him with attention, but no fried foods. He needs to stay light on his feet."

She could swear her dog gave her the side-eye after that comment. Then she was up the stairs and back again, her laptop and other materials under her arm. She returned to find Cookie with one hand typing on his laptop and the other in a basket of fries. The waitress had brought him an appetizer.

"I'm good at multitasking," he said, noting her attention to his snacking.

She settled in and took a few fried delights for herself. The two worked on their computers, searching for any information on Ormond and Leah.

"No luck yet finding anything on Ormond. And it's not the most common name."

"He might be the kind of guy that thinks having social media is a bad idea," Cookie countered. "No need to share information about where you are and what you do if where you are and what you do is…"

"Illegal?" *Good point.*

Cookie stopped typing. "Hey, I think I might have something." He swiveled his laptop toward Jamie for her review. "You think this might be the guy?"

She leaned closer. The screen showed a photo of Leah with another girl, tagged as CarmenElectric, and a man who fit the description Renata had provided. She couldn't tell if he had a tattoo, though, with the way his shirt fell.

No name or tag was attached to him.

The other girl's profile showed her name to be Carmen Evans—not many details other than the fact she lived in Austin. Cookie continued digging until he found more information for her. Then he sent her a direct message from his fake account, Don Ho Forever, saying he was a friend and was looking for Leah.

"I can't believe so many people actually respond to you at that account," Jamie said.

Cookie polished off the last of the fries. "What can I say? People love 'Tiny Bubbles.'"

"You can't sing. Hawaiian shirts are the only thing you two have in common."

He gave her a shrug. "I've just got it." His wink resulted in her slapping his shoulder.

The pair continued working but found little else that would prove useful regarding Leah and her whereabouts. Whether due to design or indifference, Leah seemed to prefer living her life in the real world, which was possibly a dangerous one.

Cookie checked his cell phone and handed it to Jamie. It showed a response from Carmen: "Haven't seen Leah in a while. Sorry. Did you try her work?"

Jamie returned the phone. "Well? You got her on the line. Keep reeling."

Cookie typed a response. Several minutes passed before Carmen replied, "She used to work at StorSmart."

Jamie searched for StorSmart in Austin, and a link came up. "It's a self-storage facility. Do they even need employees?"

Cookie closed his laptop. "According to Carmen, yes."

"Let's give them a call in the morning," Jamie said. "Until then, I'm a little worried about Renata's visitor."

Cookie asked, "You want me to call Erin to see if she can spare Becky for a bit?"

Becky was Erin's right-hand woman, the kind who would punch someone if they breathed wrong on her boss. Becky's primary role was to track down delinquent clients to make sure they settled their bets, but she was handy in a number of other areas that required persuasion or force. Erin never used her with her seniors. They were never the problem in the first place. But her strength was well-known around town. One rumor claimed Becky had once made two Marines cry. No one would talk about the details, but she'd clearly made an impression.

Jamie nodded. "I think so. The guy may be here just to scare her, but still..."

"Say no more." Cookie typed a quick text on his phone.

"Erin said no problem. She'll go keep an eye on her at work and then follow her home. I'll send Renata a message to let her know Becky is going to be tailing her so she doesn't get freaked out."

Jamie closed her laptop, and Cookie followed suit. "You know," she said, "we still need to decide what to do about the El Camino."

Cookie smiled. "Maybe we take it out for a spin?"

Jamie cocked her head to the side, considering. "Let's put a pin in that." She felt a buzz and checked her phone—another message from Alex. She couldn't keep a poker face.

Cookie asked, "Lemme guess. Alex?"

She nodded. "I still need to take care of that... thing... for him."

"You want me to go with you?"

"Nah," she said, wrinkling her nose as if the offer was insulting, as if the idea that she couldn't handle the task solo was offensive. In truth, she knew he just didn't like her going to Riley's on her own. Scuffles happened now and then—mostly low-level stuff. Still, because the mess was her parents', she felt she needed to handle it by herself.

"I'll give you a high sign when I go in tomorrow, okay?" she said.

"Arnold likes to sleep in. You know that."

Arnold, Cookie's Smith & Wesson .357, had seen very little action since it came into his care. Weapons tended to complicate things, getting people in trouble with the cops. Since Jamie and Cookie preferred to work without that kind of additional attention, weapons were a last resort.

"I'll keep working to see if I can get some traction with Ormond in the morning while you handle the parent thing."

Jamie smiled and reached over to give her friend's hand a pat. "Once I handle this thing, Alex and Stella will be gone for good."

"How do you feel about that?" he asked without a hint of sarcasm. "Are you sure you're ready for them to be gone for good?"

Jamie considered the question. "Can't miss what I never had."

CHAPTER TWENTY-ONE

Jamie pondered how many daughters had been tasked with obtaining new identities for their parents. She guessed that was a pretty short list. She wondered if a support group existed out there for such things and if she would even attend. Maybe if the beer was good.

The reality that Jamie had relationships with those who could help people disappear was not lost on her. She just hoped that how she wielded those resources would offset the bad karma her family had accumulated over her lifetime. That said, karma might poke her for using said skills to help her parents flee after stealing money from a well-connected crime boss.

Taking complicated family dynamics to a new level, she thought.

Kingsland was a small town an hour from Port Alene whose claim to fame included being adjacent to a famous large cattle ranch. Famous with a lowercase *f*, sure, but those in the state knew the ranch well. Some people even came for tours to learn about its history and the skilled vaqueros who managed the ranch's resources over its 800,000 acres. It was a tourism draw for south Texas.

Jamie drove several miles down a farm road, FM2140 to be exact, noting a right turn at the old Dobson cemetery, and following it until she came upon a shopping center that had seen its glory days decades prior. The white brick showed its age and weather spots, with large patches peeling in a random pattern, and the roof, while still covering the surface of the building, looked as though it might back out of the arrangement at any moment. Most people would assume the place abandoned, which is why Jamie figured that Riley had picked it in the first place.

She checked her watch—just past eight in the morning. Jamie was grateful that Riley liked to start early. She'd heard him mention once that he could never sleep longer than four hours at night so he might as well make money off his insomnia by taking on more work.

After parking in the mostly empty lot, she walked up to the front door, the glass so fogged from age that she could only faintly see her own silhouette in reflection. She pulled it open, and when she did so, a collection of bells tied to the top of the door announced her arrival. The sound reminded her of an antique shop, but Riley's couldn't have been more different.

She looked up at a fluorescent light on the ceiling, its flickering a tentative promise to do its job—much like the roof—and Jamie glanced around the room to see if anything had changed since her last visit.

Nope.

Three metal desks took center stage in the room, each with a rolling chair. The surfaces served as storage space for random auto parts, screws, tools, and other metal fittings used to fix who knew what—definitely not a lot of paperwork happening there.

Jamie moved toward the back of the room, and as she did, a man appeared from the hallway. He grazed six feet, with colorful tattoos down both arms and dark hair cut short, and he wore a plain black T-shirt and jeans. He squinted at Jamie through the dimness of the back hallway.

"Hey, Riley, how's business?"

He walked closer, his scowl turning into a smile. "Pretty good still. People like you keep finding me out here in the middle of hell's belly." He reached for her and gave her a quick hug. "How are you doing, Jamie?"

"Better than you, maybe," she said, taking note of a purplish bruise traveling down his neck and disappearing into his shirt. "What happened?

"Take my advice. Don't get in a fight with a dude swinging a metal chair."

"Did you win?"

He pulled his head back and smirked. "Are you serious right now? What do you think?"

"That I should see the other guy?"

"Good answer." He touched the bruise gently. "Shit hurts, though. Not going to lie." He glanced around the empty space. "So what brings you here?"

"I have a couple of people in need of your unique skills."

"Figured you wouldn't drive all the way out here for my company, although it is one of the most underrated treasures the world has to offer."

Jamie winked at him. "Well, that's up for debate."

"Come to the back," Riley said. "We can talk more there."

Jamie followed Riley to a room in the back of the building, and after she stepped inside, he locked the door behind her. She instinctively turned around. She and Riley had always been on good terms, but his security protocol still made her nervous. She'd had enough bad childhood experiences to make her wince any time she found herself locked in any space. That still made her flinch.

Riley seemed to note her discomfort. "Unlikely to get more drop-ins, but you never know."

His office was a stark contrast to the front room, which really was nothing more than a decoy for anyone who came in without the proper references. His work desk was organized, stacks of paper in neat piles and a couple of composition notebooks and digital cameras on its surface. Off in the corner was a mini portrait studio, complete with a white screen, lighting, and a posing stool.

"What can I do for you? You have another special case?"

Jamie shook her head. "Not in the way that you mean."

Riley sometimes offered his services at a deep discount for clients who needed to escape dangerous situations or spouses. She appreciated his generosity in the times she'd come to him, and in reality, no one in the state was better than Riley in the "fresh start" business.

"This one's a little tricky," Jamie explained. "I need a full set for my parents."

Riley let loose a low whistle. "Wow. Big responsibility for you, then."

"I need your best work on this, but on the upside, I want you to charge them retail plus rush."

"Family feud?"

She shot a smirk his way. "Think of it as a 'thank you' for all the cheap work you've done for me and Cookie in the past." She smiled. "And they have plenty of money. They won't feel a thing when they pay you." She didn't know if the last part was true, but the words leaving her lips gave her satisfaction.

"How is that handsome Hawaiian-shirt bastard?"

"He'd love to hear you describe him that way, and he's great. Still trying to find Mrs. Right Now."

"Aren't we all?" Riley moved behind his desk and sat down. He picked up a pen and reporter's notebook, folding the paper over to a clean page. "Okay, give me the details."

"Names are Stella and Alex Rush. They need the full set, generic names, plus a bit of online history, backstory. Nothing major."

Riley nodded as he took notes. "Okay, so we'll go age plus three either side, height within two inches, and identities that don't show much travel and only domestic. Plenty of people who live mostly off the grid that we can use, maybe blend a couple of backgrounds, but make sure the socials pan out on basic databases."

"I don't know if they plan on traveling again once they get to their final location, but let's say my father is stupid enough to keep bouncing, maybe with an itch to go to Europe, so let's make sure he can pass for the ten years the passport's active."

"Finding the right marks is going to take a little time, but I can put a rush on it."

Jamie nodded her head. "If you do, bill the hell out of them for it."

"Please make sure to refer any other relatives you dislike my way."

Jamie laughed. "Our relationship is... complicated."

"You don't have to explain anything to me, Jamie. Every person who comes in here is complicated. They wouldn't need me otherwise."

"So you want me to send them your way for the photos and payment?"

He pulled a piece of paper. "Give me the cell number you want me to use for them." He then added, "I'm not here on Fridays. Other aspects of the business keep me occupied."

"Ooh, international man of mystery." She pulled her cell out and checked Alex's number then wrote it on the paper and returned it to Riley. "Can you give me a heads-up when they're coming in?"

"Of course," he replied. "I'll take good care of them so you never see them again."

Jamie smiled. "That's the nicest thing anyone has ever said to me."

Confident that Stella and Alex would be covered, Jamie left her parents in Riley's skilled hands. Her thoughts turned to Grace and whether she yet knew their parents were planning to leave the country.

This is their mess to clean up, Jamie thought. *Let them handle it.*

She'd done her part, working to get her parents out safely. She would take care of Grace later. She remembered the Rush family motto: "Safety first, honesty later."

And they wondered why both Rush women had trust issues.

Just when Jamie got into her car, her cell rang.

"Hey, you doing okay?"

"Yes, Cookie. All good. Very quiet this morning. Just finished up. What's up?"

"I did a little back-and-forth with Carmen, and she told me where Ormond works."

Finally, some good news. "So what's the story?"

"How do you feel about a road trip to Austin?"

She looked at her watch. "Okay. Meet me at Hemingway's in an hour."

Jamie hung up the phone, a new surge of energy flowing through her system. Finding Ormond meant they were one step closer to finding Leah or at least learning more about what had caused her to drop off the map, if she had done so by choice. Jamie wasn't completely convinced of that yet, but that didn't matter. Jamie set her GPS for Port Alene to meet Cookie at Hemingway's. With a bit of hustle, they could be in Austin before three in the afternoon.

CHAPTER TWENTY-TWO

J amie smiled as she pulled into Hemingway's parking lot. Cookie had reclaimed his prized space, complete with orange cone, and was leaning against his truck. She kept the engine running as Cookie walked over. He opened the passenger side door and handed her a brown bag from San Juan's and a large iced tea in a Styrofoam cup.

"And I also took Deuce out and walked and fed him, so he's back upstairs snoozing," Cookie said with a smile.

"Best partner ever."

"You know that's right" was his reply.

"I called Maggie, so she'll take him out later."

"You're nicer to Deuce than you are to people."

"Present company included," Jamie joked.

"You may need therapy," Cookie said.

"I've tried it. The therapist told me I used humor to deflect dealing with trauma." Jamie took a sip of her tea. "Like I needed to pay someone to tell me that." She held up the drink. "Thanks for breakfast."

Cookie climbed into the passenger seat and put his backpack by his legs before getting his own breakfast on the go sorted. He then checked his phone. "I'm thinking that we should go to Ormond's place first and then the storage place."

"Where is he?"

"Carmen said he was a mechanic at Mikey's Auto Shop. We need to make him priority in case we run out of time or run into trouble."

"That sounds like a lot of running," Jamie answered.

The pair left Port Alene's slow and steady pace to travel north four hours to Austin. The capital city's allure wasn't lost on Jamie, although she'd long eschewed big cities for the comfort of Port Alene's shores. Austin's unique culture was a chameleon of sorts. The city offered anonymity and community. Its vibrant tech economy coupled with its long history of launching musical talent made it desirable to all kinds of hustlers, artists, and entrepreneurs. And the restaurants served some of the best food in the state.

Its cost of entry—aside from some of the priciest real estate in the county—included horrific traffic. Those two factors alone kept Jamie from ever wanting to call the city home.

"And this is why they call I-35 the parking lot," Jamie said as brake lights in front of her blinked on and off as traffic went from a slow crawl to a stop. Cookie glanced at the exit overhead, noting the name.

"Slaughter Lane. That one always gets me." Cookie said. "I don't know how it got past the naming committee."

"Maybe it's meant to keep other people from moving here," Jamie mused. "I read that over a hundred people a day relocate to Austin."

Cookie gestured toward the traffic ahead. "Maybe they need a scarier name to slow the population growth."

"Death City?"

"We should come up with some names and send them to the city council."

"I'm sure they'll get right on that."

Jamie continued to inch her Tahoe along through traffic, one foot on the brake and one on the gas, as Sammy Hagar recommended. She finally caught a break with a line opening up before the next backup. At least that time, she had a better view of Town Lake. The lake boasted a pristine mirrored surface, undisturbed by paddleboarders or rowers. The frigid temperatures had chased off even the most dedicated water-sports enthusiasts.

Jamie exited onto Congress Avenue then followed Cookie's interpretation of the GPS instructions, for which he tried and miserably failed to impersonate Morgan Freeman.

"Just stop, Cookie. It's painful."

Her partner smiled at her disdain. "This is all for your benefit, you know."

"I appreciate your sacrifice."

As she drove farther from the interstate, the density of buildings lessened, easing from an onslaught of standalone and strip centers and giving way to more neighborhood sprawl, with small businesses dotted along the main roads and tucked off turns. Five miles later, Jamie and Cookie had located their destination, Mikey's Auto Repair.

Mikey's was set back in a lot with little next to it, no businesses other than a drive-through burger place on the next block. It was unremarkable in the way that most repair shops are unremarkable. That was what gave them credibility with the locals. A flashy place with a nice waiting room was probably the kind of business to overcharge in order to pay for said waiting room.

This was not that.

Mikey's was a metal building that had seen better days. The red paint on Mikey's name, written in script, flaked in several spots, and the black border on the sign suffered the same damage. The main entry included a simple glass-panel door, and the side of the building showed a row of three garage bays, with only the last bay open. Jamie spotted two men standing outside, smoking cigarettes, engaged in conversation. The taller of the two waved his hands in an animated fashion as he spoke. They wore light-blue shirts, dark-navy pants, and work boots. She was too far away to read the names embroidered on their shirts. When Jamie pulled into a nearby parking spot, the duo gave her a quick glance, stubbed their smokes on the ground underneath their boots, and retreated inside.

Jamie cut the engine and waited for Cookie, who was also giving Mikey's the once-over. "So should we just go in and ask for Ormond? Just straight out?" Jamie asked.

Cookie straightened his beanie on the center of his head, tucking in a few short stray hairs. "Might as well. If we act shady, we're probably not going to get far."

Jamie and Cookie exited her Tahoe in tandem, with Jamie taking the lead at the door. When she stepped inside, she spotted a small greeting counter and a man behind it, maybe midtwenties, with black-rimmed glasses, a small ponytail that worked for him, and a light-blue work shirt. His name, Jeremy, was embroidered on the patch. Those glasses seemed all the rage lately.

The man looked up from his computer screen. "What can I do for you today?"

"Hi, Jeremy," Jamie said. "Is Ormond here?"

He typed something on his computer. "Do you have an appointment?"

She shook her head. "No appointment."

"What's your name?"

"Jamie Rush."

Jeremy then looked at Cookie, who said, "I'm with her."

If Jeremy was annoyed by Cookie's lack of introduction, it didn't register on his face. He turned his attention back to Jamie, nodded slightly, then turned his back and disappeared through a door, leaving Jamie and Cookie alone in the "lobby." A minute or so later, Jeremy returned.

"Uh, he said he'll be out in a minute. Just finishing up with an engine."

"Sure, no problem. We'll wait... right here," Jamie said with a gesture toward the lack of chairs in the small space.

Cookie offered a stoic nod, all chin, no smile.

Jeremy busied himself on the computer, although Jamie wondered if he was actually inputting any important data or squeezing in a quick game of solitaire. Cookie exhaled deeply, encouraging a brief look from Jeremy, who then returned his attention to his screen.

The door behind Jeremy opened, and a man emerged. Jamie hadn't been sure what to expect, but Ormond, at first sight, was a formidable stack of a man, taller than Cookie and lean in the way a man becomes when he spends a substantial amount of time lifting heavy weights. Clearly, Ormond loved the gym. His hair was dark and cropped, and the veins of his neck resembled a roadmap leading from under his chin into the neckline of his shirt, a garment that felt the strain of covering his chest. No nameplate was on his shirt.

He wiped his thick hands with a rag and looked at Cookie then Jamie. "Can I help you with something?"

Jeremy made himself scarce at a single glance from Ormond.

Cookie straightened up, ready to respond, but Jamie stepped in first. "You Ormond?"

He nodded. "What do you need?"

"We're looking for Leah."

"Join the club," Ormond said. "I haven't seen her."

"For how long?" Cookie asked. "When was the last time?"

"And who are you?"

"I'm her partner."

"And you do what?"

"I do a lot of things." Cookie leaned on the bar, closing a bit of space between him and Ormond. "We were hired by Leah's sister to find her. Seems she's gone quiet, and your name came up."

"Oh really?" He shrugged off the comment as if it had no consequence.

Jamie gave Ormond a hint of a smile, an effort to cut the testosterone standoff she found herself in. "Listen, we know you two were dating for some time. Her sister believes she's missing, and we're looking for her."

Ormond held up a hand. "I don't know what to tell you. I haven't seen her. She left one day, and I haven't heard anything since."

"Well, it sounds like you want to hear from her, too, since you sent one of your guys to scare the holy hell out of Renata." She shook her head. "Having a guy intimidate a woman at work isn't cool. Must mean you want to see Leah too. Pretty badly."

"Maybe you're the reason she left," Cookie added.

Ormond clenched his jaw and tossed his cleaning rag on the counter, streaks of black patterned on the white fabric. "What's going on between me and Leah is between me and Leah. It's none of your business." He reached toward his face and rubbed his eye. "And I wasn't trying to scare her. Wally just has that way about him."

"Maybe someone with a lower scare-the-shit-out-of-the-sister factor next time?" Jamie asked. "You're a smart guy. I think you chose Wally to do exactly what he did."

"Like I said," Ormond replied. "It's between me and Leah."

"Disagree about this being only between the two of you," Cookie said. "If her family is worried that something has happened to her, and you show up threatening a family member, that's absolutely our business."

"'Threaten' is a strong word," Ormond replied. "And clearly, I had nothing to do with it, since you now know I'm looking for her too."

"So let's say that you didn't," Jamie said, "although it looks bad. I mean, the boyfriend is usually the main suspect. Add the scare tactic, and it looks like you're involved."

Ormond took the rag, wiped his forehead, and stuffed the rag into his back pocket. "You can think what you want. I don't know where she is."

"Is there somewhere else we should be looking?" Jamie asked. "Someone who might want to hurt her?"

Ormond glanced down at the ground then back at Jamie. "Leah is her own person. No idea what else she has going on. She had her secrets."

"But you're her boyfriend, right?"

"Not anymore."

Cookie replied, "Maybe you want her back?"

Ormond ignored the comment. "I haven't seen her, but if you find her, tell her to give me a call."

Jamie glanced at her partner. "So you can't name anyone else that we should be talking to? No friends, nothing?"

Ormond shook his head. "Sorry. Guess you'll have to do more investigating." He smiled as the words left his lips. He had no interest in helping them find Leah. Jamie considered leaving him a card but figured that he wouldn't call regardless. Plus she didn't want him to have her number. She figured if he was going to be an unhelpful ass, she would return the favor.

Jamie nodded at Cookie, and the two left Ormond behind the counter. She could almost feel the heat of his glare on her back. They remained silent until they got in her car and started the engine.

"What a waste of time," Cookie said as he slammed the passenger door shut.

"Not a complete waste," Jamie said. "We know he's looking for her and he's unwilling to tell us anything about her, which means he wants to get to her before we do. His supposed girlfriend is missing, but he's not interested in her safety. He's got to get to her for some other reason."

"Maybe," Cookies said, but his words lacked conviction. "Well, we're in Austin, and we're going to need to eat soon."

"I can't believe you're hungry again."

"I'm always hungry. You know that."

"I tell you what," Jamie said. "You can pick where we eat, but we've got one more place to go first."

"The storage facility? You think we'll find anything?"

"It's all we've got."

Jamie glanced in her rearview mirror as she pulled away from Mikey's Auto Repair. Ormond was standing at the window, peering out as she pulled away. Cookie glanced at his mirror too.

"Hey, if he were my boyfriend, I'd run too."

"The question is why, Cookie. Why didn't she at least tell Renata she was leaving? And why is Ormond looking for her if they broke up?"

"Maybe she needed to get away from Ormond for her own safety. Maybe he didn't want their relationship to end."

"That's a possibility," Jamie said. "She's definitely running, either from Ormond or from something to do with him. And if she's smart, she's not reaching out to Renata because the less her sister knows, the better." Jamie knew the lengths a woman would go to protect her sister.

She glanced one last time at Ormond's figure in the window as she turned onto the main road. She wondered how much of a threat Ormond would be, not only to Leah but also to her family.

A chill ran through her, and it had nothing to do with the weather.

CHAPTER TWENTY-THREE

According to the omniscient GPS, the StorSmart facility was located in East Austin, and as they traveled past Riverside Drive and toward Montopolis, Jamie entertained what living in the big city once again might be like. She had landed there briefly as a kid, pulled by her parents' con jobs and relocations, and much of her time there remained a blur. Her memories were less of landmarks and schools and more geared toward the apartments she briefly called home and the bars and racetracks her father chose as his work spaces. Someone likely to gamble at a track or spend all night on a barstool might be more open to a new business endeavor or opportunity. Her recollections, save for a select few, were jumbled and messy. She often remembered street names and attributed them to the wrong cities, relationships that were real to her but imagined or wrong when she recalled them aloud to Alex or Stella. Over time, she stopped sharing her memories entirely. She couldn't even be right in recounting her own experiences when she was in their presence.

Cookie tapped her shoulder. "Dreaming of leaving the hustle and bustle of Port Alene for the relaxing calm of Austin?" He smiled at catching her in a rare state of quiet.

"A very cool city, no doubt," Jamie replied, "but I'm good with island life, if not island time. At least for now." She reached over and tapped him on the forearm. "Besides, you'd be lost without me. You don't have to admit it. We both know it's true."

Cookie shrugged. "It's the other way around, but you know, whatever helps you get through your day."

The GPS announced that Jamie had arrived. Jamie looked at the StorSmart sign and shook her head. "Why do people intentionally misspell names on businesses? I don't get it. They couldn't fit all the letters on the sign? Is there a discount for fewer letters or something?"

"Okay, grammar police, take a beat and settle down." Cookie nodded toward the building. "Doesn't look like a big operation. Maybe that's the office?" He pointed at a side building with a front door. One window was off to the side, but the blinds were closed.

Jamie nodded, and they walked to the front door. Cookie pulled on the door, and as it opened, a litany of bells rattled, announcing their entry.

"Very high tech," Cookie joked.

They looked up to see a young woman sitting at a metal desk. Sparse, pretty industrial—the desk, not the woman. Small white wires snaked from the woman's ears to a phone on the desk.

"Hi, can I help with a storage unit?"

Jamie shook her head. "Not at the moment."

She took a seat in the metal chair across from the woman's desk. Standing over subjects while questioning them often put them on guard. Cookie reached for a nearby chair and placed it next to Jamie.

"We're looking for someone who, we were told, works here or used to work here?" Cookie flashed his high-wattage smile, and Jamie had to admit, it was pretty good. The woman tapped her phone, possibly to cut the sound from her headphones. She smiled at them both.

"I'm sorry. Really addicted to this podcast. Say again?"

Cookie gave her a second pass. "We're looking for a friend who used to work here." He was clearly stuffing his annoyance at having to repeat himself. He hated wasting charm, as it was a valuable, precious commodity.

She tilted her head and said, "Ummm... okay. Not sure I can help you. I've only been working here for a couple of months." She glanced around the spare office. "It's pretty boring, really."

"You hiring?" Jamie joked. "I could handle being bored and getting paid for it."

She smiled. "If you'd like to leave an application, I'll pass it along to the boss."

The poor girl had a sense of humor like a tree stump—another quip wasted on an unappreciative audience.

"I'm Jamie, and this is my friend, Cookie. What's your name?"

"Callie. Callie May."

"Our friend's name is Leah Sandoval. Does that name sound familiar?"

The blank stare on her face told Jamie it didn't. "Never heard of her, but like I said, I'm pretty new here. Maybe I can look her up in our database?"

Jamie and Cookie exchanged a quick glance.

"That would be great," Jamie replied, reaching into her back pocket and pulling out a business card. She placed it on the desk in front of her. "Just in case you need it."

Callie leaned closer to the computer monitor as her fingers tapped the keyboard. After a few moments, she said, "Oh, yeah. I see her in here. She used to work here." Her eyes scanned the computer screen, which Jamie, unfortunately, couldn't see. "She's a customer too. She's got a unit at our Corpus Christi location."

Jamie and Cookie exchanged a look. "You have a Corpus Christi location? Good to know." She pointed at the back of the monitor. Do you have the unit number?"

Callie hesitated. "You know what? I don't think I was even supposed to tell you that much, honestly. Please don't tell my manager."

Jamie leaned forward. "Of course not," she replied. "We're trying to help a friend. What you've told us is a good thing."

"Maybe so," she said, "but I don't think I should share anything else. I need this job."

"Understood. We'll keep this conversation to ourselves." Cookie pretended to lock his lips together, making Callie smile.

They both thanked Callie for her help and left her to return to the comfort of her paid podcast-listening job. Once inside the Tahoe, Jamie sighed and rubbed her eyes. She'd driven a solid six hours between Riley's and Austin, and she felt she had little to show for it.

"So now what?" Jamie asked. "We know she's got a unit back in Corpus. We can't just break into it."

"Not only that," Cookie replied, "but maybe she just moved her apartment furniture and things into it when she left Austin for Port Alene. Renata said that Leah told her that she wasn't planning on settling in there. It was just a stopping point before deciding where to move to next."

"So we don't know much more than we did before we left this morning, other than Ormand is unhelpful and menacing and that we had to drive to Austin to find a storage unit back in Corpus."

"We did make progress," Cookie said. "We have more information. We just don't know what it means yet." Cookie was always clutch for bringing in a pep talk when a case hit a roadblock.

"Okay, what's next?" Jamie asked. "We're going to drive home right in the middle of rush-hour traffic."

"I need food," Cookie said. "My blood sugar's low, and I can't think straight now."

"So a stop at El Arroyo for an early dinner before we head back?"

Cookie grinned like a kid who'd just been told he could stay home from school. "I haven't been there in years."

As she navigated the Austin traffic, Jamie's mind turned over the events of the day. Ormond could be simply a jealous boyfriend or something more nefarious. Leah had a storage unit. Jamie was working on a high-stakes jigsaw puzzle, and not only couldn't she see the full picture, she didn't even have all the pieces. They had driven to Austin only to return home with more questions than answers.

CHAPTER TWENTY-FOUR

Austin traffic proved lighter going south, with cars spending less time traveling bumper to bumper at twenty miles an hour. By the time they arrived back on the island, the time was close to eleven in the evening. The fatigue of having driven more than four hundred miles in a single day, coupled with the realization that she would soon say goodbye, possibly forever, to her parents, settled in her bones. The adrenaline rush that had fueled her at the beginning of the day's trip was long gone, replaced by the kind of fatigue she hadn't known since pulling a string of all-nighters in the Theakston case the previous year.

As Jamie turned the corner to pull into her parking space, she spotted a black dually parked in her spot, and Cookie's orange cone was tossed onto its side. Cookie shook his head at the toppled cone.

Alastair was back.

"Okay, that's some bullshit right there," Jamie said as she maneuvered to another space farther away from the entrance. She jumped out of her Tahoe and walked over to the truck.

Cookie got out of the Tahoe and followed her, putting a hand on her shoulder. "Don't get all bent on my behalf," he said. "That's what he wants."

Jamie took a beat to catch her breath. She knew she was spent, and walking in half-cocked was a bad idea even if it would've felt good at the moment. "I'm fine, I'm fine," she said, holding a hand in the air. They both knew better, but she would fake it for now.

Cookie put an arm around her and pushed her toward the door. "C'mon. That truck isn't going to quiver from the side-eye you're shooting."

Jamie leaned into him, his arm still around her shoulder, and let him guide her into Hemingway's. Spotting the cone-crushing culprit didn't take her long. Alastair responded with a wide grin and held up his beer glass in a toast.

Asshat.

Jamie felt the pressure of Cookie's hand on her shoulder. "Careful there, cowboy. Don't let him get under your skin. That's how he owns you."

"Nobody owns me," Jamie replied under her breath.

"Damn straight," Cookie replied. "Let's make sure we don't reward his bad behavior."

Jamie straightened her posture and focused on her breathing. They walked toward the far end of the bar, and Cookie waved at Marty for a drink. All she wanted was to power down from a very long day with a beer and some fried snacks without Finn in her space. *Is that too much to ask?*

Alastair made his way over to the duo, beer in hand, smiling wide.

"Didn't expect to see you here," Alastair said.

Marty, with his usual impeccable timing, brought two draft beers and, with his offering, delayed Jamie's instinct to knock the smile off Finn's face and the beer out of his hand. "Here you go," Marty said, placing them on the bar. "This one's on me."

Alastair held his hand up. "What? I don't get free beer?"

Marty shook his head. "Sorry, bud." Marty knew how to read a room, and in short order, he disappeared to the other side of the bar to handle his other waiting patrons, leaving Jamie and Cookie to deal with Finn and his smug mug.

"You really don't want to park where the orange cone is," Jamie said, taking a sip of foam off the top of her draft. "You'd be amazed how many door dings and scratches you can get from… things." She smiled at Cookie then continued, "I mean, my Tahoe's got some miles and wear on it, but that shiny dually of yours seems like it needs more babying."

The smile slipped from Finn's face, and he glanced at Cookie, who responded with a shrug.

"She's right," Cookie said. "Wrong car in that space could end up with some damage. It'd be a real shame."

Finn seemed to consider his next comment but kept his mouth shut. Instead, he took his beer and made his way back to the opposite side of the bar. Jamie and Cookie watched in unison as Finn wiggled his way through the crowd, back to less hostile company.

"Well played," Cookie said to his partner.

"Same to you," she replied, holding up her glass for a cheers. "And I'd never damage such a fine ride, but he doesn't know that."

She glanced around the bar, looking for familiar faces, and spotted a couple. Bob Mandel, Bob the Builder to his friends, was a local contractor who could claim dozens of local businesses as customers. He shared space with Sparks, an electrician who had survived an unhealthy number of electrical mishaps and one rumored lightning-bolt strike. Sparks was a nice enough guy but unusually forgetful, his voice often trailing off before he could finish a sentence. Sparks possibly hadn't yet found his calling or at least a profession that would better guarantee his safety—friendly enough but as sharp as a Q-tip.

"You need to check in with Becky?" Jamie asked. "Just to make sure no other excitement happened while we were gone?"

Cookie nodded and pulled out his phone and sent a text to Becky. Jamie knew Ormond had likely sent word to his handler, Wally, who he had following Renata, and Jamie was worried a bit for her safety. The response came a few minutes later.

"Becky made her presence very well known and made sure Renata got home, so if Ormond's guy was in the background, he stayed there. At least for today." Cookie's vibe was one of cautious optimism—a shrug and a nod—but Jamie knew their visit to Ormond's garage might stir up some activity. On the one hand, it could prove helpful in finding Leah. On the flip side, it could also put both Renata and Leah in danger. Working cases meant kicking over rocks, and sometimes what was under those rocks proved dangerous.

Jamie's mind drifted back to Leah. She believed Leah was alive but wondered if Ormond was the reason she was on the run or if some other event or threat was still covered. And the money was a huge question mark. She didn't know if that was her money to start a new life or if it belonged to someone else.

Alastair, still at the far end of the bar, waved a hand to get Jamie's attention, which she reluctantly gave. He smiled at her with his annoying shit-eating grin then disappeared out Hemingway's front door. Jamie glanced at Cookie, who had witnessed the wordless exchange.

"You think I need to go check on my car?" Jamie said, reading his mind.

"Nah," Cookie replied before taking a long drink from his draft.

"If there's a scratch on my Tahoe..."

"Jamie, you've got tons of scratches... and dents." Cookie smiled at his friend. "If he did something, you probably wouldn't even know."

"Those are all work related. That guy"—she pointed toward the closed door Alastair had gone through—"is another issue entirely."

"Ignore him," Cookie replied. "Finn is a lot of things, but he's not stupid."

"Debatable."

"I mean not stupid in starting a war for no good reason."

Jamie trusted Cookie's advice, and the truth was that her partner knew Alastair Finn far better than she did. Hell, she hadn't even known he existed until a few days before, and she wished for nothing more than to banish him from her memory and her physical presence forever. She imagined stealing some of his clients, and a smile crept across her lips.

"Dreaming of crashing Finn's dually?" Cookie said, noticing her grin.

"Something like that."

She felt her phone buzz in her back pocket and checked it. She groaned then returned the phone to her pocket.

Cookie tilted his head towards her. "Who's calling?"

Jamie took a long draw from her beer. "That would be Grace." A second long draw. "I don't have the energy to talk to her right now. She needs to be handled carefully, and I'm not in top form." Jamie sent her little sister a quick text saying she was in the middle of a job and would call her back.

"Did you tell her about your parents' plans to skip the country?"

"Negative," Jamie replied. "That's not my job. They need to at least have the decency to tell their own daughter that they plan on leaving and aren't sure if they will be back."

"You trust them to do that?" Cookie asked.

"Absolutely not." Jamie sighed. "And not to be soft, but it breaks my heart to think of them running out on her. But I think she needs her heart broken so she won't keep hanging her hopes on them. They string her along and treat her with kid gloves. And I do, too, but she's going to need to get stronger." She took another sip. "Like the caring parents say, 'It's for your own good.'"

"That must be hard," Cookie said.

"I hate it," Jamie said more bluntly than she intended. "If I step in, I'm the target, and it all gets directed toward me, and they get off easy." Jamie rubbed the corner of one eye. "This time, Alex and Stella need to come clean. I'll be there to pick up the pieces, but I'm not swinging the hammer. That's on them."

"I'm sorry your family's a hot mess." Cookie moved closer and gave his partner a small side hug. "You can borrow mine anytime."

"Would love to," Jamie said. "I'll mow your mom's lawn for her homemade enchiladas."

"She'd take that deal."

Jamie gave Cookie a quick squeeze. "I'm going to turn in." She leaned back to check a nearby crowd of patrons, noting that Deuce was sitting on his special high-backed chair, basking in the constant attention of strangers. If a bulldog could smile, Deuce would have been grinning from ear to ear. She pointed toward her beloved pooch. "I bet he made more money in tips than we made from billable hours."

Jamie parted ways with Cookie, leaving him to finish his beer. He'd already turned to talk to someone at the bar. He could hold a conversation with a telephone pole. He had the gift of gab.

Jamie gathered Deuce from his fawning fan club, scooping his squatty body up in her arms. She caught Marty's eye, acknowledging that the transfer of custody had taken place. After one last pat from the group, Jamie made her way up the stairs to her loft. She felt a little guilty for having been gone all day, although she doubted Deuce felt the same, with all the adoring attention he'd received. She carried him up the stairs and put him down to unlock the door. When she did, Deuce made a beeline for his dog bed, at the foot of Jamie's own.

She was facedown in her bed a few minutes later, her mind drifting off, mulling over Leah's whereabouts in her consciousness. She turned the options over in her mind, like a rock tumbling in a river, slowly smoothing the surfaces, dulling the hard edges, searching for the truth.

CHAPTER TWENTY-FIVE

Call me when you get this.

Jamie rubbed her eyes as she looked at the text from Cookie. The time was just shy of seven, which in her mind was two hours too early, but she'd forgotten to close the blinds by her bed, so the morning sun saw fit to greet her by squeezing through the slats and shining in her face.

Jamie hung her head over the side of her mattress to check on Deuce, who was snoring so loudly that she was reminded of her ex. Jake was the best relationship Jamie had ever had. He was charming, funny, and stable in a way that made her nervous, with sarcasm skills well suited to her own. He was reliable, honest, and in search of something that would last for life.

In short, he was too good for her, and she told him so. He thought she'd warm to the idea of settling down and taking different work. He worried about her hours, her clients, and the dangerous skips and surveillance. When she had to choose her work or Jake, she chose the former. As much as she loved Jake, she could imagine her life without him. The same didn't hold true for the job. It was her security blanket, her way of making sense of the world, trying to bring closure to others searching for their own version of it. The work allowed her to take her childhood and all the nefarious things she'd learned as a kid on the run and turn those skills into something that benefitted others rather than taking from them. That was her small repentant offering for her family's legacy.

And besides, once Cookie joked that "Jake and Jamie" sounded like a John Mellencamp song, she knew the relationship was doomed.

Deuce had begun to stir and quickly went from full snooze to standing by the front door. She'd rarely seen him go from dead sleep to outdoors, which could only mean one thing. Someone had given him Marty's famous jalapeño poppers.

Once they were back inside, she gave him a bowl of water, deciding to hold off on his breakfast for a bit to give his digestion time to work itself out. They'd been down that road before, and even though Jamie knew it was best for him, Deuce snorted at his empty food dish then returned to his corner. She was getting tired of doing things that were best for others but made them resent her for it.

Jamie plopped back down on her bed, her mind alert but her body still tired. She wondered if she could steal another hour but knew she wouldn't be able to fall back asleep. The morning walks down the stairs often stole any potential extra slumber.

She turned back to her phone, checking for messages and ignoring her emails. Her brain wasn't quite ready, the fog of the morning still clouding her grasping for clarity. She called Cookie, who answered almost immediately.

"Surprised you're up already," Cookie said.

"Deuce needed to go outside."

"Someone gave him jalapeño poppers again?"

"Yep," Jamie said. "I'm going to have to hang a sign around his neck, forbidding it." She turned and checked on Deuce, who was back asleep. "So what's going on? Why the early text?"

"I got a message from Renata," Cookie said.

Jamie sat upright in bed. "Everything okay?"

"I don't know. She said to tell you thank you but that she didn't need us on the case any longer."

Jamie crossed her legs on the bed, her forearms resting on her thighs. She rubbed the morning sleep from her eyes. "That doesn't make any sense. Did she say why?"

Cookie sighed into the phone. "Not really. She just said that she shouldn't have come to us and that she couldn't pay us anyway, so we needed to just let it go."

"That's what she said? Let it go."

"Yep."

"That sounds like maybe someone said those same words to her."

"Maybe," Cookie said. "I think she's working this morning."

"So... tacos?" Jamie said. "And you're buying, right?"

Cookie laughed. "Meet you there in twenty."

JAMIE PULLED INTO THE San Juan's parking lot and was greeted with a steady stream of people with the same idea. She scanned the area, looking for Cookie's F-150, but didn't see it. After a minute or so, she spotted him pulling in and parking in the side lot, away from other vehicles. He was still in that prudent honeymoon stage. Jamie couldn't relate, having never owned a new car. Cookie stepped out and emerged around the corner.

"Okay, let's go easy on her to see what she says, " Jamie said. "She's probably scared."

"Soft touch. Got it."

"Like your favorite blanket soft."

Cookie smiled and opened the front door for her. They stepped inside and glanced around then took a booth by a window. Jamie gave the indoor dining area a scan, looking for Renata, but didn't see her. A waitress came by and dropped off menus they didn't need. They knew it by heart.

"Can I get you some coffee or tea?" She was young, pretty, and unfamiliar.

"Yes, please," Jamie said. "Is Renata here?"

The waitress shook her head. "No, she called in sick this morning. I'm working her shift. I'm usually over at the other location."

Ah.

Cookie glanced at Jamie then turned to the waitress. "Can we get three bean-and-cheese and three bacon, potato, and egg? Flour tortillas. Extra salsa verde. And two large unsweet teas?"

"Sure," she replied. "I'll get these going for you."

Jamie held up her hand. "And make it to go, please. Looks like something just came up."

CHAPTER TWENTY-SIX

With a paper bag in hand and iced teas to go, Cookie followed Jamie to her car, leaving his truck parked at San Juan's. Jamie pulled out of the parking lot and onto Avenue A.

"Did you send Renata a text?" Jamie asked. "Should we send her a message?"

"Yes and yes."

Cookie sent another text message, his third since she'd contacted him the previous night, with still no response. It was possible that Renata really was sick and wasn't answering the phone because of that.

But unlikely. She'd asked them to find her missing sister then told them to forget it and called in sick. Jamie feared something worse than a sour stomach had befallen their client.

Cookie continued to check his cell in the hopes of receiving a text from Renata. An uneasy energy hung between them as they drove in silence. Jamie considered reaching for the radio to search for anything to dull her concern, to take the edge off, to offer a slight distraction, but she knew that coping mechanism was a mistake.

Those particular moments, when she didn't know what she would be walking into, demanded she remain on edge. The edge kept her safe.

Renata's house was just outside Port Alene's tourism row, a small neighborhood with houses dotted in random order along winding and poorly paved roads. The county had done a piss-poor job of taking care of the area, although it was clear from driving into the entrance of the neighborhood that the houses, for the most part, were handled with care. The lawns were tidy, bushes were trimmed, and front porches were decorated with rocking chairs, small tables, and potted plants, as well as a few Farley boats.

"Two streets down, take a right?" Jamie asked Cookie, who was checking his cell phone for GPS instructions as well as a response from Renata.

"Yep. Right on Driftwood and then a left on Shelltower." Cookie pointed out the window. "Not too many cars parked out here right now, early in the day."

Renata's neighborhood was one of the few areas populated mostly by locals, who needed inexpensive rent and weren't interested in paying for views they wouldn't enjoy since they would likely be taking care of people who paid more for those beachfront properties. A town that relied largely on the tourism dollar could be tricky for the people who served it. Housing was scarce—most developers wanted to buy up land for pricey homes and attractions—leaving local folk the challenge of searching for affordable housing. Jamie knew that required a lot of digging, like putting a hand down a sand-crab hole in the hopes of pulling out gold coins.

Jamie followed Cookie's instructions and, after a couple of turns, found herself on Renata's street. Whispershores Avenue offered no whisper of any shores, and the road itself had fewer homes but more land between each one. Jamie took her foot off the gas, coasting as she continued down the road as she eyeballed the house numbers in search of 607.

Cookie craned his head to the side. "We're getting close. Odd numbers on my side."

He read numbers as they passed each house. As they neared the end of the five hundreds, Jamie slowed down further, glancing through the passenger window.

Jamie approached number 607. It was a small single-story ranch-style home with a trimmed, albeit brown, front yard. Yard décor included a Farley boat planter and other potted shrubs. Her front porch was tidy, with a wood railing, two weathered rocking chairs, and a potted cactus in a colorful ceramic pot.

Jamie didn't immediately stop but kept driving past the house instead. "What kind of car does Renata drive?"

"A small blue Toyota Corolla."

No Toyota Corolla in the driveway.

Jamie drove to the end of the street and circled back toward Renata's house. She parked by the neighbors' house, which had no cars in the driveway, reducing the possibility that someone would come out and complain.

"If she's sick, why isn't her car here?" Cookie asked. "She should be resting. At home."

Jamie looked around. "I don't see Becky anywhere."

"She's good at surveillance, so that doesn't mean she isn't here. If we can't see her, that's a good thing, right?"

Cookie had a point.

The pair walked to the front door. They decided Jamie would take lead on that particular call, as they didn't know much about her home life aside from the fact that she had a missing sister. She knocked on the door.

Nothing.

A second knock.

Still nothing.

"Maybe she's at the doctor's office?"

"I don't know," Cookie said. "My gut tells me no, but what else is there to do? She's either here and someone has her car, or she's at the doctor and will be back later."

"Still doesn't explain cutting us loose on Leah's case."

The two stayed on the front porch for another minute. Jamie leaned forward, her hands cupped on a nearby window. No movement in the living room. *However...*

"Cookie, look." She gestured at the window.

Inside and off to the right was a dining room table. Two chairs lay sideways on the floor.

"Maybe some sort of struggle?" she asked.

"What now?"

They returned to the car, and Jamie started her engine.

As they left 607 Whispershores in her rearview mirror, Cookie asked, "So Renata probably isn't at the doctor's office."

"Send a message to Becky," Jamie said. "See what she knows." Jamie took a deep breath and tapped the steering wheel. "I hope this doesn't mean we now have two missing people."

As soon as those words left Jamie's lips, her cell phone buzzed.

Jamie picked up and asked, "Hey, did you get my text?"

"You need to come over here," Erin said. "Becky's here, and we've got a problem."

Jamie pressed End on her cell and turned to Cookie. "Becky is with Erin."

"Not a good sign," Cookie said.

Jamie cocked an eyebrow.

"Definitely not a good sign."

She pulled onto the main drag and turned toward Erin's warehouse.

CHAPTER TWENTY-SEVEN

Jamie and Cookie arrived at Erin's warehouse to find Erin and her bodyguard sitting on a bench out front. Becky was holding an icepack over her eye, head down, forearms resting on her knees. That was the first time Jamie had ever seen Becky looking anything close to vulnerable.

"Becky, are you okay?" Jamie asked as she and Cookie rushed to her side.

Erin waved them off, signaling to give her space.

"Can you tell us what happened? Were you at Renata's?"

Becky nodded. She cleared her throat and took her time sitting upright. When she released her hand from her eye, she revealed a cut at the crest of her cheek and a brownish bruise spreading across her eye socket and below. "I can't believe I let them get the jump on me," she said.

More than anything, Becky's ego seemed the most bruised. As a woman confident in her bodyguard skills, she would certainly berate herself for some time over someone getting the upper hand.

"Take me through it," Jamie said.

"They pulled up in a black Suburban. Didn't know if it was family checking on her or a threat. Two guys got out of the car, both tall, heavyset, one blond, the other black hair. They moved quickly. Knocked on the door, and Renata opened it, and as soon as she did, they took her. She ducked into the house for a moment, and then they brought her out. After that, she didn't resist. I was on the side of the property and tried to catch them off guard. The blond guy clocked me hard. Definitely knew how to get me to the ground."

"How many people total?"

"At least three. The driver in the Suburban never got out of the car. Didn't get a good look at him. The other two took Renata in her car, one in the back seat with her. It was precision. She didn't have a chance."

"Hey, I've gotten an ass kicking now and then," Cookie offered in an effort to soothe her humiliation. "It happens."

Becky nodded. "I didn't see anyone in the house. They moved fast. She was out of the house and in the car before I could get back up."

Erin told Becky to take the day off with pay. Becky pulled herself off the bench. "I'm sorry I failed you," she said.

"You didn't fail us," Jamie said. "You were outmanned." She glanced at Cookie. "I think we all are right now."

Becky disappeared inside the building, leaving the trio to figure out their next step. Jamie took Becky's place on the bench next to Erin while Cookie stood next to them. She leaned forward, her forearms resting on her thighs, cradling her head in her hands.

"This has to be Ormond, right? He's the one who sent a guy to intimidate Renata at work."

"But where do we look? He was in Austin yesterday."

"Maybe our showing up escalated things," Jamie said. "He knew he wasn't the only one looking for Leah."

"Who is also still missing," Cookie said. "All of this leads back to Leah."

"So now what?" Erin asked. "Is there any lead that you can go back and revisit?"

Jamie stood up from the bench. "I think it's time for another trip to see Ronnie Arroyo. We're pretty sure he was seen with Leah at least once at Vince's Comedy Club."

Erin gave Cookie and Jamie a quick hug. "Let me know if I can help," she said. I'm going to go check on Becky, but I'll be here if you need me."

As Erin walked back into the warehouse, Jamie thought about what could've been so important—and to whom—that it meant two sisters were now in jeopardy. She willed her mind to put the pieces together, to find the connections, to work faster.

Jamie, like the missing sisters, was running out of time.

CHAPTER TWENTY-EIGHT

Jamie had made good time from Erin's place to IslandCraft RV &
Marine. Her driving strategy had balanced being in a hurry with
not getting pulled over for speeding. Only five miles out, she was
thinking of Renata and where she might be, of Leah and if she knew
her sister was in danger. The car had been quiet. Cookie, skilled at
noticing when his partner was too deep in her own head, broke up
her angst with his observational minutiae.

"It is said that the best two days in a fisherman's life are when he
buys a boat and when he sells it."

Jamie never understood the appeal of owning such a vehicle. A
boat, unless one had the funds to pay someone else to handle the regular hassles of cleaning, fueling, docking, and such, seemed an enormous headache. Cookie had once owned a boat—rather, it had been
given to him by a cousin who later asked for it back—and while he
enjoyed it for the occasional scuba adventure, he, too, found it much
more trouble than it was worth.

"I'm not saying I wouldn't mind getting another one," Cookie
explained as the two of them sat in her Tahoe, parked a distance away
from IslandCraft RV & Marine. "I would need a lot more free time
first. Seeing a boat reminds me I don't have the time or the money to
use it."

Jamie smiled. She knew his strategy. She needed to bring her energy down a notch. Too much angst meant more possibility for mis-
takes. She leaned in. "Lots of charters around here if you want to go
fishing," Jamie said.

"Cheaper than a boat but still pricey. Those rates are for tourists with good jobs. I think I need to make friends with more fishermen, trade some surveillance work for redfish."

"Note to self: make lots of money. Buy boat."

"Actually, you can get a good deal on a boat, but you're going to throw a lot of money into repairs and maintenance—"

Jamie tapped Cookie on the forearm. "I know seeing these boats gives you some FONB, but you've got to let it go..."

"FONB?"

"Fear of no boat." Jamie smiled at her cleverness but was alone in being impressed by her acronym skills.

Cookie wrinkled his nose at her. "That's not a thing."

"It's absolutely a thing," she replied. She pulled into the lot and parked a few empty spots away from the entrance. She took a deep breath to settle her nerves. "You ready to see if Ronnie wants to share today?"

Cookie nodded. "I think I can be pretty convincing, given the circumstances."

The pair walked into the front office to find a different man behind the office counter. She smiled at him and gave a half wave.

He glanced up from his computer screen. "Hi, can I help you?"

"Yes, we were working with Ronnie on a project. Is he in today?"

He nodded. Then shook his head. "Yes, he's here, but he ran out to pick up a part that came in. Should be back any minute. You want to wait here?"

"We don't want to be in the way," Jamie said. "We'll go wait outside for him. Thanks."

Jamie and Cookie returned to the Tahoe and turned on the heat. They were a week into the island's icy temperatures, and her patience, like Cookie's winter wardrobe, was wearing thin.

Cookie rubbed his hands together. "Is your heater working?" he asked, holding his hands in front of the vents.

"Yes, but she's old, so give her a minute to warm up."

Jamie turned on the radio. Selena's "Como La Flor" filled the cab.

"How long you think we're waiting?"

The words had barely left Cookie's lips when a truck emerged on the gravel road to the boat repair building. The pair instinctively ducked down in their seats as he came closer and parked on the opposite side of the building. Jamie and Cookie immediately stepped out, picking up their pace in the hopes of catching him still by his truck.

They caught him just as he slammed his door shut. Ronnie Arroyo made eye contact and immediately tried to get back into his truck. Cookie pushed forward, jamming an arm between the driver's side door and Ronnie, who was sizable in his own right. The two men stared at each other, faces close together, eyes narrowed, in a standoff. Ronnie finally relented.

"What you two want?" he asked, wiping a dark patch of hair out of his face. "I already told you that I don't know anything."

"That's funny," Jamie said, "because we know someone who told us that they saw Leah here. With you."

Ronnie shook his head and held his hands up. "Look, I don't want any trouble, and I'm not saying anything," he said.

"Well, you need to tell us something, because now it's not just about Leah. Her sister, Renata, is in trouble. Like, forcibly-taken-from-her-home in trouble."

From his expression, that was news to him. He softened his stance. "I don't know anything about that." He took a step back, his hands on his hips, eyes studying the ground by his work boots. "I'm sorry about Renata, but I don't know her or anything about who might have taken her." Ronnie seemed shaken. He took a second step back from Cookie and leaned against his vehicle.

Jamie moved closer to him. "Ronnie, here's your chance to do the right thing. It's clear that you do know something about Leah, and you need to tell us because we need to get her sister out of this. If Leah's taken on some trouble, that's on her, but Renata is innocent. She's just caught in the middle. Guilty by association. And Leah may not even know her sister is in trouble."

Ronnie laced his hands behind his head and stretched his back. "Look, I might have been doing something that's not exactly legal. I mean before." He crossed his arms, his eyes still studying the ground.

Jamie pushed a little more. "We don't care what you were in or what you're doing," Jamie said. "You're not our priority. Renata is. And Leah is, if she wants our help."

"You'll keep me out of it? Don't use my name, or I'll deny all of it." Ronnie had gone from avoiding eye contact to having a conversation.

Negotiating. Progress. "Done," Jamie said.

Cookie nodded in agreement.

Ronnie took a moment before speaking. "So maybe, just maybe, Leah had a business boosting cars and selling parts," he began. "And maybe I used to help her scout for cars a while back in Corpus."

When he looked at Jamie and Cookie, both kept stoic expressions—no tells, no shock. They knew better. Jamie called it the "brace face."

"Okay, so she's stealing cars and selling parts. So far, it doesn't sound too dangerous. Illegal but not that uncommon."

"Right," Ronnie continued. "So she was making pretty good money but also taking some extra jobs on the side and not sharing it with her boyfriend."

"Ormond?"

Recognition washed across his features. "You know Ormond?"

"We met once. Not a fan. We know he's looking for Leah," Cookie said.

"Yeah, well, you don't want to cross Ormond, but that's not her biggest problem." He paused, looked back at the ground, and shook his head. "I can't believe I'm telling you this."

"You're telling us so we can help Renata."

Ronnie nodded. "So, she stole a car that she shouldn't have, and she's getting heat from it. This car is going to be a real problem."

"Ormond's angry about her boosting the wrong car?"

"Ormond is the least of her problems now," Ronnie explained. "She'd be lucky if she only had to deal with him. No, this one... She's in deep. She might not get out. I just helped her with a place to stay while she figured out what to do."

"What's the deal with the car?"

"I can't give you details. All I can say is if you want to save Renata, you're going to need to get to Leah first—before anyone else does. Because this thing she's in? I can see them going after family to get to her."

"Anything else?" Jamie asked. "You can't tell us who's coming for her?"

"That's where I end it," Ronnie said, shaking his hands in front of himself. I got my own people to take care of, and they need me. Not putting my neck out any further. That's all you're getting."

Jamie could tell from the tightness in his jaw that Ronnie was done. They'd been lucky that the man had a conscience at all and gave them anything. Many in his position would've told them to shove it. Jamie offered her hand.

"Thanks, Ronnie," she said as she shook his hand. "You're a good guy."

"Don't spread that around, please," he said and shook Cookie's hand. "I hope you find Renata okay. And Leah. She's solid. Just too ambitious for her own good sometimes."

Jamie could relate more than she wished to admit.

Ronnie left them alone in the parking lot, and as they walked back, Jamie glanced over her shoulder. "So who do you think is after Leah?"

"No idea," Cookie said as he reached the Tahoe and opened the passenger door. "The fact is our missing, now not missing, person is being chased by two people and has a sister as collateral." He shook his head. "Not a good thing."

"So someone with money," Jamie said. "Someone with power who's not afraid to use it."

Leah had taken her skills and reached for more than she could handle, much like Jamie's parents. The greed always got the better of them. Jamie wondered if she would be able to save any of them.

CHAPTER TWENTY-NINE

Jamie and Cookie returned to Erin's warehouse and found her inside, perched in the middle of a row of boxes, her body bent over a cardboard container. She stood up to greet them.

"What are you doing?" Cookie asked.

"Nervous energy," she said. "When I got this place, it was still full of a lot of random crap, so whenever I'm anxious, I come over here and dig through stuff and throw things out. It's my therapy."

"Sounds like a good strategy," Jamie said. "Find anything good?"

Erin stood up to stretch, arching backward and extending her arms outward. "I found some divorce papers and an old watch. Doesn't work. Probably not worth anything." She walked closer to her friends. "How are you two holding up? What's next?"

"Ronnie Arroyo was helpful. I mean, helpful to a point. It sounds like Leah's in deep with some pretty connected people." Jamie sighed and rubbed her eyes. "But we don't know where she is or where Renata is."

"Now what?" Erin asked.

"I sent a text to Detective Herrera to let him know about Renata. Don't worry, I didn't mention Becky or any witnesses, but I did tell him that it looked like she had been taken with her own car. Maybe a BOLO could help find her." Jamie knew that escalation meant she needed to alert law enforcement. She also knew she was in a position to investigate in a different way than he would be—she didn't have to follow the same rules. And with so much at stake, she would need to take some chances. Some dangerous chances.

"I think it's time to pull our big card," Jamie said.

"Take the El Camino out?" Cookie asked. "As bait?"

Erin crossed her arms. "Are you sure that's a good idea?"

"I think it's the best chance we have for drawing out whoever took Renata. They took her as a way to get to Leah, right? And if they think we're her, then…"

"This could go sideways. You know that, right?"

Jamie nodded. "It's already sideways, Erin. We've got to get Renata back, and if pretending to be Leah does it, well…"

Erin said, "One condition. You take Becky with you."

"You really think Becky wants another go?" Cookie asked. "She's already had a tough day."

"She'll jump at the chance to help on this one," Erin said. "In fact, she'd be pissed at all of us if we didn't trust her enough to ask." She signaled to the opposite door. "I'll go get the keys to the El Camino and let Becky know she can be the tail."

THE EL CAMINO CUT A sharp contrast in the setting sun. Cookie hunched over, his backpack balanced on his legs, and dug until he retrieved his "surveillance beanie," which promptly went on his head.

"Feel better now?" Jamie joked.

Cookie straightened and adjusted his beanie. "Damn straight. I can't believe how cold it gets when the sun goes down."

They'd decided Cookie should drive this job. Jamie considered herself equally capable, if not better, at evasive maneuvers, but she was fine riding side for the lure. She needed a break from being behind the wheel. Cookie had all kinds of pent-up energy that needed an outlet. Becky would tail them in Jamie's car since it was nondescript and blended easily into a sea of traffic.

Cookie left the warehouse and made his way into town. They figured the best tactic was to give the car a basic run down the main streets first before breaking off into neighborhood patterns. Reaching Avenue A took only a few minutes, and Cookie made tracks a solid ten blocks back and forth.

Jamie trained her eyes on the traffic, scanning any cars that seemed to have paid them unusual attention. So far, other than a few glances of general interest from other drivers, nothing seemed to register. Cookie monitored his speed, careful not to tempt the local authorities into pulling him over. Jamie knew Cookie longed to put the car through its paces, but that could attract the wrong kind of attention.

He continued driving up and down the main drag, taking detours off to side streets where he knew locals hung out. He turned and passed Slices Pizza, a popular take-out joint known for its Chicago-style pizza. The El Camino got a few admiring looks as they drove by but nothing else. Cookie wouldn't admit it, but he enjoyed the attention.

Port Alene was surprisingly busy that night, a regular stream of cars driving up and down Island Main and turning off to local watering holes, bars, restaurants, and liquor stores. The island had seen a crop of new liquor stores pop up because the tourists seemed to need only three things: sunscreen, seafood, and alcohol.

"What do you think?" Jamie asked. "Keep cruising?"

"Why not?" Cookie replied. "The longer we're out here, the more likely we are to get lucky." He shrugged. "Let's take a run by Alibi Alley."

Jamie glanced in her mirror and spotted Becky safely back but in view. She continued to study cars in the next lane, taking in car models and any other descriptive elements she might need to recall.

Cookie made a run by the Tarpon Taproom parking lot, passing two cars coming in. It was a decent crowd for so early in the evening. Jamie looked over her shoulder and checked the crowds.

"Think of all the people lying about where they are tonight," she joked.

"And that's different from our job how?"

"Good point."

Cookie took one last tour down Alibi Alley then made his way back into town. He noticed a set of headlights in his rearview mirror, two cars back. Jamie caught his rapid mirror checking.

"The one two back?" she asked.

He nodded. "Could be nothing. Some people like to leave the Alley early."

"Ri-i-ight. Lots of people worried about being up at the crack of noon tomorrow."

"Uh... fishermen? Guides? Hello?" Cookie checked the mirror again and saw the car was still there. "That reminds me. I need to get Paulo to take me out for a day when it warms back up again."

Jamie resisted the urge to look over her shoulder at the car. The one directly behind them peeled off to take a right, and their car of interest, an unremarkable black sedan, held back, adding more space between the two cars.

"Can't see what the driver looks like," Cookie said. "Whoever it is knows how to position headlights in my eyes. Or is just damned annoying. Could go either way."

Cookie took a left, and the car behind him followed, still keeping a careful distance. He continued working his way toward the main intersection, curious to see if his new tailer would follow. He then stepped on the gas.

"Bold move," Jamie noted as the speedometer crept up toward the speed limit, something they both knew carried a risk, as locals knew the town loved few things more than a good speeding ticket on the main tourist drag.

The sedan, an older-model black Chrysler, was speeding up at a measured pace, wanting to keep them in range but not too close. Cookie played with the pace, a test of how committed the other driver was to staying near. He drove the length of the main drag and decided to take a turn leading toward a neighborhood of older rental houses and an RV park.

The sedan followed.

Cookie kept his eye on the car tailing them. He'd chosen to lure their unwelcome guest toward Mallard Bay, a small area with open fields and a small inlet that sometimes served, in the daytime, as a host for people fishing and crabbing. Becky remained in the distance, behind the sedan tailing the El Camino.

The sedan sped up, working its position in the left lane of the old road. No traffic was coming on the other side, and the driver continued until the sedan passed the El Camino then swerved sideways and cut them off. Cookie slammed on the brakes, saving the car from T-boning the offending sedan. Both cars stopped, engines still running.

A woman stepped out, gun drawn on the El Camino. Her black hair, pulled back in a ponytail, disappeared down her back, and her clothes and boots were also black.

Leah.

Cookie kept his hands on the wheel. "Put that shit down. Right now," he commanded her.

She did no such thing.

"Leah, you know me. My mom took care of you when you were a kid."

"Cookie?" she asked, her eyes studying his face. "I thought you looked familiar." She shook her head. "Wow. All those days I spent trying to climb your mom's fence."

"Not much has changed," he said.

Sure it has," she said. "I'm faster now." Leah lowered her weapon and tucked it behind her back. "Sorry, I didn't know it was you."

Jamie opened the side door of the El Camino slowly. "Hey, Leah, I'm Jamie. Cookie's partner."

"Sorry to meet under these circumstances," Leah said, her eyes shifting between Jamie and Cookie. "How did you find him anyway?" she asked, pointing at her vehicle.

Becky pulled up behind them, diverting Leah's attention. She reached for her weapon.

"It's okay," Cookie said. "She's with us."

Cookie stepped out of the car, prompting Leah to take a step back. He held his hand in the air. He called to Becky, "It's okay. Stand down."

Becky stayed in the Tahoe but kept the front headlights shining in their direction.

Cookie said, "We're on your side. And we don't have a lot of time."

"Give me the keys first, then we'll talk."

Jamie could see Cookie's disappointment. He hadn't ever expected to keep it, but his joyriding days were officially over.

"You know, you could get hurt driving this car around. People are looking for me."

"No shit," Jamie said. "That's why we're doing it. We were hoping to lure the people who are looking for you."

"Well, surprise. Now you've made it worse because I'm out in the open."

"We had no other choice, Leah, and you know it."

Leah studied them the way a parent does her children after catching them in the act of something dangerous, exasperated by their momentary carelessness—running with scissors or playing with matches.

"You know Renata is missing," Jamie said. "She called in sick today, and when we went to check on her, we found out she'd been taken. Whoever took her did it to get to you."

"So you're good at connecting the dots," Leah said.

"All dots... and roads... lead to you," Jamie replied.

"Renata doesn't deserve this, and we aren't letting go of this case until she's home safe," Cookie said.

Leah's guarded stance softened slightly, her expression less tense. "I'm taking care of things with Renata. I know who has her, and as soon as I handle my end, they're going to let her go," Leah said. "It's safer for all of you if you're not involved." She held her hands out to Cookie. "Hand them over."

"He really loves this car, you know," Jamie said.

"He's got good taste" came her reply. Her hand remained out to receive the keys.

Cookie walked toward Leah, and she took a step back. He slowed his pace, slowly extended his arm, and dropped the keys into her outstretched hand.

"Does she have a name?" Cookie asked. "She really needs one."

"His name is Frankie. After my uncle, God rest his soul." She made the sign of the cross and kissed her finger. "Apologize to Miss Yvonne for me. I left some money for her in her cat-treat jar in the kitchen. Let her know if you see her."

"That's a new thing, the housekeeper paying?"

Leah shrugged. "I wasn't very good at it, but she didn't mind. She really just needed the company. Nice lady."

"Your sister was really worried about you. Enough to hire us to find you."

Leah nodded. "It looks like you're good at your job."

"Our job isn't done until Renata is safe," Cookie said.

"Mine too," she replied. "She's my sister. This is my mess. I've got it covered."

"My number is in the glove box," Jamie said. "You're going to need it."

"Don't follow me," Leah said. "I know you're already thinking about it, but I promise you if you do, it's going to put Renata in danger. She's okay right now. I'm handling it." Leah walked to her El Camino and slipped into the driver's seat. She pulled away, her arm out the window with a wave. "See you later," she called as she disappeared into the night.

"Yes, you will," Jamie said, moving toward the sad sedan. "Well, I'm not touching this one." She signaled to Becky, who drove the Tahoe over to the pair.

"This doesn't feel right," Cookie said. "What if she can't handle this on her own?"

Cookie was right. Leah's approach might work for her, but she was no longer the primary concern. Renata was the one in danger, the one who needed rescue.

They still had one piece of leverage.

"Don't worry," Cookie said. "She'll be back. And soon."

CHAPTER THIRTY

One hazard of the work of skip tracing was that losing oneself in the pursuit of finding others was easy. The hunt, the puzzle, the study of another's motivations—a person not known outside of a case file, some photographs, and a personality analysis from the client with their own cloudy lens—could be wonderfully consuming. A case was an opportunity to tuck away relationship issues, family drama, and all the small but hard daily-life struggles that showed up.

But that day, the shield that Jamie's work provided against her own personal traumas—most notably, being born to parents she would never be able to trust—would do no good. She had to face them and to say goodbye. They never would have agreed to a last meeting, which was why she'd asked Riley for help. Having lived a life under their loose care, Jamie knew that if Stella and Alex had a chance to slip away into the darkness without having to answer for their choices, they would do so in a minute.

That's why she'd asked for the call.

Riley sent her a text once he set an appointment with Alex to pick up his new documents, the things that would help them forever leave this life behind and begin anew, free from bad bosses chasing them or daughters asking them to be parents—all the hassles of a con man's life.

Jamie had known that day would come. It was inevitable. At some point, Stella and Alex would overplay their hand, and the rightful owner of those stolen assets would claim repayment and possibly something more personal. Their ambitions always reached further than their abilities, substantial as they were, because they kept raising the bar. Once they reached above their station, well, everything would go south.

And soon, so would they.

Jamie made sure to leave well in advance of Alex's appointment to give her enough time to lie in wait for their arrival. She parked at the back of the building and waited for the message that they had indeed entered. Stella, in particular, was never one for confrontation. She much preferred to use Alex for those messy entanglements, to let him go out in front while she pulled the strings in the background, always getting what she wanted while never getting her hands dirty. All Jamie had wanted as a child was an ordinary mother. Stella had never intended to have a family. She told her daughters as much. She'd been talked into it, and Alex was very persuasive when they were younger. Most people thought having a family was everything, the American Dream.

Not if your parents are grifters.

Jamie's phone pinged.

Stella and Alex had arrived.

Jamie sat in her car, hands folded for a moment, and inhaled deeply. She walked to the front of the building and waited outside the doors, leaning against the battered brick of the long-forgotten shopping center.

Jamie checked her watch a number of times, a reminder of how seconds could feel like hours when waiting for bad news. When she got to the number ten, she told herself she had to count to a hundred before she could check her watch again.

Seconds later, the door swung open, and Stella came through first, with Alex right behind. When she turned to her right and saw Jamie, surprise flickered on her face before her features turned pleasant, as though she was seeing an old friend.

"Jamie, sweetie, so good to see you," she said, her voice soft and soothing. She was proficient at smoothing the jaggedness of the many lies that had passed through her lips over the years.

Jamie knew it well. To that day, it almost still worked—almost.

Alex moved closer and interjected himself. "Hey, Jamie. We didn't expect to see you."

"I figured as much," Jamie replied. "Were you planning on saying goodbye?"

"Of course," he said.

Jamie knew neither of them believed that.

"We just wanted to get settled first."

"Well, I'm glad I served your purposes," she said. "And Riley too."

"I know you don't believe it, but we are grateful," he said. "And Riley is top notch. Expensive but worth it."

Jamie held a hand up to him as he spoke, keeping her eyes on her mother. "Have you told Grace what's going on yet? Does she know you're leaving? Because I'm guessing that she would expect to be going with you, but you didn't ask for new credentials for her."

Stella reached for Jamie, who took a step back, so Stella took back her outstretched hand then laced her fingers together in front of herself. "Look, you know how your little sister is. She hears what she wants to hear." She glanced at Alex and said, "We've both tried to start the conversation about how we might need to leave one day if it became too dangerous for us to stay..."

"I'm pretty sure Grace thought she was included in your plans," Jamie said. "I talked to her recently, and she was upset because you weren't answering her texts."

"I did answer her texts," Alex said, "and I told her we were in the middle of something and we would fill her in soon."

"When?" Jamie asked, holding her arms wide. "When you're safe and settled in Belize? How is she going to take care of herself? She makes her living off of the jobs you give her." She looked directly at her mother. "How can you just leave her like that, without any answers?"

Alex clenched his jaw and glanced away. He didn't have an answer, and they both knew it. He stood quietly and let Stella take the heat. For once, she had to answer to Jamie for her choices, had to look her daughter in the eye and tell the ugly truth. And the truth was that Stella and Alex were a tight union, so much so that they simply didn't have any room for their daughters. Jamie knew it. Grace didn't.

She just wanted Stella to say it out loud.

"You have no intention of telling her, do you?" Jaimie asked. "You two are going to, what, slip out in the night, leave her a note saying that you'll send for her soon, and then just drift away? A long goodbye?"

Jamie wanted to hear the words. She would make her say the words.

"Jamie, you have to understand..."

"Tell me the truth for once," Jamie demanded. "You're going to leave and not tell her."

Stella dropped the concerned-parent facade. Her eyes narrowed. The charade was over. "No, I'm not going to tell her. She'll want us to take her, and we just can't do that right now."

"Can't or won't?"

"That's not fair," she said.

"Don't you *dare* talk to me about fair," Jamie replied. "Not one fucking thing that's happened here is fair."

"So why did you agree to help us in the first place?" Stella asked. "So you could tell me off before we go?"

Jamie glanced around—still not another soul in sight. A gust of cold air whipped at her face. She looked at Alex then back at Stella. "Maybe I just wanted to make sure that you'll be gone for good. The truth is that it's better for all of us. Let's cut that last string."

Alex took a step forward. "What are you going to tell Grace?"

Jamie shook her head. "I'm not telling her a damn thing."

"Nothing?" Stella asked. "She's going to need you once we're gone."

"Oh, I know, and I know that you're counting on that," Jamie said. "She's my sister, and I'll take care of her, but I'm not making any excuses for you."

The three of them were in a standoff in front of Riley's secret disappearance factory. Jamie took one last look at her parents, keeping her father's gaze then her mother's. She didn't offer any parting words, no "good luck" or "have a nice life." She walked away, leaving them in silence, letting them feel her back turned on them.

Not that it mattered.

The ties had been cut. She would need to figure out how—and when—to tell Grace the truth. And as painful as that personal entanglement had been, Jamie had bigger concerns. Leah was in the wind, Renata was in danger, and Jamie had no idea what to do about either one of them. She would keep her energy focused on those who truly needed her.

Alex and Stella were officially on their own.

CHAPTER THIRTY-ONE

Jamie was three shots of tequila in before Cookie arrived. Marty walked by and placed a tall glass of ice water on the bar for her. "Pace yourself," he said. "You remember how bad you felt last time?"

She nodded. "I know. It's important to hydrate while you scrub your memory."

Cookie made his way from the front door to Jamie's stool, stopping first to stoop down to give Deuce a proper greeting. "You're not doing a good job keeping her on the wagon, you know that?" After another rub of the jowls, he took a seat next to his partner.

"Why didn't you let me go with you?" Cookie asked. "I could've stayed in the car. Moral support, you know."

Jamie shook her head. The tequila had kicked in, and her voice sounded loud as she spoke, like screaming to be heard at a rock concert. "No, no, no. I had to slay that dragon alone."

"I don't know what it is with you suffering solo, but it doesn't make you noble."

"No?" She held up a finger and thumb in a pinching symbol. "Not even a little bit?"

"Maybe if your life becomes a cheesy TV movie one day, but no."

"Mine would definitely be a cautionary tale."

Cookie countered, "Nah. You've done a lot of good, and let's face it, your upbringing could have put you on the fast track for earning a rap sheet longer than the Jetty walk. I think you're a damn success story." He put an arm around her shoulder. "But you're still young, so there's still time to screw this up if you really want to."

Jamie rested her head against her friend's shoulder. "I appreciate your faith in me. Maybe you can get a side bet with Erin on my odds of staying on the right side of the law."

"I'd take that bet."

Marty brought Cookie a beer and another water for Jamie. He said, "Drink that."

"Do I have to remind you that I'm part Irish?" Jamie said. "I may not be big, but I can hold my liquor. It's in my DNA."

"Bullshit is in your DNA," Marty joked.

Cookie gave Jamie's shoulders a bit of a shake. "You gonna be okay?"

She nodded. "Yeah. I mean, not right now, but you know... It's a big day, getting my parents new identities and saying goodbye to them, possibly forever."

"You don't really think that you'll never see them again, do you?"

She spoke more softly. "I think they're gone for good. I do." She took a sip and put the glass down. "It's okay. I think it would be better for me and Grace if those two just went off and we didn't hear a word. Every time they show up, they just tear little pieces of us apart and toss them in the wind."

"That's very dramatic," Cookie said.

"It's the tequila. I'm more eloquent when I have a good buzz going."

"Apparently." Cookie waved a hand under his neck at Marty, a signal to cut Jamie off.

"I saw that," she said.

"I know you did."

"By the way, I'm not so drunk that I can't feel your patronizing stare. I'm just going to go upstairs and fall facedown in my bed. No problem."

"I know, but I think you could use some more water. It'll make tomorrow morning easier."

Jamie glanced down at Deuce, who was sound asleep on the floor. "He's drunk off dog treats. Marty keeps spoiling him with bacon."

Cookie said, "We need to get Renata back. You can drown your sorrows later."

The sound of Renata's name stuck in Jamie's ear. She straightened up, left her beer alone, and reached for her water. "Okay, you've got me. No more feeling sorry for myself. I have more important things to do."

"Yes, you do." Cookie gave her a hug. "Get some sleep, and I'll see you in the morning." He gave her a once-over. "You need help up the stairs?"

"Nope," she said. "I've been in way worse shape than this." She started to leave and stopped. "But if you hear me rolling down the stairs, come get me?"

"Will do."

Jamie followed her partner's advice, giving Marty a wave and taking Deuce upstairs. She crawled into bed, images of her parents fading in the distance in her mind. She pushed them away, the way they often did her. Her eyes closed, and she took comfort in the darkness.

Tomorrow would be different.

CHAPTER THIRTY-TWO

Tequila is never a good idea.

Jamie shifted her head on her pillow, her left arm tingling from having slept at an odd angle, her eyelashes pressed into her sockets. She moved her head slowly to the side, blowing a patch of stray hair stuck to her lips.

Going to be a rough day.

As she moved her head off the mattress to peek at Deuce, she was greeted by the sound of snoring and his pudgy face plunged into the side of his dog bed. From the looks of it, they'd both had too much of a good thing last night.

Note to self: Tell Marty to lay off the dog treats.

She pulled herself up in her bed, her head against the pillow, knees up to her chest. The day before returned to her in small pieces—confronting her parents, walking away. Whatever small shred of hope Jamie entertained of having parents who acted like… well, parents… had disappeared with them.

Good riddance.

She reached for her phone and deleted their contact information. Their numbers wouldn't be active anymore anyway. Maybe that was a ceremonial task, but it felt good. She would still need to take care of Grace, but she wasn't going to rush into that crisis. She wouldn't realize their parents were gone for a while—a small reprieve.

Jamie heard a knock at the door and the turn of a key. Cookie opened the door, coffee and a brown paper bag in his hand.

"I should have never given you a key," Jamie said as she rubbed a temple. "What if you walk in someday and I'm with somebody?"

"Who are you kidding?" Cookie replied. "When was the last time you were with anybody?"

She shrugged. "There might be one day." She then rubbed her face. "But probably not."

"Hmm." He handed her the coffee. "Here, this might help." He put the bag on the table.

"What's in the bag?" she asked. "I don't smell tacos, which is why Deuce hasn't bothered to wake up."

"I didn't think your stomach would be up for it. There's some cinnamon bread in there from my mom. She said to tell you to lay off the tequila."

Jamie smiled. "Tell your mama I hear her." She sniffed the coffee, took a small sip, and grimaced. "Don't think I'm even ready for that yet. Doesn't even smell good." She lay back down and pulled her bedsheet over her head. "To what do I owe the pleasure of this visit?"

Cookie walked over to her bed, pulled up a chair, and sat next to her. Jamie moved slowly over to the edge and put her head on his shoulder.

"I'm a good pillow, right? I've helped many a woman with a hangover. It's like one of my superpowers."

"You're wonderfully fluffy. I'll give you that. And you always smell good. Except when you smell like tacos. And then you still smell good."

Cookie gave her a pat on the head. "I know yesterday was hard on you. Wanted to make sure you're okay." He waited a moment then said, "I wish you had let me help you with it."

Jamie tilted her head up toward her friend. "You giving a shit helps me."

"I'll always have your back. You know that."

"I do. You know what else will help?"

"What?"

"Promise me that you won't ask me about them again."

Cookie nodded. "What were we talking about?"

She smiled at her friend. "We were talking about what's on our schedule today."

"James Brown asked if we wanted to take a surveillance case for him. I told him we had a priority case right now but maybe another time."

"Once we get Renata and Leah in the clear, let's book a year of boring, high-paying surveillance work."

Jamie rolled off the other side of the bed and walked to the bathroom. After a quick shower and change, she was presentable—mostly.

Her head still hated her. The dull ache behind her eyes made her wince, and her neck muscles were still tight with stress. She moved her head from side to side, but the movement made the room spin for a second.

No more tequila.

Cookie smiled at Jamie's momentary wobble. "I took Deuce outside while you were getting ready. He's got fresh food and water. He's not impressed with today's breakfast menu."

"I think we both need to make better choices today." She reached behind her neck and rubbed. "Don't let me drink tequila again."

"I'll try, but you're pretty stubborn sometimes."

Jamie grabbed her bag and reached for her phone. As soon as she slipped it into a pocket, she felt a buzz and checked the message.

"Change of plans," she told Cookie. She handed him the phone for him to read. "Looks like Leah wants to meet."

Jamie grabbed her bag and gave Deuce a goodbye pat. "You know," she said as she opened the door, "one of these days, we're going to land a huge payday job."

"Maybe," he said as he followed her and turned the lock. "But not today."

CHAPTER THIRTY-THREE

Jamie had instructed Leah to meet them at the Jetty.

The Jetty served as a long walkway along the coast, fashioned from substantial blocks of granite placed in a haphazard position, a walking trail of sorts, but one treacherous to the uninitiated. Traveling the Jetty was not a leisurely stroll. It required some focus and awareness of the water, the surface, and the gaps. The jagged blocks were mottled in places by dark-green algae, and when the surface was wet, it could prove dangerous. Many a fisherman had turned an ankle traveling that path in search of his daily catch.

Port Alene's winds traveled across the Gulf, the waves fierce as they crashed against the granite rocks lining the Jetty path. Jamie and Cookie walked across the uneven length, at turns hopping over open dips between the large slate blocks that led to the water's edge. As they came closer to the far corner, Jamie spotted a lone figure at the end, but she couldn't yet focus on the face.

"Slow down," Cookie said as Jamie's pace quickened a bit across the rocks.

"I am going slow," she replied. "The wind is rough right now. Just want to get off to the side, toward some shelter."

Jamie glanced up and spotted Leah waiting for them. Cookie was by Jamie's side, the two walking together.

"Good to hear from you," Jamie said.

"You knew you would," Leah replied. "Once I realized something was missing from my car."

"Nice smuggler's box, by the way," Cookie said. "Whoever did that... Quality work."

"Where's the money?" Leah shifted her weight from side to side, her energy anxious.

"Where's Renata?" Jamie asked, ignoring Leah's question. "Is she safe?"

"Yes, she's safe, but I need the money to keep her that way."

"I think you're in a lot of trouble," Cookie said. "Like, someone-might-get-killed trouble."

"I've got things under control." Leah said, a hint of hesitation in her words. Maybe she didn't truly believe it either.

"Really? Because it kind of feels like you don't." Jamie took a step closer. "Why are you shutting us out? Renata came to us for help, and now she's in danger. We can't walk away from this. And you can't do this alone. You're going to need reinforcements. Let us help you."

"If you want to help, give me my money back." Leah looked away in the distance, studying the waves as they traveled to the rocks. A small crack formed in her voice. "I can't get Renata back without the money." She glanced down at her shoes. "I'm trying to protect you too. The less you know, the better."

Cookie shook his head. "You can't protect us. We're already in it. We need to know everything."

"At least tell us about the money," Jamie said. "I'm guessing it has something to do with your car-boosting hustle?"

Leah's eyes flashed in recognition, her jaw clenching. "What do you know about that?"

"We know more than you think."

"And we know about Ormond. We took a little road trip to Austin. Not a nice guy, really. You could do better."

Leah's body stiffened at the mention of his name. "You talked to Ormond?" She put her hands to her face. "I wish you hadn't done that."

"We had no choice. He sent some guy to stalk Renata at work and scared the shit out of her. We decided to go right to the source."

"You shouldn't tangle with Ormond," Leah said. "Where else did you go?"

"We stopped by your old job at the storage facility," Jamie said.

Leah was visibly uncomfortable, shifting from side to side. She reached inside her jacket pocket and pulled out a pack of cigarettes. She tapped the pack on the heel of her hand and took one. She struggled to light it in the wind. When she did, she took a deep drag.

"We also know that you stole something you shouldn't have." Jamie took a step closer. "Leah, we don't have time to play games, and I don't think you have time either. Who knows what's happening with Renata?"

"I talked to Renata this morning," Leah said. "She's okay. She's scared, but she's okay."

"And the girls?"

"Out of town, still with their dad. Safe."

Leah tossed her cigarette into the ocean, the white filter disappearing quickly in the current.

She pulled another cigarette from her pocket. "This is where I give you the chance to opt out of the rest of the information. The more you know, the more danger you're in."

Jamie glanced at Cookie, who nodded.

He said, "We'll take our chances."

"Okay, but I can't tell you. You're going to need to see it. And then you're all in. Last chance."

"We're all in," Jamie said. "Let's do this."

CHAPTER THIRTY-FOUR

The Sparkling City by the Sea was well short of dazzling that morning. South Padre Island Drive was filled with three solid lanes of traffic. Thankfully, they could exit to StorSmart after only another three miles.

Jamie did the driving, and Cookie retained his post in the front passenger seat. Leah sat in the back, quiet, her eyes fixed on the passing roads outside the car window. Jamie glanced at her now and again in the rearview mirror. The sound of the road and the low hum of Jamie's Stevie Ray Vaughn playlist played in the background.

"So you miss Austin?" Jamie asked.

"I do," Leah said. "Great food and the best music. The tech execs have been very good for my business." She sighed. "I do miss the work. I'm good at it, and now I'm kind of... on hiatus."

Jamie made eye contact with Leah in the mirror. "Tell me more about Ormond," she said. "He's pretty intense. At least, he was when we met him."

"He doesn't like strangers poking around in his business. He and I have that in common," she said, though a small smile emerged as she spoke.

"His approach with Renata was... questionable," Cookie added.

"Ormond didn't use very good judgment, I'll give you that. He was just trying to get my attention."

"He certainly got ours," Cookie said. "She was pretty scared."

"Yeah, I gave him an earful for that. I mean, he figured if he scared her, she'd tell him where I was, but she didn't know because I

216

hadn't told her anything. She'd be safer that way, and if Ormond had any sense, he would've known that I wouldn't have told her anything. I'm not going to run to my sister. She has zero skills to help with my current situation." She shrugged. "He's hot-tempered, and he doesn't think things through. That's why I don't tell him everything about the business."

"So you were keeping some things from Ormond?"

"Hell, yeah," she said. "The money, for one—the money you took from me? I didn't take that from him. I earned that on the side, but in his mind, it's stealing because I used his crew even though I did all the work and paid them from my share. He didn't like me doing that, but he said I was taking too many risks."

"So why do you need that money if it doesn't belong to him?"

Leah turned her attention to the passing scenery outside her window. "Because now the money does belong to him. In his mind, I stole it by using his resources, and now that I have this other... issue, he's requiring it as payment to help." She shrugged. "I'm out of options. I've got no choice. And we have history, so I trust him."

Ten minutes passed, and they arrived at the StorSmart. The building exterior was unremarkable in the way that storage units were unremarkable. It certainly didn't seem to have a regular cadre of visitors coming and going. If anything, it appeared to be the kind of place that could end up on one of those reality storage shows where people buy abandoned storage units in the hopes of finding items worth thousands of dollars, as if someone who had things that could be converted into stacks of cash would leave them languishing in a storage unit for someone else to take. Jamie made that observation to Leah.

"Yeah, it doesn't happen like that in real life," she said. "From what I've seen, the only time someone ends up with something good is if the original storage owner dies, and then it's taken over."

Cookie looked over at Jamie. "Never had a client leave us a storage unit, right?"

She shook her head. "Nope."

"With our luck, we'd just end up with a bunch of broken fishing poles and dusty particleboard furniture from the nineties that we'd have to haul to a dumpster and then set on fire."

Leah pointed toward the road running alongside the storage facility. "Keep going. There's another building farther back, on the left."

Jamie raised an eyebrow at her partner. "Is this part of the place?"

"It's a kind of special off-the-books cluster for people who have more security concerns," Leah said. "Probably don't want to know what's in those. I know this from working there."

Jamie followed Leah's directions and, sure enough, came upon a stretch of metal buildings, squat and uniform, off to the left and tucked back in some trees. A scattering of car parts and other metal castoffs from mechanical projects were littered around one side of the building. It resembled the yard of a small-scale hoarder or tinkerer well on his way to creating a private junkyard.

"Go around the backside. Just watch for metal in the road," Leah instructed. "Don't want to drive over it. It'll shred your tires."

As Jamie navigated around the back, the structure of the building came into view, a row of metal garage doors in a line, all uniform. Leaves gathered in piles on the ground as they had fallen in response to the cold weather.

Leah waved her hand. "Go to the very end."

As they pulled up, Jamie took note of the number on the door. The numbers made no ordered sense, more of a random system.

"Yours is thirteen thirteen?" Cookie asked. "You just like a whole lot of bad luck or something?"

Leah said, "I like all symbols of bad luck. Keeps me on my toes."

"I don't understand you at all," Cookie said.

"You're in good company," she replied.

Jamie pulled to the side and parked the Tahoe. She cut the engine and turned to look over her shoulder at Leah. "Okay. Big reveal time."

"Last chance to bail," she said.

"There's not a dead body in a freezer, right?" Cookie asked, his expression one of both joking and concern.

"No, no," Leah said, "although what's inside makes things complicated. For all of us now."

Leah reached inside her jacket pocket and pulled out a small keychain. A small religious medallion dangled from the silver ring. "St. Anne," she explained, noting Jamie's gaze. "My mother gave it to me. It was her mother's."

"I'm familiar," Jamie said. "Catholic grandparents. They tried, but not much stuck."

Leah stepped out of the car. Jamie and Cookie followed, staying a step behind. She bent down to the pull handle and latch, inserting a key into a lock on Unit 1313. She turned the key, gave it a strong yank, and squatted to push the door upward. The sound of scraping metal disturbed the quiet. She continued pushing until the door disappeared into the ceiling bay.

The unit was much deeper than it appeared from the outside. A wide, empty space greeted them, and the trio stepped inside onto the concrete. A few boxes lined each side of the metal walls—cardboard, unmarked, not uniform in size. Jamie looked toward the back of the storage space and noticed a black tarp over a vehicle. At least, the outline looked like a vehicle. Leah caught Jamie's gaze.

"There's the source of all of my trouble," Leah said. She took several steps toward the back and stood in front of the draped object. "If there is one job I wish I hadn't done, it would be this one."

Jamie exchanged a glance with Cookie. She waved at the tarp. "Let's see it."

Leah reached for the tarp and bunched a corner of the fabric in her fist. With the flair of a magician, she yanked the black material, which cascaded toward her, revealing a black Mercedes E350 class sedan. It was attractive in a uniform sort of way. Not flashy—in fact, quite the opposite—like a nicely tailored black suit that one would notice for its quality before forgetting entirely.

"Okay, you've got a nice, standard black Mercedes."

She nodded toward the car. "Look in the back seat."

Jamie took several steps closer. At first, she didn't notice anything out of the ordinary. She stared again and spotted, on the floorboard, what appeared to be a camel-colored jacket, expensive. Then she saw it—a patch of dark brown on the fabric.

She looked up at Cookie and signaled him over. He took a glance, and Jamie watched as he came to the same realization that she had. His eyes widened, but he kept his expression solemn.

"Um... is this from a hit and run or something?" Jamie asked. "The outside doesn't show any signs, but..."

Leah shook her head. "No, no hit and run." She walked over to the back of the car and looked inside as though checking to see if it was as she'd left it. "This is what happens when you boost the wrong car."

"So you think you've got evidence of a crime in a car you stole?"

She nodded. "You watch the news?"

"Now and then, but not really."

"You familiar with the Elizabeth Van Zant case?"

Jamie let loose a low whistle. "Oh, shit. Are you telling me that this car is somehow involved?"

Cookie said, "I thought the authorities checked all their cars—hers, his—and there was no evidence there."

"I think this is a fleet car," Leah said. "I looked up the VIN, and it's registered to Woodbridge Investments." She waited a moment then added, "One of Van Zant's companies is Woodbridge Investments. He has about twenty of these cars, from what I could find. Older models, easier to boost, don't have all the electronics to circumvent."

"But we don't know that this"—Jamie signaled toward the back seat—"is linked to the missing Mrs. Van Zant."

"There are photos of her wearing a coat like this one," Leah said.

"So you stole a car that's linked to a high-profile missing person case?" Cookie asked.

"That about sums it up." Leah exhaled, her arms crossed in front of her. "This is my problem."

"You really should rethink your numerology, because that's some pretty shitty luck."

Jamie took another glance inside the car. "So you brought the car back personally? Or someone on your crew?'

"This one was mine. I like to keep my skills sharp now and then, even though Ormond says it's an unnecessary risk. And this was a risk."

"I can't believe I'm saying this, but you should have listened to Ormond," Jamie said.

"Yeah, probably, but I've always loved that part of the job. It's how I started, and then I worked my way up to management and distribution."

"You make it sound like a manufacturing job," Cookie said, only half kidding.

"It is, isn't it? I mean, same business principles apply, with a few specialized concerns for illicit goods. I'm actually very efficient."

Jamie held a hand up. "Let's start from the beginning. Walk us through this job."

Leah touched a finger to the bridge of her nose as if shunting an oncoming headache. "It was a lucky break. At least, that's what I thought at the time. It was parked behind an old Italian restaurant that went out of business last year, and I happened to be driving by when it caught my eye. I was with one of my scouts."

"Ronnie?"

Her eyes flashed recognition. "You two are good." She looked back at the car. "I thought it was odd. Like, why would you put a nice car in that old place? No lights on, the place has been closed for a long time. I pulled in behind the car to check it real quick. It was locked, but that didn't take long. Older model, no digital starter. I did my thing, and before long, I had it started. I drove it, and Ronnie followed with my car. No big deal."

"Except that it was."

"Except that it was."

Jamie stood quietly, thinking through the options of what to do next. "So you've got evidence of a crime—a big one—and now you can't dump the car because..."

Leah hedged. "I might have sent out a message saying I had some evidence that was worth something."

Jamie couldn't keep her jaw from dropping. "You blackmailed a possible murderer with evidence of the crime?"

Leah nodded with hesitation. "I regretted it immediately. But I knew I was already in deep, so..." She put her hands over her mouth. "I knew it was stupid as soon as I did it, but something like this? I was already in trouble. We could use the money. Not just me, but Renata and the girls."

"She'd never take the money if she knew where it came from," Cookie said. "You know that."

"Yeah, but I wouldn't tell her. I was just going to put some away for them. For later."

"You ever done anything on this level before? I mean, you know what kind of resources this family has?" Jamie asked. "That's a big step up from boosting cars."

"Momentary lapse of judgment. I figured an even mil would be small time compared to what he keeps in the bank." She glanced down at the ground. "And now I can't get out of it."

"Can't you just dump the car and call it in? Or give it back to the murderer who lost it? Leave it somewhere and call the cops? Anything?" Cookie was clearly having trouble connecting all the dots. "Wipe it down for your prints and just put it where you found it."

"That's kind of the problem now," Leah said. "Who do you think has Renata? It's not Ormond. Ormond is trying to help me get her back. The money is for the risk he takes, being the middleman. Van Zant's people found Renata before I could get to her." She pulled the car tarp back over the Mercedes, carefully covering each corner with fabric. "This car is my only leverage. It stays here. Safe. Until Renata is safe."

Jamie agreed but needed to think through their next moves. With one misstep, Renata would pay the ultimate price. Jamie looked at Cookie, who offered a small nod.

"I think we may have a way out," Jamie said. "But you have to trust me."

She gestured toward the car. "I think we've established that."

"Okay, let's go."

"Where?"

"To see a friend."

CHAPTER THIRTY-FIVE

Jamie returned Leah to the Jetty to pick up her El Camino. "So you aren't worried about driving this now?"

She shook her head. "Not really. I'm watching for tails, but now that we've negotiated the terms of the arrangement, they won't come for me. Van Zant really doesn't want to hurt Renata. He just wants his car back."

Jamie hoped Leah wasn't giving her nemesis too much credit, especially with so much at stake. After watching the El Camino disappear into the distance, Jamie wondered if they should tail her. She'd had her eye out for any possible tails on Leah and, so far, hadn't seen anything unusual.

"If you're thinking of tailing her, you know she'd lose us," Cookie said. "So don't even think about it."

"Quit taking up space in my head," she replied. She rubbed her temple in an effort to ward off a headache. "I hate this, having to wait."

"Not being in charge?" Cookie asked. "Yeah, that's a new one for you. He surveyed the Jetty, watching a group of fishermen begin their journey across the granite. "We're going to meet her at Erin's soon. We just need to be patient."

A vision of the camel-colored coat in the back seat of the stolen Mercedes flashed in Jamie's mind. "I think we need to read up a bit more on the Van Zant case. It's no longer just a news story playing in the background of a bar."

Cookie searched the latest on the case on his phone. "Not too much here. She's his second wife, he's offered a reward for information on her disappearance..."

"That's rich," Jamie said. "Like he doesn't know anything about it."

"Has one daughter from his first wife," Cookie continued. "First wife passed away years ago. She came from a wealthy family. No new leads."

"Well, I can tell you that I didn't expect the case to take this particular turn," Jamie said.

What had started out as a small-time missing person case had quickly escalated into an entanglement with a possible murder involving one of the most powerful businessmen in the Lone Star State.

Edward Van Zant, a titan of local industry and a man known for using his considerable power to shape the landscape of the state, was not Jamie's average foe. He had money, access, and countless resources at his disposal.

All those things would be threatened due to one fateful night when his second wife disappeared. The car provided proof of his possible involvement, and Van Zant, it seemed, would do anything to keep that evidence hidden.

Jamie's cell phone rang. She checked the screen and put her finger to her lips in Cookie's direction. She rubbed her temple with a forefinger again then answered.

"Good morning, little sister," Jamie said, trying to put a lift in her voice that only fell flat.

"You doing okay?" Grace asked. "You sound like hell."

"We're in the middle of a really ugly case." Her dark hair fell to the side of her face as she tilted it toward the window. "Thanks for calling me back after you called me. Now I don't remember who started it." She sighed. "You doing okay?"

"I don't know. You tell me."

Here we go.

"What is it?" Jamie asked, the sigh in her voice coming through loud and clear.

"Don't do that," Grace chided. "Mom and Dad aren't returning my calls again, Jamie. Mom sent me this lame text saying she was busy and she'd get back to me. I'm still waiting."

"This is how they do things," Jamie countered. "I mean, what's different now?"

Jamie leaned her head against the window, the grime of the island's salts and winds coating the view with an opaque film. She glanced at Cookie, who pretended not to be paying attention to the call.

"I'm worried they're on the run again," Grace said, her voice laced with a hint of a quiver, the tone softer, the edges dulled by the familiar fear of being abandoned by their parents.

Again.

Jamie wanted to soothe her little sister, to relieve her own conscience of the burden of carrying the truth of her parents' plans alone, but she knew it would be the wrong choice. Stella and Alex ran from many things—debtors, double-crossed business partners, marks—but most of all, the suffocating needs of being attentive to their daughters.

Jamie redirected Grace's fears. "Okay, let's think this through. Didn't you tell me that they had a deal that looked like it might fall through?"

A small sniffle through the phone. Jamie hated to hear her sister in such a way. "Yes, but they told me not to worry."

"Okay, then, if they said you don't need to worry, then take them at their word. This is normal for them. They fall off, they show back up, usually without any explanations or apologies, and almost always longer than we expect. Right?"

After a momentary pause, she replied, "Right."

"Look, for all their skills, when it comes to staying in touch with us, those two are remarkably predictable. Just let them lie low for a while, give the phone a break, and let them get in touch. You know the more you hound them, the deeper they go down the rabbit hole."

"That's true," Grace conceded.

"Besides, when they do come up for air, they're going to come to you first."

Jamie was attempting to make Grace feel better. Grace had always strived to be favored, to find a way to turn the Alex and Stella show into a trio. She never understood that the Kelly and Astaire of small-time cons simply didn't have room for a third dance partner.

Jamie wrapped up the call, feeling a twinge of guilt laced with relief that she'd been able to calm Grace down and buy a bit of time before heading feetfirst into the dumpster fire that was the aftermath of her parents' planned skip.

"Wow," Cookie said, his expression tinted with sadness. "That must have been hard."

"It's going to get worse before it gets better," she replied. "I feel terrible not telling her, but if I do, it's actually going to be harder on her." She held her hand up. "Hell, I don't even know if they've left yet."

Cookie leaned over and offered an awkward side hug. "I got you. You know that, right?"

She nodded. "I do. And I'll have Grace when the time comes."

As she placed her phone in the car's cupholder, she noticed a new text from Leah. She picked it back up. "Okay, she's ready."

THE MEETING COULD GO either way.

Jamie lingered outside the back of Erin's brick building, her arms crossed as she leaned against the driver's side of her Tahoe. A flicker of movement caught the corner of Jamie's eye, and she turned to spot Cookie's F-150 pulling into the back lot.

He stepped out and gave the parking lot a once-over. "No sign of our girl yet?"

Jamie shook her head, pushing herself away from the Tahoe. "Nothing yet, but don't worry. She'll be here."

"We'll see."

No sooner had the words left Cookie's mouth than Leah pulled up and chose a spot several slots away from the other two cars. Jamie could see Leah typing on her phone. She stepped out of the car and tucked the cell in her back pocket after glancing at the screen.

"So this is it?" Leah asked, glancing at the building. "It's nice. Not what I expected."

Erin opened the back door and stepped outside. She was a stark contrast to the functionally casual trio of people in front of her. Her long blond hair was pulled back in a high ponytail, and she wore a teal-blue jumpsuit with a matching jacket, pointed toes peeking from the hem of her pants. She resembled Island Business Barbie.

Jamie registered Leah's judgment as she glanced at Erin. Many others had made the same mistake, assuming her pretty packaging held little else of value. Erin Clay had made a fortune off similar opinions. Jamie was pretty sure she dressed that way just to elicit such a response, an invitation to further lean into one's own biases.

"You want to come inside to handle business?" Erin asked. She winked at Cookie before waving them in. "Come in from the cold."

Cookie held out an arm toward Leah. "Guests first," he said, signaling her to move toward the door.

Erin stepped aside, out of the way of the open door. Leah moved toward her, a hint of caution in her steps.

She smiled at Erin the way one smiled at someone for the first time when one couldn't quite size them up and wasn't sure what to say. In that particular moment, Jamie enjoyed seeing that Leah had a lousy poker face.

Jamie moved to walk behind her, greeting her friend as she walked through the door. "Nice jumpsuit," she said, noting the contrast between Erin's polished style and Jamie's current uniform of well-worn flannel and jeans.

Erin reached for Jamie and gave her arm a squeeze. Cookie was last and was greeted with a hug. He always thought he was Erin's favorite and loved to rub it in every chance he got. Erin locked the door behind them with her key, twisting the deadbolt until it clicked.

Fluorescent lights shone down to reveal a largely open industrial space, the roof panels mostly clean but a few cockeyed and bent, with an occasional wire peeking through. It was in no shape to house tenants but was the perfect locale for stashing vehicles, stolen goods, and the occasional missing person.

"Follow me," Erin said as she walked toward the far end of the building.

Leah held back, letting Jamie and Cookie walk ahead of her.

Jamie sensed Leah's hesitation and turned over her shoulder. "Don't worry, we aren't going to bury you in some concrete blocks in the back," she joked, pointing at a stack of concrete blocks in the corner.

Jamie had meant to ask Erin what the hell those were doing there but decided against it. Messing with Leah's head a bit could be a benefit. It could keep her on her toes.

Erin walked through another door, which revealed another room that screamed business-office potential. While the main area resembled an open garage or storage, the next area seemed perfect for a call center or hot desking. Erin held a hand up, signaling them to wait as she walked through yet another door, presumably into a private office of some sort. She returned with a black duffel bag. She looked at Jamie, who nodded. Erin handed it to Leah.

"I heard you were looking for this," she said. "You can count it if you need to. I won't take it personally."

Leah took the bag by the short handles and put it down on the ground. She knelt down, unzipped it, glanced at the contents and moved a few stacks around, then zipped it up.

"It's fine," Leah said, standing back up, leaving the bag at her feet. "If I'm short, you'll hear from me."

Erin smiled at her, completely unintimidated by Leah's response. "As expected."

Leah didn't smile, exactly, but a small curl crossed her lips. "Thank you," she offered.

"So we good?" Jamie asked.

Leah waited a beat then glanced at Cookie then at Erin. "We're good."

"Let's get Renata home," Jamie said.

"I just hope she'll forgive me when this is over." Leah reached down and picked up the black duffel.

"That one's out of my hands," Jamie said.

The fact wasn't lost on her that they were two women both hoping for a sister's forgiveness.

CHAPTER THIRTY-SIX

Leah's El Camino pulled out of the parking lot as Erin, Cookie, and Jamie watched. The trio stood together silently until the car was out of view.

"So what do we think of our girl?" Jamie asked.

"Tough one," Erin replied. "She took one look at me and thought I should be working the cosmetics counter at Nordstrom."

"Well, I'm sure you'd do a fabulous job," Jamie said. "If I bothered with makeup, I'd trust you."

Cookie wrinkled his nose." You think that's why you don't date much? Because you don't..."

"Try harder?" Jamie joked. "No, I think it's because I have zero interest in being worried about what some guy thinks of me."

"I hear Alastair is single..."

"I can see why," Jamie said. "Not my type." She wrinkled her nose as if she was smelling rotting garbage.

"Definitely your type," Erin said a second time.

"No. He. Isn't." Jamie pretended to shudder as the words left her lips. "But I can see why Marty goes to bat for him. I've heard he has some redeeming values buried deep, deep below his many annoying layers."

Cookie added, "As much as I hate going toe-to-toe with Finn on the work stuff, from what I know of him, he's a stand-up guy personally." He clutched a hand to his chest. "I can't believe I just said that."

"Wow," Jamie said. "That's pretty big of you."

Cookie waved off her comment. "Okay, back to Renata's safety. That's a common goal, so I'm sure that she's going to do whatever it takes to make that happen," Cookie said.

"The key is whether she's up to the task," Jamie said. "Let's face it. She's out of her league with the Van Zant family. Hustling and boosting cars is good money, dangerous even, but she's batting with the Little League kids against some very heavy hitters."

"I didn't know you watched baseball," Cookie said.

"I don't," she replied, "but I do love a good sports analogy."

"She's not alone, though," Cookie reminded her. "Ormond is the middleman negotiating the return of the car to Van Zant. And he has his own crew, so Van Zant will take him more seriously. He keeps Leah safe, gets Renata back, and gets paid for the exchange in evidence."

Jamie walked to her Tahoe and leaned against the side, feeling the cool metal through her shirt. The winter winds had relented for the time being. "I hate to bring this up, but I think we also might need to bring in some additional help." She looked at Erin. "I don't think Erin is up to doing surveillance."

She held her hand up. "Count me out. Not in my wheelhouse."

She looked at Cookie and waited for him to register. She widened her eyes his way and tilted her head. He finally got it.

"Oh no," Cookie replied. "You don't mean Finn?" He looked like he'd sucked on a sour lemon.

"Good idea," Erin replied. "You just said he was a stand-up guy on the personal level."

"Not so fast," Cookie counted. "He'd steal your clients the moment you took your eyes off him."

"I don't think my clientele gets in enough trouble to use his services," Erin quipped.

Cookie shot some quality side-eye. "You know what I mean." The small vein in his neck flinched as he spoke. "Ugh, I hate this."

"Only as a last resort. I'll hit up James Brown first, but he just asked us to cover a job for him, so I'm not confident he's available." She put a hand on his shoulder. "Alastair's not my first choice, either, but he's good at his job." She wrinkled her nose. "And we're out of options."

"I don't know. I feel like this case is really going off the rails," Cookie observed. "Do we even know if Leah is going to keep us in the loop? She might try to do this exchange herself now that she has the money."

"I don't know," Jamie answered honestly. She turned her attention back to surveillance. "I'm not saying that we show Alastair all our secret files. I'm saying that we use him for some surveillance. Think of it as an opportunity for him to build some goodwill after stealing money out of our pockets. I get the feeling that he'd like to make amends in some way."

"What makes you think that?" Cookie asked.

"Just a hunch," Jamie replied. "We're going to need someone with skills, and let's face it, Alastair Finn has them. Just because we don't like him doesn't mean he's not a good investigator. I think he's already proven he is. Even you have to admit it."

Cookie wouldn't admit it, but he did shrug in concession. "I'll think about it, but I still hate the idea."

Good enough.

"Why don't I reach out and see what he says?" Jamie offered. She knew that while Cookie might concede to working with Finn, no way on God's green earth would he himself ask for help.

Again, he nodded with no verbal response.

"I wonder where Leah is going," Erin said. "Any guesses?"

"We don't have to guess," Cookie said, pulling out his phone. "I know exactly where she's going."

"What do you mean?" Jamie asked.

"Well, you know I love that El Camino, and since I got to spend a little time with her, I might have placed a tracking device on her. Just to keep her safe."

"By her, you mean Leah or the car?"

"Both." The sour pill of Finn had been swallowed and followed by a sweet chaser. "Plus, Leah was always on the run when she was little. It doesn't look like much has changed." Cookie held his phone out to Jamie to show a small red dot moving slowly across a map. "This tells me she's still on 361."

"You clever bastard," Jamie said. "Why didn't you tell me you did this?"

"Oh, didn't I?" Cookie feigned forgetfulness. "I thought I did."

"I love you—you know that?"

"Of course you do." Cookie checked the phone one last time before walking to Jamie's car. "Let's go see where our friend is headed."

Jamie reached for Erin and gave her a squeeze. "Thanks for your help." She then turned to Cookie. "Let's go."

Jamie started her engine and turned on the heat. She thought of Renata and wondered if she was scared, if she was truly safe. Most of all, she wondered if Edward Van Zant would let her live once he got what he wanted from Leah.

The odds weren't in their favor. Men of his stature rarely left loose ends.

They would have to change the rules of the game.

CHAPTER THIRTY-SEVEN

J amie despised asking for help.

Trust was something to be bestowed only in the rarest of circumstances, upon as few people as possible. With Cookie and Erin as confidantes, Jamie had little trust left for anyone else.

But in the Van Zant case, with Leah's unpredictable nature and Renata's safety in doubt, Jamie knew she'd have to reach out to the one person she didn't want to ask for help.

Jamie had asked Marty to give Alastair a heads-up that she needed to speak to him. He responded with a text stating Alastair would be at Hemingway's in an hour. So while Alastair Finn's presence could feel like a sunburn on the back of the thighs, at least he wasn't stringing her along and making her wait.

When Jamie arrived at Hemingway's, she found Marty behind the bar, engaged in deep conversation with one of his regulars about whether the Cowboys would make it to the postseason that year.

"My money says that they make it through the first two rounds," Jamie said over her shoulder.

"Guess you don't like your money much," the man quipped.

Jamie smiled. *Well played.*

She took ownership of a barstool at the far end of the bar and studied the people on the opposite side. Marty had a bartender's gift for gab, an ability to engage anyone who walked through his doors. Sometimes, she just watched him in her peripheral vision as he reeled in one fish after another.

Alastair appeared at the front door and, after a quick scan, made eye contact and threw her a nod. She cringed. He seemed even taller than when she'd seen him last. He wore a motorcycle jacket, faded jeans, and black work boots, the Alastair Finn standard uniform.

Marty glanced at Jamie, caught her eye for a moment, and tossed her a wink. Jamie pretended not to see him, but they both knew. Alastair pulled up a stool next to her, sitting a smidge too close, and put an arm on the bar.

"Did I understand correctly? That you actually wanted to see me?" He slapped the bar. "You missed me. Knew it."

Jamie resisted the urge to slap that self-satisfied smile off his face. She bowed her head, unable to make eye contact. "Well, it's kind of a necessary evil, but yes, I do... need your help."

Finn's smile expanded further. He leaned in on his forearm, pressing it onto the bar. "You need *my* help?" He was enjoying being in his position, which made the interaction even worse than she'd imagined.

She wondered if she and Cookie could perhaps handle things on their own.

"Don't make this any harder than it needs to be, okay?" Jamie said. "I need you to do something, and I'd appreciate it if you didn't turn the screws while I subject myself to this."

"I'm sorry, Jamie," he said, "but I can't go out with you."

"Never mind," she said, deciding against it. She would rather do surveillance solo for several nights on end. She couldn't imagine having to deal with him like that for days. But then she thought of Renata and decided to roll back her attitude.

"I'm sorry," he said. "I just needed to get that last one in. I promise—no more rubbing whatever this is in."

Jamie glared at him for several seconds. His expression turned more serious. He waited quietly for her to speak.

She rolled her eyes and sighed. "Okay, here's the thing. We have a case, and our client is in some serious trouble. Cookie and I need an extra resource for surveillance. And there's no money in this job. This is for good karma points only."

Alastair's eyes widened as if he'd seen Sasquatch. "Wait. Cookie is on board with this?"

Jamie shrugged. "We're kind of out of options."

"Clearly," Alastair noted. "How dangerous is it?"

"It could be a simple exchange. It could also go bad really quickly."

"What can you tell me?"

Jamie leaned in closer, in an almost conspiratorial manner. "Do you know much about Edward Van Zant?"

Finn cocked his head and clicked his tongue. "You really go for broke, don't you?"

CHAPTER THIRTY-EIGHT

Cookie walked through Hemingway's door just as Finn was making his way out. The two men acknowledged each other with a stiffness that would make a prison warden seem relaxed. The union would need work. With Finn out of the building, Cookie was at his partner's side.

"So AF is on board?" Cookie asked, smirking at the acronym.

She rewarded his joke with a thumbs-up. "Yep, he's on our team. He likes the high stakes of this case."

"I guess he's not so bad," Cookie replied.

"He's going to do some recon on Van Zant," she continued. "I'm going to put together some of my resources and send them to him so he can get up to speed—at least what I've been able to gather since we realized that Ormond wasn't the mastermind behind Renata's kidnapping."

She placed a finger on the paper file in front of her on the bar. "Finn and I worked on this during our meeting. Just a quick outline of what we know about Van Zant from online resources."

Cookie leaned forward to read over Jamie's shoulder as she tilted the file toward him. He took in a few things then asked, "You really think we can do this without any collateral damage?"

"I don't know" was her honest answer. "I checked in with Leah, and she said she's waiting to hear from Ormond on next steps. Are you still tracking her?"

"Of course," he said. "She hasn't moved since she parked at her shack hideout. I have an alert on my phone for when she leaves."

Jamie nodded and turned her attention back to her scribbled notes. Van Zant Enterprises was one of the most influential and powerful property developers in the state. Edward Van Zant wasn't known to covet the public eye, but his only child, Chloe, seemed to be on every social media platform in existence.

"It says here that they have almost six million square feet of retail, industrial, and mixed-use real estate in their portfolio. I don't know much about real estate, but it sounds like a hella lot."

Cookie pulled up his phone and searched for Chloe Van Zant's social media. He tilted the phone toward her for inspection and was greeted with a grid of squares, each featuring Chloe, her friends, and her travels. She, too, seemed to fit the stereotype of the only-child rich kid. Her long blond hair was styled as though she had stepped straight out of the seventies, blue eyes highlighted by perfectly shaped eyebrows. Her social media accounts bragged that she had recently returned from a vacation in Hawaii. In one photo, her tanned, toned skin contrasted with a carved gold bangle on her wrist. Jamie reached for Cookie's phone and scrolled through a few of the images. Her friends could have been sisters. They all looked the same.

"You'd think with that much money, you could branch out a bit, you know? Make friends that don't look exactly like you?"

"Maybe she's so amazing that she needs to be around others that remind her of herself." Cookie wiggled his fingers at her in an effort to get his phone back.

"I guess," Jamie said, returning the device, "but that shit depresses me."

"Agreed," Cookie said, "but you know I have a thing for brunettes."

Marty made his way over, carrying two glasses of iced tea. "I can tell you're working, so the beer can wait till later. Gotta keep sharp," he said. "And I'll bring some food when Dig has it ready."

Dig was Marty's new cook. Jamie had once heard that skinny chefs shouldn't be trusted, but she had to admit Dig knew his away around the kitchen. He'd been experimenting with some of the seasonings on the jalapeño poppers, and Jamie was a fan.

"Can you ask Dig to throw some extra fries on whatever you've got coming?" Jamie asked. "Cookie always steals mine."

Cookie shot her a side-eye and said, "Yeah, throw some extra so I can steal them. I'm hungry."

Marty nodded and left to wait on two new patrons that had appeared. Jamie glanced at Cookie and watched him scroll through Chloe's social media feed. He paused to pull a notebook and pen out of his backpack then wrote down dates and locations of where Chloe had been, along with notes on other people tagged in her photos.

"Anything interesting?" Jamie asked.

"Other than the fact that her life is much more glamorous than ours?" He scribbled down a date and wrote "Maui" next to it. "It looks like she was on vacation when her stepmother disappeared."

"What else can you tell me about Chloe?" Jamie asked. "Please tell me she's one of these trust fund kids that puts her life online for us to consume. Anyone in particular that she's close to? That we should be taking a closer look at?"

Cookie continued scrolling through Chloe's feed while Jamie mined news articles and resources regarding the Van Zant family. As she expected, the bulk of the links pertained specifically to the disappearance of Elizabeth Van Zant.

"Hey, hey, I think I may have found something," Cookie said, pointing at his phone.

"Let me have it, Sherlock," Jamie replied, her eyes moving from her laptop to his small screen. She leaned in and squinted. "So this is from Socialite Scoop. Okay. Looks like it could be from inside any nightclub in the country."

"But it isn't." Cookie tapped the screen to reveal a tag. "You see that? Check the date. The location."

Jamie scanned the post and the connected the dots. "This place is in Corpus. I hear it's impossible to get into without knowing somebody." She shrugged. "Not that I'd ever want to be caught dead in a place like that."

"But look who does care." Cookie tilted the phone back and forth for effect.

"So this shows Chloe in Corpus at the same time her own posts claimed she was in Hawaii."

"Or maybe she just missed it." Cookie shrugged.

Jamie tapped a finger on the table. "Maybe she was here helping her dad clean up his mess and was trying to establish an alibi that she was out of town?"

Cookie's phone pinged, and he turned the screen to check it. "Looks like Leah's on the move," he said.

At that exact moment, Marty showed up with two large plates of fried heaven. Jamie immediately grabbed a fry to pop it in her mouth before reaching over to shut her laptop.

Marty sighed at the tell. "Let me guess. You need this to go?"

Jamie nodded. "You know us too well."

Cookie smiled at Marty and stood up from his stool. "You know we appreciate all the psychic work you do. You anticipate my needs better than any girlfriend."

"Well, if I'm going to keep cooking for and taking care of you, you'd better start putting out, Cookie," Marty joked. "I mean, a man's got needs." He then turned on his heels to pack up the food, returning soon with two paper bags. "I just dumped it in there. Napkins on top."

"Who needs napkins when you've got jeans?" Cookie quipped, taking custody of the food.

"Oh, and can you—" Jamie started before Marty put up a hand.

"Yes, I'll take care of Deuce. But I'm keeping his tips."

"Fair." Jamie followed Cookie, who smelled of chicken strips and fries, out the door of Hemingway's. She opened the door to her Tahoe and slid into the passenger's seat. "So I guess you're driving this time. Where are we going?"

"Seems like she's headed toward Bellamy's on the Boardwalk."

Jamie grimaced at the location. "That's a pretty rough place, from what I've heard."

"Chances are she didn't find the place by herself, so whoever she's meeting is probably who chose the meetup spot."

Jamie reached into the paper bag and popped a fry into her mouth. "Let's go. We've got some miles to make up."

CHAPTER THIRTY-NINE

Bellamy's on the Boardwalk, from what little Jamie had heard, was once a ritzy hot spot with an ocean view. In its heyday, Bellamy's hosted well-traveled guests and influential businesspeople from all across the state. Notable musicians packed the place on the weekends, and the daily seafood buffets were events of local legend. It was the kind of place where people dressed in anticipation of a night to be remembered.

Then the shooting happened.

That was all before Jamie's time. "What a tragedy," people would say. "It was such an important part of the community. So sad to see it go that way."

She prompted Cookie to give her more details.

"Bellamy's was one of the hottest places in town," he explained. "Ocean view, big dance hall, weekend brunches, all kinds of people coming and going. That was what made it so special. The owner, Rick Bellamy, really made an effort to get different kinds of people in each week. He was interested in interesting people. Wouldn't let it become a highbrow hangout exclusively for money people."

"Sounds like a cool guy," Jamie said. "And a shrewd businessman. I'm guessing that was part of his success?"

Cookie nodded. "Yep. Rick wasn't impressed with celebrities or local bigwigs, but he'd definitely use them to get some good press for the place. He did really well until the shooting."

"Were you around when it happened?"

He nodded. "Oh yeah. It was huge news around here. Apparently, Rick got in a bad way over his wife's relationship with Jeddy Junior. Word was that they were having an affair, although she denied it."

"Not a big fan of country music, but I know the name," Jamie interjected. "Don't hear much from him these days on the radio."

"Yeah, I don't think he's recorded anything in years. Yeah, so Jeddy's wife shows up to confront Delilah—"

"That's Rick's wife?"

"Yep. They'd only been married a year or so. They should have still been in the honeymoon stage. So Jeddy's wife—I think her name was Lorraine—showed up and planted herself at the bar with several dirty martinis until Delilah showed up. From what they said, she was saying all kinds of things, threatening to tear Delilah in half."

"Wow. This all sounds very dramatic."

"It was. Better than any telenovela, my mom used to say. Anyway, she got kicked out of the bar because she was drunk and angry. No one realized she was hiding out in the parking lot until the place closed for the night."

"Keep going," Jamie said, realizing she actually knew very little about the Bellamy event. "You should have your own true-crime podcast. You're very good at this."

Cookie smirked. "So anyway, Rick and Delilah lock up the place and leave, and a very drunk Lorraine is lying in wait behind a dumpster. She jumps out, pointing a gun, and Rick immediately goes for it. From what I remember, Lorraine shoots Rick, Delilah lunges at Lorraine, they struggle for the gun, and then Delilah gets shot. She leaves them both to bleed out in the parking lot and goes to Jeddy for help. He turns her in to the police. Says she doesn't remember any of it during the trial. The whole thing was just one big train wreck."

"That's a very apt description," Jamie said. "So what happened to the place? No one wanted to buy Bellamy's?"

Cookie looked at her as if she'd gone mad. "Would you want to sink a lot of money into a place where the previous owners were murdered? What kind of sad story would keep that business going? One guy tried to take it over, but he just ran it into the ground, and now, it's really cursed. I wouldn't want to have a drink there. I'd just be thinking about those two poor people dying in the parking lot out back."

"At least they were together."

"Well, aren't you a hopeless romantic?" Cookie turned his attention to the window. "So now, the place is up for grabs, depending on the day and who makes a move for it. One time, a local gang tried to take it over, and their attempts to claim ownership resulted in the leader's disappearance. Several people bragged about getting rid of Jagged Jermaine—"

"Jagged Jermaine? What the hell kind of nickname is that?" Jamie wondered if her friend was making things up. "There are a lot of *J* names in this story."

He held a hand out and moved his finger in a zigzag line. "JJ, as he was known to locals, had a very specific knife with a jagged pattern, a kind of calling card."

Jamie still had doubts, but she kept them to herself. "So now what? There's a daily booking setup between small-time bad guys to take the place over for a night?"

"I think it's a three-day maximum, from what I hear. No more squatting. It's bad manners."

Even some of the most ruthless players still abided by their own set of rules, strange as they might be. She once knew a small-time burglar who had an agreement with his competitors that they wouldn't hit homes on a holiday. Bad karma, he said. The goods weren't worth it, and people were usually home anyway. Knowing that was an odd comfort.

"Your tracker still showing Leah going towards Bellamy's?" Jamie asked. "Don't want to drive all the way out here and miss her."

Cookie nodded. "Yep. She's there now."

They turned onto RM 628, a farm road that, if followed, would eventually lead to Bellamy's, which overlooked Baffin Bay. Jamie could see the structure at a distance. Several cars there had headlights on, although she couldn't tell if they were on because they'd just arrived or needed the light source. She imagined no one had stepped up to pay an ongoing electric bill. As they got closer, she realized she was wrong.

"How the hell did they get power out there?" Jamie asked. "I thought the place was abandoned."

"Maybe some sort of nefarious bad guy electric co-op?" Cookie leaned closer to his window and squinted. "I expected the place to be in worse shape. I mean, it's been closed for a decade. Maybe someone's still taking care of it."

The place was indeed dilapidated, but signs of repair were also evident on the wooden structure, and the main sign appeared to have been repainted in an attempt to restore some dignity.

Cookie glanced at his phone. "She must be inside." They avoided getting too close to the entrance, although they knew their presence would be known any minute, even with their headlights off. The Tahoe lacked the silent stealth-motor mode so often needed in such circumstances. That was the one technique that eluded her in her surveillance toolbox, especially when the target location was in the middle of nowhere.

"We're going to get picked up any minute," Jamie said. "Should we roll up with the lights on or leave 'em off?"

"On. If we try to be sneaky, they might think it's some sort of sting. Might draw fire, and I'm not a fan of that."

Jamie agreed. As they got closer to Bellamy's, Jamie steadied her gaze in search of Leah's El Camino—no sign of it, but they were still a bit of distance away. She counted half a dozen cars, then she saw it. The El Camino was off by its lonesome on the other side of the parking lot. Jamie stopped short before reaching the cars in the lot. She could see two figures lit by her headlights and knew treading lightly would be best. She parked, giving herself some distance to cut a quick corner and turn if she needed to get away, and killed the engine. She stepped out first, with Cookie following right behind her. She was careful not to make any sudden moves and kept her hands visible.

"I think you're lost," a man called out, his face obscured by a car's headlights. He had a stocky build, not more than five foot nine, and a bald head—zero sense of humor.

"Looking for a friend, and I heard she might be here," Jamie replied, taking her time to walk toward the man.

The man moved toward them. Cookie kept pace at her side. She glanced his way then back at the man.

"Maybe I can just step inside and take a look?" Jamie tilted her head and waited for his response. He moved several feet in her direction, putting a halt to her forward momentum.

"We're not looking for trouble," Cookie said, holding a hand up. "Just need to talk to Leah." Cookie pointed at the front door. "We'll be five minutes and out."

He held a hand up. "I don't think so," he said. "You can't show up here uninvited. Rules, you know." The man took another step. "You should leave now."

"We're not leaving until we see Leah." Cookie's voice had taken on that edge that Jamie knew all too well. He didn't use it often, but when he needed to, he could be convincing.

If only it had worked this time.

The man stepped forward and swung with this right, catching Cookie's jaw, his head snapping to the side and pushing him onto his back foot. Cookie reached for his jaw and rubbed it. No expression. He checked his nose for blood—none. The punch had landed low.

He opened his mouth and moved his jaw to one side, working out the shock of the blow.

"You're not very good at making friends," Cookie said, giving the guy a wink.

"I don't need more friends" was his reply. "And you don't have any friends here, so you should get going. You have no business here. Leave before I make you disappear."

Jamie caught the reference. The bay nearby had been rumored to be the final resting place of a few people who'd crossed the wrong paths or the wrong people. She ventured a guess that at least half a dozen missing person cases could be solved in those waters, if only the evidence hadn't been reclaimed by nature. The Gulf Coast and her channels were experts at keeping secrets.

"We just need two minutes with Leah," Jamie said, one last attempt at reasoning with a man who had no interest in being reasonable. "What harm is there?"

A door slammed, and Jamie, Cookie, and the gatekeeper turned to look toward the clatter. Jamie had hoped to see Leah coming through the door, but in the darkness, the figure was masculine. Then, in the light, his face became visible.

Ormond.

"What are you two doing here?" he asked, looking around. "How did you find me?"

"We're looking for Leah," Jamie said. "We just need to talk to her for a few minutes."

"I know she's here. We saw her car," Cookie added.

Ormond's expression turned from confusion to understanding. "You two were tailing her?"

"Maybe," Jamie said.

Ormond thought for a moment then tipped his head back and rolled his eyes. "That's why she wanted me to drive her car tonight. I gave her my truck instead."

Jamie and Cookie exchanged a glance. She couldn't believe Leah had been onto them.

"Do you know where she went?" Cookie asked.

"No, she wouldn't tell me. I kept trying to get her to let me help her, but she said she had to handle this on her own."

"That doesn't make any sense," Jamie said, struggling to put the pieces together. "Where would she go?"

Ormond's bodyguard waved at his boss. "You okay here? I got that thing I need to handle."

Ormond dismissed his right-hand man with a nod of the chin. The bodyguard disappeared in a small Hyundai that seemed poorly suited for a man with his rough demeanor. Jamie had pegged him for a muscle car guy. Ormond glanced back toward the building.

"I have some stuff to handle here, so good luck with Leah. Let me know if you hear anything."

Jamie and Cookie took the hint and went back to her Tahoe. She didn't know where Leah was at the moment, but the pit in her stomach told her something wasn't right. She drove off, leaving Bellamy's in the rearview mirror.

CHAPTER FORTY

Whatever business had been going down at Bellamy's, Ormond claimed it had nothing to do with Leah. Jamie still wasn't completely sure, wondering what other motivation he would have that far south. She left him and betrayed him before asking him for help. He didn't seem like the kind who forgave easily, but for the moment, she had to take him at his word.

Jamie drove away, her eyes on her rearview mirror, watching as Ormond turned and disappeared back into Bellamy's.

Cookie shook his head. "This doesn't feel right. Where else would she go?"

Jamie's cell rang, and she tapped the button on her steering wheel to answer. "Whatcha got for me?"

"Straight to the point, I see," Alastair replied. "Van Zant's on the move. He's got another guy with him. Security, maybe."

"You see anyone else with him?"

"Negative. Just those two. Hi, Cookie," Alastair sang over the car speaker.

"Hi, Alastair." Cookie's response was as enthusiastic as a disgruntled teenager's.

Jamie glared at Cookie and mouthed, "Be nice."

She then said, "Thanks for the help, Finn. Really."

"No problem."

"Where are you?" he asked. "Just in case you need me."

"We're leaving Bellamy's. Trying to figure out our next move."

"Oh, wow. That place can be rough. Be careful."

Jamie ended the call with a tap of her finger and looked at her partner. "He's really not that bad," she said. "He's helping us."

"Don't go to the dark side," Cookie replied. "Their cookies aren't your Cookie."

"You're my ride or die. You know that, but we need him right now, so let's play nice, and then we can say snarky things behind his back when it's over."

"Deal."

Her phone rang. She touched the screen.

"Alastair, are you close?"

"Negative," he said. "Maybe we misread this thing."

She corrected him. "Maybe I misread it. Where are you going now?"

"Looks like I'm going toward Bellamy's."

"Okay," Jamie said. "Whatever you do, don't go inside. Hang back." She ended the call and turned to her partner. "Where is Leah if Ormond's here and Van Zant may be on his way?"

JAMIE CONTINUED DRIVING away from Bellamy's. As they did so, two cars passed them, one Mercedes and one Suburban, both driving at a decent clip in the dark.

She said, "Let me see if I can turn around," and before she could pull over, Cookie sat upright in his seat, his eyes searching the darkness through the passenger-side glass. "Look up there," he said. "Is that…?"

They spotted a dually ahead, pulled off on the right side of the road. Jamie could make out a figure leaning against the outside of the vehicle. Jamie pulled over and parked behind him, her engine still running. She leaned out her window.

"What the hell happened?" she called out.

Alastair pointed at his back tires, which were quickly going flat. "They objected to my following them. Shot out both tires. Damn good shot. Was trying to keep my distance, but on this road now..."

"I know. He must've gotten nervous about anyone following him out here. Not much to draw traffic out this way." She waved an arm at him. "Leave it. You can come with us."

"You know how expensive this truck is?"

"You got insurance, right?" Cookie asked, his body leaning over Jamie as he asked. "It'll take a day before you get a tow truck out here."

Alastair reached inside his truck and grabbed a backpack then jumped into the back seat of Jamie's Tahoe. As she turned to maneuver around Alastair's injured ride, a spray of gravel shot out from under her tires.

"You better hope that didn't damage my paint," he said, catching her eye in the rearview mirror.

"It's fine."

Jamie continued down the road, unsure of how much pressure to give the gas pedal. She didn't want to tear in and announce her presence, but she knew she might have lost time with Alastair being stranded. The threat to Renata only increased as the minutes ticked away.

Cookie turned to her and said, "Fools rush in."

"Yes, we do."

When she clocked a half mile out from Bellamy's, she slowed down and cut the headlights on the Tahoe, a difficult move with only the moon providing hints of light. Jamie could see the front of Bellamy's, but distinguishing details was still difficult. She then cut the engine.

She reached behind her seat and pulled her bag to place it on her lap. Her Glock 19 felt heavy in her hand, and she sighed before tucking it into her jacket pocket. Cookie retrieved Arnold from his backpack and tucked it behind himself in his waistband. She looked over her shoulder at Alastair.

"I'm good."

"You bringing a knife to a gun fight?" she asked.

He shook his head. "Nope. I've got my piece on me... and a back-up." He winked at her. "And a knife just in case."

Cookie scowled at him.

"No offense, friend, but I've probably been in a few more violent situations than you have. I can take care of myself. Don't worry."

"Maybe being in violent situations isn't something to brag about," Cookie countered. "The best work is done without blood-shed."

"I agree," Alastair said. "But it's the nature of the work. The dangerous stuff pays better." He then said, "Except this job."

Jamie held a hand in the air. "If we could all take a break from this manhood-measuring contest, that would be great." She knew those two would go at it for hours if left unattended. Under normal conditions, she'd be front row with popcorn, but more urgent matters demanded their attention.

"Just this once, we're a team," Jamie said. "Let's get the Sandoval sisters back."

CHAPTER FORTY-ONE

Jamie restarted her engine and drove at a crawl, the Tahoe inching toward Bellamy's in as stealthy a manner as it could, aided mostly by the desolate darkness of the South Texas terrain. She was close enough to see the building at a distance, the lights in the lot serving as a small beacon for the trio in wait.

"How do we want to play this? Stay here and go on foot or crash the place? Once we get close enough, my engine's going to announce our uninvited arrival."

"If we leave the car here and we need it, we're too far away. Competitive disadvantage."

Alastair leaned forward, his face close to the back of Jamie's neck. She could feel his breath on the fine hairs of her nape. "Cookie's right. We might need the car, and it can provide some shielding just in case someone shoots."

She nodded but didn't turn to face him. Instead, she put her Tahoe back in drive and looked at Cookie. "Hang on."

Her foot pressed down on the gas. Small gravel kicked up from the Tahoe's rear tires, and the SUV fishtailed to one side before finding its center back on the road.

"She loves this shit, so get ready," Cookie warned Alastair.

"Good to know," Alastair replied, leaning closer to the back of Jamie's headrest. He tapped her on the back of the head. "Maybe you should look at doing off-road competitions when this is over. I bet you could do real damage in a monster truck."

"Maybe," she replied, her eyes on the road and her knuckles showing white stress from gripping the steering wheel to keep the Tahoe steady as she barreled down the gravel path. She raised her voice, struggling to overcome the sound of her increased speed and loose rocks humming underneath her wheels. "And don't tap my head again. I'll cut your finger off. Maybe more."

Alastair laughed but leaned back slightly, his body bouncing in response to the rough ride. "You think you can stop this thing in time?"

Jamie ignored the question. Bellamy's came closer into view. She took her foot off the gas to slow down then hit the brakes and pulled the Tahoe to a stop just feet away from Leah's El Camino. She took note of the two vehicles that had passed them on the way out, the white Mercedes and the black Suburban.

A figure came running out front.

"That's Van Zant's guy," Alastair said as he ducked down in the back seat.

As Security Guy moved closer to the Tahoe, he squinted as he looked inside the front windshield. Leah quickly emerged from the front door behind him, with Ormand popping out right behind her. Jamie got out of the Tahoe, as did Cookie, both of them careful to show their hands in full view, unarmed. They didn't need to set off a shooting match in the first minute.

"Leah, Ormond said you'd left with his truck," Jamie said. "Were you here the whole time? What's going on?"

Ormond moved closer to Leah, his grip now around her forearm. Leah flinched at his touch. "It's not a good time, Jamie. We need to take care of some things first."

"Where's Renata?" Cookie asked.

"She's safe. But she won't be if you don't get out of here." Ormond's voice was harsher than before, his demeanor rough like the gravel underneath Jamie's boots. He had morphed from the concerned ex-boyfriend to something more sinister. The mask had slipped.

Jamie's eyes stayed on the grip on Leah's arm. "Oh," she said, feeling a dark tingle at the back of her neck. "I'm so sorry. You really trusted him, didn't you?"

Leah's eyes met Jamie's for a second, but she didn't move. The betrayal she felt showed on her face and in the slump of her spine.

"I've always been good to her, and she used me." Ormond turned his head to look at her, and Leah cast her head downward when he spoke. "Did you really think I was going to take that lousy cut when you had the keys to a seven-figure payday? I'm taking all of it."

Cookie's stance stiffened, his eyes narrowed. "You're not really going to escalate this into murder, are you?" he asked Ormond. "That doesn't seem your speed."

"You'd be surprised" was all he said, the edge in his voice cutting through the space between them. "I've done more for less."

Another man emerged from the building. He was tall and thin, and his clothing moved in a way that signaled money, even in the dark. Waves of gray hair wisped across his forehead. He kept his hands inside his tailored black dress coat—Edward Van Zant. "What's going on here?" The question was asked to no one in particular.

"Just a small complication, but don't worry," Ormond said. "We can handle it."

"This is not a small complication," he replied, his voice wavering ever so slightly. "We weren't expecting company, and now we have an issue." He turned to face Ormond. "This is now your problem."

A small vein bulged underneath Ormond's clenched jaw. "You weren't supposed to be here," he said. "I gave you an out. Why didn't you take it?"

"Where's Renata?" Cookie asked again, this time his voice louder.

"It's not your concern," Ormond said.

"She's our client and our friend, so yes, it is our concern." Jamie's correction hung in the air as the group stood, almost as if stopped in time, in a children's game where someone had yelled the word "freeze."

Van Zant addressed Ormond. "You told me you could deliver the package I'd lost and handle the sisters, so handle them." He looked toward Jamie and Cookie. "And these two just make things messy." He rubbed his head. Apparently, getting rid of two people seemed fine, but four had become a burden.

Ormond nodded, and Jamie looked at Leah. Never once had she seen naked fear in the defiant woman's eyes—until then.

A loud banging of metal cut through the silence. Jamie tilted her head to the side, her senses seeking out the source of the sound. Cookie rotated his gaze from one parked car to the next—the Suburban, the El Camino, Van Zant's white Mercedes. A second set of metal clangs led Jamie's eyes to the Mercedes.

Ormond kept his grip on Leah with one hand while the other hand pointed a gun at Jamie.

Van Zant turned to him. "I'll leave my associate here with you to make sure everything is tied up properly."

Ormond nodded but said nothing more. Leah looked off to one side, and Jamie recognized not fear in her eyes but sadness. She had betrayed Ormond, but Ormond had double-crossed her, willing to end her life and that of her sister for money—a lot of money, to be sure, but money just the same—a simple transaction.

"So that's it?" Jamie asked, struggling to ignore the weapon he was pointing her way. "This is how you solve your relationship issues?"

Ormond smiled with his lips but not his eyes. He looked at Leah, but she kept her face turned away. He squeezed her arm more tightly. "I trusted Leah. Completely. And she was stealing from me all this time. Using my people, my resources, to make money and keep it for herself?" He shook his head. "No. She chose this. So when I heard from one of my guys that Leah had accidentally boosted Mr. Van Zant's vehicle, I reached out. Figured it was time to repay the favor. And I told her I'd be her middleman."

"And make a hell of a lot of money at the same time.'"

"Of course," he said, his grip still firmly on Leah's bicep. "This is business. I mean, personal, too, but business first. The revenge is a bonus. No one treats me that way."

Cookie shook his head and nodded toward Van Zant.

"Why did you do it?" Cookie asked. "Why did you kill your wife?"

Van Zant's expression softened. "I didn't kill my wife. I loved her."

"But you know she's gone. That's why you want the car back so badly. The evidence speaks for itself."

"It isn't what you think it is," he said, his voice taking on an unexpected sadness. "It was a horrible accident. I wish I'd been there to help. Maybe things would have turned out differently."

Jamie studied his face, the sadness and regret on it. He didn't seem like a man acting out of jealousy or anger. She thought of his daughter.

"You'd do anything to protect Chloe, wouldn't you?" she asked. "Any parent would."

A flicker or recognition flashed in his eyes. He looked toward the sky, as if the answers would be found in the heavens, a place he would likely never see, given his transgressions. He then returned Jamie's gaze. She felt the tremendous weight of both Van Zant's solemn stare and Ormond's pointed weapon.

"Chloe has her whole life ahead of her, and as much as I loved Elizabeth, I can't fix things now. She's gone. But I can protect my daughter. I owe that to her."

"But don't you owe Elizabeth's family some closure?" Cookie asked.

"I loved Elizabeth!" Van Zant snapped. He had morphed from calm and precise to angry, unsure of himself. "It was just a stupid argument. Elizabeth tried so hard to support Chloe, but it was tough love. Chloe was so angry at Elizabeth for trying to replace her mom." He took a deep breath. " It doesn't matter now. Sometimes life often takes unexpected turns." He waved toward Jamie. "Like yours, for example. Is this where you imagined yourself when you woke up this morning?"

"Definitely should have stayed in bed," Jamie quipped.

"Ditto," Cookie replied.

Van Zant looked at his security guard. "Gary, you're going to drive our guests here in their car. Let me know when all the loose ends have been tied up."

"Your name is Gary?" Jamie asked. "I expected something more ominous, to be honest."

Gary shrugged. "Sorry to disappoint."

Gary the henchman had a sense of humor, something Jamie would normally have appreciated except for the fact that he was in the process of trying to put her in an early grave.

"It's clear that you don't know what you're doing," Jamie said.

"I disagree," Van Zant responded and looked at Ormond. "He knows what he's doing, and I'm paying him a small fortune to clean this up. My part in this is over."

"I'm worth every penny," Ormand said.

"Finish this," Van Zant commanded as he walked to the black Mercedes. He glanced briefly into the back seat before slipping inside.

Jamie couldn't fault the man for not staying until the end. Men with his means often paid handsomely for others to do their dirty work, and from the looks of it, things were going to get messy.

CHAPTER FORTY-TWO

Gary extended an arm as though he was a chauffeur guiding his guests to a car for an evening out. Being told to get into her own car, possibly for the last time, was not something Jamie had anticipated. She reached for the back passenger door and opened it, and when she did, something caught not only her eye but Gary's.

Alastair was still hunched in the back seat.

Gary's eyes widened, and Jamie seized his momentary confusion by landing a solid sucker punch. Gary stumbled back, his hand reaching behind his back. Cookie lunged forward, and the two stout men struggled for the weapon. Alastair pulled his lanky body from the back of Jamie's Tahoe, rushing toward the two men battling for control of Gary's gun. Cookie threw his elbow into Gary's stomach, causing him to fold over, but the gun was still in sight.

In the confusion caused by Alastair's surprise appearance, Leah swung a forearm backward into Ormond's face, knocking him off balance. A quick turn and a kick in the groin toppled him to the ground, his weapon dangling from his loose grip. Leah lunged toward him, scrambling for the weapon as the two fell to the ground, her atop him. She claimed his gun and pointed it at him.

Behind her, a single shot went off, piercing the night air and momentarily stopping the sounds of struggle. Alastair fell a few steps short of Cookie's feet. The struggle resumed, with Cookie using his elbows again, then in Gary's face. Blood trailed from Gary's nose as he fell backward onto the gravel. Cookie gained control of the gun, holding it on the henchman. Jamie ran to Alastair, who remained on the ground. He groaned as he held his leg, a dark-red stain spreading on his jeans above the knee.

"I'm okay. Just a flesh wound," Alastair said, his voice confident. "Go get Leah. I'll be fine. Not the first time I've been shot." He grimaced at Cookie, who shrugged.

"Technically, Gary shot him," Cookie said.

"Uh huh" was all Alastair could muster.

Jamie rushed to Leah's side, her own weapon now also trained on Ormond, who remained on his back in the gravel. Leah held her left hand out.

"The keys," she demanded. "Both sets."

"You aren't going to get away with this," Ormond said. "A man like Van Zant has resources. He will find you."

"I'll take my chances," Leah said. "I'm not asking again." She leveled her weapon at his leg. "The keys."

Ormond leaned to one side, covered by the two women with weapons, and slowly fished two sets of keys from his jeans pocket. He held them up gingerly and tossed them onto the ground. Jamie reached down, weapon still trained on him, and picked them up.

"What now?" Jamie asked her.

She handed Jamie the keys to the white Mercedes. "Pop the trunk. Now." Her eyes never left Ormond's, and the weapon remained steady in her hand as she pointed it at him.

Jamie walked over to the vehicle and pushed the trunk-release button on the fob. The trunk lid opened.

Renata was lying on her side, a bandana tied around her mouth, her hands secured with duct tape in front of her. Her eyes registered fear then relief after seeing Jamie's face. Jamie glanced at Leah, who was keeping her attention completely focused on Ormond. She pulled the bandana away first, and Renata gulped for air. Jamie took the keychain and used the metal end to cut the tape, pulling it away from her skin. She reached down, giving Renata leverage to pull herself from the trunk. Renata stood on shaky legs and scanned the scene around her. Alastair was on the ground, bleeding, with Cookie pointing a weapon at Gary. Leah's gun and attention were still completely trained on Ormond.

"You've been busy while I was in there," she deadpanned. "I guess my Leah doesn't need me to protect her after all."

Alastair adjusted his weight on the ground, moving his leg to one side. "Texted Detective Herrera while I was sitting here bleeding," Alastair said. "I'm an incredible multitasker."

For the first time, Cookie and Alastair shared a laugh. Maybe Alastair wasn't so bad after all.

No sooner had the words left Alastair's mouth than Jamie spotted small red and blue lights in the distance, followed shortly by the sound of sirens. Ormond dropped all the way back onto the ground, resting his head on the gravel. Leah remained steadfast, not taking any chances. Jamie reached for Renata and gave her hand a squeeze.

The distant lights drew closer and brighter. Sirens rang louder as the police cars approached. Jamie walked over to Cookie and Alastair. Gary had given up, defeat written on his face and in his posture. Alastair winced, still holding his leg.

"You two owe me dinner at Hemingway's for this. And an open tab for the night."

"I'll spot you six drafts." Cookie said. "How's that?"

Progress.

CHAPTER FORTY-THREE

Jamie could imagine few things more uncomfortable than attending a child's birthday party, but she stood with Cookie at the back gate of Renata's house, surveying the landscape. Several children ran in a circle over and over, colored balloons trailing behind them as they finished laps. A little girl in a party dress contented herself with a cupcake. Jamie liked cupcakes. Maybe it wouldn't be so bad after all.

"The look on your face is priceless," Cookie said. "You actually look a little scared."

"Kids make me nervous," Jamie said, a small bag decorated with balloons and yellow paper dangling from her hand. They're unpredictable, and I don't like baby talk."

"Well, Sophia is ten, so I think you just talk to her like a regular person. But without swear words."

"I know that."

Cookie raised an eyebrow as if he weren't quite so sure. He reached for the back gate latch and swung the wooden gate open. Renata walked toward them as they entered the backyard.

"So nice to see you!" Renata grabbed Jamie and hugged her tightly.

Jamie handed her the birthday gift. "For Sophia. Don't worry. Cookie helped me."

"I told her Sophia didn't need a lockpick kit," Cookie said.

"Although they come in handy." She glanced around the yard. "I'm glad the weather finally warmed up. That cold snap was brutal."

"Can't imagine anything less fun than twenty little kids in the house," Renata joked. "They need to be outside, for sure."

A young girl dressed in a long-sleeved T-shirt and jeans walked up next to Renata. The resemblance to her mother was striking.

"Sophia, this is Jamie and Cookie. They came by to wish you a happy birthday." Renata handed her daughter the gift.

"Thank you," she said.

"I like your Converse," Jamie said. "I've never seen the green ones."

"Thanks. I like yours too."

Renata brushed her daughter's hair with her hand. "Go have fun with your friends."

Sophia nodded and disappeared back into the crowd of kids and party favors.

Jamie craned her neck to search the crowd. "Is Leah here?"

Renata shook her head. "Not now, but she was here earlier. Spent some time with the girls. Said she had some things to do. She's working with the investigators, and Detective Herrera has been giving her some support. I think it's going to work out, especially with Ormond in custody."

"Glad to hear it," Cookie said. "My mom sends her best. Said she'd drop by later."

Renata pointed over her shoulder. "We're cooking burgers, if you're interested. Plenty of food to go around."

Jamie shrugged. "I mean, I like a good burger." She glanced at all the kids in the backyard enjoying their self-created chaos. "We can stay a bit."

Cookie smiled at his partner. "There's hope for you after all."

CHAPTER FORTY-FOUR

Alastair Finn lumbered into Hemingway's with a limp and a smirk. He glanced around the interior, an eyebrow above the crowd. Jamie waved him over from her stool at the bar, and Cookie elbowed her.

"What?" she said. "You shot the guy. We owe him."

Cookie grudgingly nodded. "Fair."

Jamie reached for her beer glass and took a sip, returning it to the battered bar. She signaled toward a seat next to her. Cookie glanced over and gave Alastair a nod.

"I think I'm getting faster," Alastair said as he leaned back to sit on the barstool, his leg protruding straight out under the bar. "It only takes me twenty minutes to walk to the bathroom." He looked at Cookie. "Thanks, by the way."

"Couldn't have happened to a nicer guy." Then Cookie smiled. "Seriously, I'm sorry about that one. Gary was a tougher wrestle than I'd expected."

"Yeah, Gary had some skills," Alastair said.

"Gary's going to sing like a canary," Jamie joked.

Cookie smiled at the rhyme.

"And I suppose you two saw the news already about Van Zant."

"How could you miss it? Alastair said. "It's the biggest news story since Bellamy's."

"I'm just glad to see that Edward and Chloe are both being charged," Jamie said. "Here's hoping all that money doesn't get them a lighter sentence."

"How's Renata doing?" Alastair asked.

"Good. Should be here any minute."

The front door opened, and Renata and Leah appeared as if they'd heard Jamie's words. Cookie waved at them to call them back. He then made a circular motion with his hand to Marty, who picked up the nonverbal ask like a true professional.

"So nice to see you," Jamie said as she extended a hug to Renata.

"So nice to not be in the trunk of a car." She turned to Leah. "She's since taught me a few things about getting out of different models. Let's hope I never need to use that information."

Leah stepped closer and smiled without hugs—not the hugging type. "Thanks for all you did," she said to the group. She looked at Alastair. "Sorry about your leg."

"It's okay. Cookie's going to be my nurse."

Cookie almost choked on his beer. "Hard pass, friend."

"Did you call me friend?" Alastair smiled at Cookie, who couldn't stifle a small smile in return.

Marty interrupted their conversation with a round of tequila shots and a second round of beers. "On the house since I hear you two did some good work this week." He gave Jamie a wink then turned to attend to other patrons calling for spirits.

"So I think I'm going to stick around a while," Alastair announced, tapping a hand on the bar. "My dad still needs me, and I forgot how much I missed this place."

Jamie could have sworn she heard a low grumble from Cookie, but when she turned his way, he just grinned. She signaled toward the shots sitting on the bar, the limes all hanging crookedly on the rims of the glasses. She reached for her glass, took the lime in her hand, and raised her glass. Alastair, Cookie, Leah, and Renata followed her lead.

"Cheers," Jamie said.

They touched glasses, and the tequila disappeared.

Jamie shuddered as she put the lime in her mouth. "I'm good for the year now."

Alastair raised an eyebrow. "Tell me about the tequila issue. I heard there are stories."

Cookie shook his head. "It transforms her from a little salty to unbearable. It's not good for anyone involved."

"Not even margaritas?"

"Especially margaritas," she said.

"I was thinking," Alastair said, leaning closer into Jamie's space, "that you and I could go out for dinner sometime."

"Like a date?" Jamie asked.

"Um, no," Cookie said. "That is absolutely not happening. She can do better."

Alastair shrugged. "Maybe, but I think I should hear it from Jamie."

Cookie tapped Jamie's shoulder and pointed toward the front door. Jamie glanced up to see her little sister, Grace, standing alone, her eyes scanning the room. Jamie needed a moment to process the fact that her little sister had traveled all that way without telling her first.

She raised a hand toward Grace and slipped off her barstool. Her eyes still on her sister, she told Alastair, "Let's talk about this later. Something just came up."

"Speaking of showing up for your sister," Cookie said.

Jamie took a deep breath before making her way to the front door. Her eyes met Grace's, who responded with a smile so nervous that she looked like she was starting her first day of school. Even in her insecurity, Grace turned heads in the bar, and Jamie instantly felt protective.

"Hey," Jamie said, reaching for her sister's hand. "This is a surprise."

She nodded. "Well, I got a surprise of my own." She handed Jamie an envelope with a letter inside. She unfolded the paper, and even in the dim light of Hemingway's, she recognized her father's handwriting immediately. She didn't bother to read it.

"I guess we have a lot to talk about," Jamie said.

Jamie handed the paper back to her sister, who folded it carefully before returning it to her bag.

Grace looked down at the floor. "How could they just leave like that? Without saying goodbye?"

Jamie put her arm around her sister. "Let's go have a drink. I'll introduce you to my people." She led her through the crowd, holding her hand the way she had when they were kids.

They reached her friends, who had all been trying not to stare but failing miserably. Marty's radar had gone off the moment Jamie left her stool, and he, too, had joined their group.

Jamie gestured toward her sister. "This is my little sister, Grace." She then waved her hand toward her crew. "Grace, this is everybody."

She glanced over and studied Grace's profile. Now it was just the two of them. Maybe their parents' leaving for the last time had made them a family. She had no idea what the future held, but that night, she had Grace by her side, and that was enough.

Jamie held up her glass. "To sisters," she said.

Acknowledgments

While I was thrilled to spend time in Jamie Rush's world as I wrote this book, the process of creating during these last two tumultuous years proved to be a challenge. I am enormously grateful to so many people who offered support and encouragement as I worked to bring this story to life.

To Austin Mystery Writers, thank you for the years of support, critique, and editing as I worked to turn ideas into words into stories. I sincerely appreciate Valerie Chandler, Kathy Gresham, Helen Currie Foster, Fran Paino, and Kathy Waller. I consider myself fortunate to be a part of this group.

To the team at Red Adept Publishing, thank you for the support you've given me as an author. A special thanks my editors, Angie Gallion and Kelly Reed, for their expertise and attention.

The crime writing community is a special one, and being a member of Sisters in Crime, Writers' League of Texas, and International Thriller Writers has given me the opportunity to learn from, work with, and support other writers in the genre. I'm looking forward to seeing many of you in person again!

Having talented writers as friends is such a gift. I'm lucky to have Andy Boyle, Micki Browning, Wendy Tyson, and Alexandra Burt in my circle. And to Sara Templeton, even though I'm a writer, I don't think I have the words to do our friendship justice.

Thanks to my THRC gym group: Trisha Taylor, Sophie Campbell, Casi Helbig, JD May, Sarah Pasemann, Danette Myers, Bruce Barnes, Tamara Keithley, Barbie Vaughn, Naomi Coleman Medina,

Wendy Shanks, Amanda Voigt, Ashley Chagnon, and Richard Comstock. This group has helped me work out countless story issues by making me run, swing kettlebells, and press heavy things over my head. I'm still a little salty about all those burpees.

A special thank you to my children, Rachel, Ryan, and William, for their love, encouragement, and humor. No one makes me laugh like this trio.

To my mother, Sharon Konvicka, thank you for instilling a love of reading at an early age and for encouraging me to continue when times were difficult.

To my sister, Anna, and my brother, DJ, I'm so thankful we have one another.

And to my husband, David, thank you for being my partner for the last three decades. I am enormously lucky to have you by my side, and since so much time has passed, it looks like you're stuck with me.

About the Author

Laura Oles is a photo industry journalist who spent twenty years covering tech and trends before turning to crime fiction. She has been widely published in numerous photography magazines and has served as a columnist for several trade and consumer publications.

Growing up in a military family, Laura discovered the frequent travels were made more enjoyable with the company of Nancy Drew. She has been an avid reader and writer of mysteries ever since.

Laura is an Agatha nominee, a Claymore Award finalist, and a Killer Nashville Readers' Choice nominee; she is also a Writers' League of Texas Award finalist. Her short stories have appeared in several anthologies. She loves road trips, bookstores, and any outdoor activity that doesn't involve running. She lives in the Texas Hill Country with her family.

Read more at www.lauraoles.com.

About the Publisher

Dear Reader,

We hope you enjoyed this book. Please consider leaving a review on your favorite book site.

Visit https://RedAdeptPublishing.com to see our entire catalogue.

Don't forget to subscribe to our monthly newsletter to be notified of future releases and special sales.